后浪

The Expedition to the Baobab Tree

去往猴面包树
的旅程

[南非] 威尔玛·斯托肯斯特罗姆 著

[南非] J. M. 库切 英译 / 李斯本 中译

四川人民出版社

目　录

那，就怀着怨憎吧。但我已禁止自己心怀怨憎。那，便怀着嘲讽吧。嘲讽就轻松多了。它透明坦率，漠不关心；我可以像一只缩进巢里的小鸟儿，退回我的树洞里，去笑话我自己。还有保持安静。也许保持安静，只是为了梦得更远吧，因为人的第七感，正是睡眠。

　　过去，我还常常为时间所困扰，当我仍然想要这日夜更迭以外的更多东西，当我执迷于计数，却不确定白日里那些我打瞌睡的时间是否该被算入夜晚，如果夜晚是平静无事，而白昼是忙碌无暇。睡眠就是夜晚。我有时是怎样将这夜晚无尽绵延的啊，在最黑暗的虚空里，尽可能地将自己蜷缩成最小的一团，额头顶着膝盖，好杀死那咬噬我五脏的痛楚；在攀缠着我的紊乱念头中，紧盯住一个颜色，并凭此固守住我自己，于是事后我便可以说，我的睡眠是蓝色的，是血一般的鲜红，又或者，是一片灰白过渡的阴影。我粉身碎骨地醒来，头晕目眩地坐起，踉踉跄跄，将一只满是尘土的脚放入长矛利刃般的阳光中。这平静而凶残的，整日不休地钻削着我居所的光束。

这是那些珠子出现以前的时间。那些珠子出现以后，时间便好打理得多了。如果我经常放纵自己睡去，那不再只是偶然，也在很长一段时间内，不再只是逃避了。那时我才是活着的，我这样告诉自己。

珠子的到来，给了我计数日期的决心。我是几天前捡到它们的，计数则是后来才有的主意。我将这些新发现归入了那一小堆陶器碎片里。那些碎片也是好奇心引领着我从各处收集回来的。那是些距离这棵树或远或近的旅途，是我偏离了原本取水的路线，抱着或犹豫、或无聊、或心灰意冷的心情走上的杂散迷途。而那段取水之路，当时已几乎要被我踩出一条清晰可辨的小径了。

我正在开辟自己的道路，一如那些荒野走兽。这也是我后来才意识到的。像马鹿，不，不像马鹿或斑马，不像水牛或任何一种群居动物。它们互为各自感官的补充，共同应对危机，共同在那些一旦落单便无力招架的凶险面前存活下来。即便如此，它们一个接一个地仍会沦为猎物，仍会孤独死去，一个接一个地，在各自的命数里。而我踩着我自己的道路，如此刻意，仿佛是要提醒自己，我已在此居住了很长一段时间，或者说，我在此住得很好。又或者我应该说：我，同样在这里存活下来了，但是我只依靠我自己，就算是在我感觉大地之下无处不是蛇蛋的日子里，就算是那时，我也必须自己照顾自己，尽量不要踩到它们。

我的小径，这条我如此轻柔地踩出的去往溪流的小径，纤细，微弯，绕过灌木丛和小树林，穿过平坦的草原——冬天正要为其染上绛红，再翻下最后一道陡坡，便可抵达阳光下波光潋滟的水面。这水面同我张开的双臂一般宽，两棵小马图米树[1]守护着的地方，是我的饮水地。往下游去，是我洗澡的地方。而上游，也就是这段支流汇入[2]主溪的地方，是大象的浅滩。

那时，我险些丧命象群脚下的时候，我想起了一个我们年轻女孩间曾会互问的谜语：什么东西把它的生命装在肚子里？想必是那一大群轰隆作响的肚子，令我不安地傻笑了片刻，后又使我的喉咙一阵干堵，因为我那可怜的藏身之处，与象群间仅隔着一块突起的石头和几株芦苇。成群的脚掌从我身旁矫健地踏过，迈入溪流。水花溅起，它们平静地沐浴着。我缩进了我自己的怀里。没有人会像一个奴隶女孩那样，在如此严密的监护之下成长起来。我还可以补充一句，也没有人会像一个奴隶女孩那样，如此愚昧无知地成长起来。就算是我，一个闪耀的特例，在面对野生动物和它们的生活习性时，依然是如此的蠢钝，因为我的知识仅限于与象牙交易有关的那点信息。每隔一季，一只大象便会吞下一颗石子，而这些石子余生都会在它们那巨大的肚子里滚来滚去，滚来，又滚去。一切令我费解的宏大的事物，到头来都会被我降作

---

1 学名 *Breonadia salicina*，英文俗称 Matumi（马图米），分布于南非东北部及邻近国家，通常生长于河流沿岸或溪流水中。
2 英译用词为"汇入"，但地理上，上游应是支流"流出"主溪的地方。

荒谬可笑的东西来消化、理解，以证明我有凌驾于它们之上的力量，然而这一个我却如此可笑地蜷缩在石头与芦苇的背后，像一只没有壳的鼻涕虫，一只不过我小指尖大小的软壳甲虫，在忐忑的假死状态里，等待这漫长而拖延的嬉戏的结束，那样我便可以像一个人类一样重新站立起来，环顾四周。最后一声大象的嘶鸣从对岸传来，我浑身僵硬地站起，拂去身上湿黏的泥沙，在轻抚着芦苇的微风中，瑟瑟发抖着。

现在，我与那群大象已经可以友好相处了，我偶尔还是会不小心闯入它们的浅滩和洗澡地点。只是，友谊这个词，总有些居高临下，并不恰当。我生活于此，它们生活于此。仅此而已。有时，从我所在的高地可以看见它们背部的曲线，在远方水面闪烁的波光中起伏、转动，我可以听见它们的嘶鸣，看见成对的象牙举起落下、一闪而过，而我仍然难以将眼前这一幕奇景，与我曾经佩戴过的光滑的镯子相连结。有些连结，仍然在回避着我。

如果我连从这猴面包树的入口到那一小堆陶器碎片和其他种种发现这短短一段路上的事情都不能悉数知晓，不知道去要这么多步，回来要那么多步，关于我的旅程，我又知道些什么呢？我有时觉得它仿佛已经持续了一生，并且仍然在继续，仍然会继续，就算现在，我只是在围绕着一个地方不停地打转而已。

去要这么多步，我的脚却已经累了。当我把它们全都带回这儿时……我知道自己在收集的是什么吗？我又要用这些破烂东西……做什么呢？时间变成了珠子，也就变成了破烂。

在我记忆的纷繁小径上，盘桓着几个阴森可怖的身影，挡住

4

了我每一次回望的目光。我认得这些身影。但我叫不出他们的名字。他们于朦胧中赫然耸现，像是人形，又像是个长满毛发的墙角，又或是一个旋转着的茅草屋，张开大口，要将我吞下、将我拖走，一个盛怒之下如暴风雨般向我袭来的大口，以惊人的速度咆哮而下，又在距离我一码开外的地方突然转向，徐徐漫步，诱我上前；我有时也会察觉到某种寂静的、扭曲的期待，随之而来的是明明白白的沮丧，当无数拧着我的尖螯变成灌木丛里松垂的卷须，当森罗万象全都消散，干脆利落，只留下一片深不可测的苍茫。我记忆里这些纵横交错的轨迹，比我一生实际所见的还要多。如果这些记忆是属于我的，如果我的探寻求索没有那样频繁地落空，以致各种蛛丝马迹都已烟消云散，我还能找到些什么吗？我无法追踪到的究竟是什么呢？

各种各样不通往任何地方的小径，从我的居所向四面八方散射开去。无人铺设它们，它们就这样出现了。当然，刚到这里时，我也借用过动物们踩出的小道，因为除却那些不通往任何地方的小径，这地方便再没什么可利用的了。只是很快我便得出结论：我的思维方式与这里的其他生物并不互通。我得去寻找、开辟一条自己的道路了。我找到了。

找到了，我说。胆战心惊。

最重要的东西，水，我无需特意去找。这一带有很多的水。你看得见，也听得到。我用我的礼物——一个鸵鸟蛋壳，盛起那溪水的涟漪。我将蛋壳捧十一弯清莹的、从一块粗糙的岩石上跳耀下来的水之弓中，以捕捉水的光泽和声音。我就这样一勺又一勺地盛着溪水，将这闪烁着、低语着的水之神灵倒入我的另一件礼物——一个陶土罐中，然后用双手慢慢举起这满满的一罐水，将其置于头顶，再屈膝拾起我的蛋壳勺子，沿着那条取水之路，走回我的猴面包树。

找到了：各种各样的稀树草原[1]的食物；也发现了当我将食物摘下、挖出、捡起之时，是在与动物们相互竞争。那些果树并不为我萌芽、开花、结果，以抚平我的饥饿；那些块茎和根茎并不为我在地下生长、膨大；不是为了取悦我，绿心树[2]才滴落它的花蜜；不是为了使我恢复精力，平冠树[3]才恰好立于那片阴影的中心；斑点兰花迎风招展，不是为了愉悦我心；紫罗兰树在初夏绽放一树的花香，也同样不是为了我。

疣猪觅食后，一个新手开始仔细搜寻这片已被专家们翻了个遍的稀树草原。她学着像它们一样跪下，没有獠牙可用，她便试着用一根木棍戳刺坚硬的地表，没有对可食用的鳞茎和根茎天生敏感的嗅觉，她便试着用视觉尽力探寻。所获寥寥，她沮丧离开。狒狒觅食后，同样的情形又再度上演了，只是她再三确认过狒狒们都已离去，才大胆涉足了它们的领地。

---

1 稀树草原是热带雨林植被与热带荒漠植被之间的过渡类型，草类高大茂密，乔木稀疏散落，主要见于非洲、南美洲和澳大利亚的部分地区，又以非洲分布最广，发育最为典型。猴面包树正是非洲稀树草原的标志之一。
2 学名 *Schotia brachypetala*，英文俗称 Greenheart tree（绿心树），分布于非洲南部，花期会产生大量的花蜜。
3 学名 *Albizia adianthifolia*，英文俗称 Flat crown（平冠树），分布于撒哈拉沙漠以南的非洲大陆，树冠扁平、宽大，具有良好的遮阴效果。

我害怕狒狒的怪相，远甚疣猪、薮猪的獠牙。他[1]太像我了。我害怕在他那张丑陋的脸孔上辨认出我自己的影子，它让我想起我在这里的劣势地位，想起我的浅陋无知。我为自己映照在他狰狞面目里的情绪与欲望感到羞耻，也为自己身形的精细优雅感到可笑，当我四肢跪地，粗野而拙劣地模仿着他的时候，我的精细优雅是多么的多余。我鄙视他，他的力量，他的狡黠，他对这世界显而易见的精通与掌控。我鄙视所有、每一只狒狒。那肥胖脸颊上的贪馋令我厌恶，那不堪入目的公开交媾，雌性那自轻自贱的乞求，她们在雄性强硬的大手和刺耳的辱骂下的躲闪，还有当你于兽群中发现他们时，他们那紧挨[2]在一起的眼睛——我认为这也是贪婪的一种表现。我对他们了解得太多了，与我的品味实在不符。如果他们被关在笼子里，我定可以好好嘲笑他们一番。而至于他们对我又了解多少，在那些斜觑的目光之中，他们什么也没有透露。我想，我对他们而言不过是一个碍眼的东西，一个局外人，远远地隔离于他们的活动范围之外。

　　只有当我入睡时，我才完完全全地知道自己是谁，因为我统治着我的梦中时光，我心满意足地占据着我的梦。只有在这样的时候，我于我自己，才有存在的必要。

　　我是在仓皇逃离一只狒狒哨兵的追逐时，闯入那块被夷平的土地的——在我看来是被夷平的。我摔倒在地，摊平四肢，大口

---

1 作者在提及动植物、恐惧和时间时，部分会采用拟人的"他"。
2 此处形容的是狒狒眼距很近的面部特征。

喘着粗气。我转过身来。我的心脏怦怦直跳，几乎要跳到我的指尖上。我鼻中呼出的阵阵气息，扑簌着干草微微颤抖的叶片。

我就那样躺了很长一段时间，仿佛一只听天由命的食腐动物——对它而言，饥饿是一种熟悉的、可以等待着被平息的感觉。然后我看到了一些闪闪发光的东西，一些小小的光珠，在我睫毛间闪动着绿色与黑色的微光，又在我指尖于草叶间翻寻、触碰到它们的刹那，化作了一颗颗真实的珠子。我坐起，将它们从泥土和干枯的草根间挖出，捧在我的掌心。两颗黑色，一颗绿色。我将这无用的发现带回了我的树。

它们像花粉一般微小。我细细检查着它们，在其数目、颜色允许的范围内，将其排列成了数量有限的各种图案。我认得它们。第二天，我还想回到发现它们的地点，但却迷失了方向，只能漫无目的地搜寻着，寄希望于我能辨认出一棵树，或者一个岩石山坡，因为那地方就紧挨着一个小山坡，这我是记得的，我还记得那些苍白的、梯子似的树根，那是一棵岩榕[1]攀附于岩壁之上编织而成的；然而我什么也没有找到。我游荡在这片稀树草原上，就像我还从未在此建立起任何系统，就像最初，我刚刚抵达这里时一样。

最初，没有时间，因为我没有时间去思考顺序；也没有类别，因为生存的挣扎消除了所有的差异。现在我可以允许自己拥有分

---

1 学名 *Ficus glumosa*，英文俗称 Rock fig（岩榕）或 Mountain fig（山榕），分布于撒哈拉沙漠以南的非洲大陆，因喜扎根于露出地表的岩层之上而得名。

类的奢侈，以及对新旧知识的判断、运用。我甚至可以反思自己在做什么。我可以让我的思想连续而有规律地运转，不起波浪，不见涟漪。我可以将我的思想聚拢成圆，就像一个陶罐，再将其设想为清凉而精确的东西，就像一罐水。我可以让这陶罐的口沿高高突起，像喷涌的水柱，好抵御那些一不小心就可能将我穿透、将我完全填满的蓝色和黑色气体的缥缈虚无。我还在我的思想里装进了各色各样的物品，一排又一排，无穷无尽，无可计数。感谢上苍，我可以忆想出足够多的物品来堙没一切，即便我记得的一切都已消耗殆尽了，我还可以杜撰出新的东西。对付虚无，我有很好的办法。

　　此时此地，这几颗无需我去想象的小珠子，和我曾经见过的、佩戴在男男女女脖颈还有手腕上的是同一类。曾经它们还可以被用于交换物品，就像曾经我也可以被用于交换别的什么东西。当然，我不知道我的价值是什么，或者我曾经可以换得些什么。一枚圆环钱币。无数枚圆环钱币。另一个我不甚了解的领域，是钱应该怎么花。我的一切都是别人给予我的，这是一个奴隶女孩的特权。我头上的屋顶。我身上的衣服。还有食物——就我而言，是非常丰盛的食物。我是多么的幸福啊。

　　这些珠子如此之小，在我存放它们的树瘤上几乎肉眼难辨；可是我闭着眼睛也能找到它们。我了解我的树，就像一个盲人了解他的家。我了解它的每一处平面、凹陷、凸起、边缘，它的气味，它的黑暗，它那巨大的光之裂隙，就像我从未了解过那些我曾被吩咐睡在其中的茅草屋和房间，就像我只能了解属于我的，且只

9

属于我的东西，我这从未有人踏足过的居所。我可以说：这是我的。我可以说：这是我。这些是我的脚印。这些是我火堆的灰烬。这些是我的磨石。这些是我的珠子。我的陶器碎片。

在我灰色的树皮之下，我是一个至高无上的存在；当我走出我的大树之时，我是骄傲地站立着的。只是后来，我怀疑自己是否又摆出了那副故作轻松、宠辱不惊的姿态——这是很容易培养的，我学会了在我的主人们面前摆出这副样子，想着留下一个好印象，会有我的好处，同时在这样的表象之下，心里却满溢自负，因为我手里握着的那一丁点琐碎的权力。

而如今我不可一世地伫立在这里，眺望着这片稀树草原。每一次我走出来，世界便是属于我的。每一次我从守护着我的树里走出来，我就又一次成为了一个人，一个强大的人。我远远眺望着这片风景，植物繁茂，动物成群，地平线上的紫色山丘斑驳零星，试图将它们围起。每一次从猴面包树的腹中重生，我都这般狂妄自大地伫立着。太阳勾画出我的影子。风为我穿上衣裳。我指着空气说：空气供养我活着。灌木莺啼叫起来，他是在啼叫着我的名字。我就是所有的一切，他啼叫着。

但我不是一切。不。如果这里还有其他人的话，我不是一切。

我寻获的这些珠子，与我早年穿戴过的相比，是多么的微不足道。那些红色的、黄色的、硕大的椭圆形玻璃珠，悬挂在我的脖颈和手腕上，宛如熟透了的浆果，与我佩戴在上臂的象牙镯子，还有我黄色印花的丝绸长袍交相辉映着。我曾经光彩照人。我曾经笑靥灼灼。我曾经是一件被拿来炫耀的物品，那般明艳的年轻，一如我最初的样子。我的无瑕，我的光滑，我曾一度完好无损的肌肤。我是人人羡慕的未受割礼的少女。我是人人心向往之的少女。我太年轻了，对这些一点儿也不在意，更不用说理解了。我只是一个孩子。那么小的孩子。那么小。当我身体里怀有一个孩子的时候，我也仍然只是一个孩子。

庆幸的是，我还记得那些女人，是她们的安抚使我逐渐适应了那里。我只能这儿一点、那儿一点地从她们的谈话中捕获一次提及、一种声调或一个重音，因为她们说的语言于我，有如瀑布倾泻，从她们口中砸落、再砸落下来。这些收留我、像母亲一样照顾我、教会我如何取悦男人的女人们，究竟是谁呢？为了使我看上去更有吸引力，她们用各种礼物将我装扮——当时，我以为它们是礼物。而我也用力地搂住她们，努力表现得更好。有时她们也会训斥我，嘴唇张开，发出嘎吱嘎吱、噼里啪啦的声音。但随后我的眼泪又会被吻去，她们又会给我喊喊喳喳的友好笑声，把我抱在膝上，紧紧地拥抱着。我爱她们，就像一个再次感受到安全感的孩子；我在她们的膝上爬来爬去，弄得那些手镯叮当作响。就这样，她们同我嬉戏，予我调教，使我直到最后仍能记起那些狂喜和折磨，但内心却没有受到任何的影响，仍然保持着完整，保持着自我。我把你们从我的记忆里召唤了出来。我记不起你们的面容了，但没有关系。我记得你们曾给过我的美妙的情感。我想知道你们如今是否衰老了，是否悲伤，是否仍然生活在那座宅子里，是否那里就是你们的终点。还有，你们是否记得我，被委托给你们以获得那份特殊的、温柔又有趣的照顾的无数女孩中的一个。以及，你们是否曾试图打探过我们的消息。你们是否在意。

我从未忘记你们的教导，就算现在，我也可以在必要时淫荡地大笑，就算现在我也可以像一只小猫，柔软地依偎着某一个人，或是随意地扭动着身体，视情况随时减轻或增加强度；只是，这些全都是多余的了。

现在我生活在虚空之中，睡眠是我浑噩的解方。我生活在由我自己衡量的时间之中，先是三颗珠子，然后是越来越多的珠子，直到我挑选出了最好的几颗绿色珠子来排列日期。就这样，一开始，我度过了一个绿色天和两个黑色天的周期，然后是一连串连续的绿色天。后来我逐渐厌倦了绿色天，又用黑色以各种我想象得到的图案和数目加以变换，全凭心情，完全偶然。我的日子逐渐有了归类和秩序。它已然是一种对抗的手段，对抗那隐匿在自然规律下的时间的混沌与虚无。时间威胁着我。它想要彻底地摧毁我。我以为只要我经常更换我的系统，便可以欺骗过它。时间永远不知道我接下来要尝试些什么，就算是清晨，当阳光和鸟鸣唤醒我的时候，我也不知道自己要用时间尝试些什么，我只是在无柴可烧时去寻找柴火，在水罐见底时去取水，在没有食物时去搜寻食物，在饥饿时去进食，在睡意袭来、四肢沉重时去睡觉。我在玫瑰色的水晶里做着梦，不时还会点几下头。

我已经快要忘记我的计数玩具了。在树内壁的节瘤上，它们最初的编号只有三，后来逐渐增多，也就逐渐使我厌倦了。有一天，我在不同的几处地方又捡到了更多的陶器碎片、珠子，还有铜丝环。我将它们全都带了回来，和剩下的碎片、珠子一起收入了那一小堆杂碎物品，那些昔日居民的遗留物品。那些昔日的居民，但愿他们遭殃吧，因为他们能留下的不过这些而已：无法拼凑完整的陶器碎片；被我不耐烦地用草秆串起、挂在脖子上的寒碜的装饰品；锈迹斑斑的铜丝环，又粗又重，像个镣铐，我拿它什么也做不了，何况在这方天地之下，更是再没有什么可做的了。再没有了——还是，我其实游荡在坟墓之上？再没有了——还是我其实游荡在被尘土、被丛生的植被覆没了的城墙之上？我是否可能游荡在庭院、广场、防御工事、露台、排水渠、宴会厅和棚屋之上，只是这些定居点和街道都已经崩塌粉碎成了无关紧要的东西，被一个又一个的冬和夏所接管了？我是游荡在我们曾漫无目的地寻找过，又在很久以前就在无情的太阳底下放弃了的地方吗？那里有一片片的灌木丛和扎人的杂草，一条一岸隐匿在小树林和藤蔓植物背后的河，一些平顶的山丘，其上是堆积成各种嶙峋怪相的圆形巨石，还有我高耸的猴面包树？场景来回穿梭，我们游荡其间，恍惚迷离，惊恐不安？那是捕猎者与猎物的地方？

我想象种族灭绝的血腥战争。旱灾。一场瘟疫。我想到不知疲倦的狂热信仰，和随之而来的崩塌与心死。然后什么也没有了，只剩下一点微小的残渣，无论我如何要自己相信，我找到了一种通过秩序来抵御永恒之威胁的方法，最终全都无济于事。因为我不愿在懒散的岁月流逝中仅仅作为一个哈欠而存在，仅仅是一缕稍纵即逝的气息，是旋律里一个次要的节拍，是永恒裂隙中的一个幽灵。

我实在缺乏构思新事物的天分，只好用那些被遗忘之人的手工艺品来消磨时间，凝固时间，同时苦涩地意识到，我不过是在虚无之中改变虚无。但这样至少让我感觉好受一些，去做些事情，去思考、琢磨，去发挥我的想象力，辅以另一种不同类型的早期记忆。

因为我刚刚抵达这里时，除了记忆，便什么也没有了。一个饥肠辘辘、衣衫褴褛的存在，挣扎着穿过平原与河谷，因一无所有而歇斯底里，跌跌撞撞地跋涉向那条永远在后退的地平线，永远的白昼的流逝，永远的周而复始，直至被一棵大树吞下，慈悲的停泊之地，慈悲而阴凉的避难之所，它使人粗略地联想到一栋大楼，有墙，有呈水柱状上升的天花板，有大地为地板，一个巨大的茅草屋，枝杈和树叶铺筑了它的屋顶。

诅咒那引领我至此的梦幻泡影吧，那个闯入我生命，还有其他人生命的旅行者，他的话语我曾出神地倾听，他的吩咐我曾奴性地遵从，因迷恋而盲目，而混乱，而丧失理智。诅咒他吧，那个以我们的牺牲成就了一台好戏的人，他妄图理解苦难、为其赋魅，那有魅力却无用处的自我认识，最终亦杀死了他。哦，那些谈话，那些谈话，那无所不知、无所不探求的大脑，到头来却什么也解释不了，最解释不了的就是同伴与跟随者们的背叛。哦，理性的无能！

穿着绛红色衣裳的异乡人，从一开始，他的机智风趣就让我着迷。他知道如何用俏皮话点亮一场过于阴郁的谈话，他比好辩的诗人、比其他诸如此类的名流通晓更多罗盘上的方位。这些人聚集在我的主人——一个富有而鳏居的商人家中，付费品尝我精心准备的宴食，也付费与主人那些漂亮的奴隶女孩交际，展开一些油滑世故的对话，即使一切仅限于注视和渴求，最多有几个冒失之徒，会趁主人看向别处时试图抚摸她们。这一个人却与众不同。穿着他的绛红色衣裳，他的水绿色衣裳，他的焰黄色衣裳，这一个戴着镶金项链和细金手镯的人，称得上是一个博览群书又见多识广的自信之人。无需提问，他便会作出他的反驳，简要地提炼出冗长言论的核心，并且一次又一次地将争辩引向荒诞可笑的结局。这让他在那些伟大的灵魂中并不受喜爱，他们虽一次也未成功，却还是一次次地挑唆他开口，想要抓住任何一个可以指责他亵渎或煽动的机会。举头三尺有神明，他们知道自己看到了什么。他坚称道。也别去打扰祖先了。当你无可指摘地生活时，他们的代祷亦是不必要的。

难道不是吗？他问。难道不是吗？

他说的话，清亮，崭新，像一道闪电。

同样的还有先知的代祷，先知家人的代祷，众神的代祷，敬畏众神之人的代祷，还有那些将他们的部落历史抬高成为宗教之人的经历留给我们的道德教训——所有这些都很有趣，但愿一直如此。每一个清晨与夜晚，召唤神的是美妙的音乐，是声音中某种共鸣的部分，一个人用它来证明，他不是满脑子只有进食和繁衍的生物，他同样认为自己是不灭不朽的，因此才想要采取适当的方法，确保自己拥有幸福的来生。让他们拥有吧。不论用什么方法，让他们拥有吧。

也让这些商人们继续吧。是他们带来了眼前所有的繁华——以一个雄辩开场的手势，他把一盘用芝麻油和椰子汁做成的虾仁烩饭递给了他右侧那位性情乖戾的诗人，同时微笑着看向我。我想他冲我眨眼了。

我主人那轻慢的目光也落在了我的身上。他示意我走近些，铜手镯从他的手腕滑落到了手肘。他的手臂已是如此的枯瘦。我捡起棕扇，为他扇风。他上唇湿润，凝结着津津汗珠。今晚，他又会因高烧而颤栗不止了。当我搬进他的房子，胆敢成为他最年轻、最宠爱的人儿时，他已然是一个病人，或许已然是一个垂死之人了。我缓慢而有规律地扇着风，试图搅动笼罩在他面容四周的沉闷空气。他没有碰过食物，只是喝了一盘水。可怜的人儿，拥有眼前如此丰裕之景象，却只能不可抑制地喘着粗气，呼吐出一个富人的生命。势力、权力，从嘴巴、鼻孔里溜走了。当他时断时续地坐着打瞌睡时——他的眼皮会微微张开一道缝隙，大抵是在观察他的宾客、他的奴隶女孩、他的儿子和女儿们齐聚在奢华与骄傲中的模样——封存已久的记忆便会重又在他浑浊的瞳孔中映现。还有他那孱弱的手指，当时是想要抓住些什么呢？一只蝴蝶？一阵海风？一个女人的笑颜？

谈话变得无趣了，他请求将他抬回他的房间。我说的是请求，不是命令。他是轻声地请求的。

只剩我与他独处了。我紧紧地搂着他，安抚他，因为他仍在顽抗着自己的日渐虚弱，显得异常地烦躁不安；只是后来，出于哀怜，我还是由着他去了。我看着他，忽然理解了他的双手想要抓住的是什么。他是在试图撕破死亡在他四周缠绕起来的精密的网。当他在痉挛中抽搐时，那张网也跟着振颤起来，在期待中狡黠地闪着微光。它缠绕得愈来愈紧了，所以房间外的嘈杂声响无法穿透、威胁到它，人们或关心或担忧的低声细语，亦被远远地挡在了他死亡的静寂之环外。

我让这病人依偎在我屈起的膝间，把他的头倚靠在我的胸前。我用他的语言耳语着下流的故事，令他在我怀里愉悦地微笑着。萎缩的婴孩，你对我而言是多么容易的分娩啊。我会喂你死亡那冷漠的乳汁，因为它不会再对你干瘪的身体有任何伤害了，相反地，或许它会是你的解脱之径，将你从所有的仁慈中释放。任何的怜悯都只会痛苦地延缓你的离去。

一天清晨，我爬上主人宅子最高的屋顶露台，呼吸黎明清新的空气，眺望城市、大海，还有那些被拉拽上岸、平躺在海滩上的小船——其中有几艘，就属于那个我刚刚才与他永别了的人。它们现在，或许也同我一样，要被处理掉了。我的未来，我奴隶伙伴们的未来，女人，男人，还有那些躺在玫瑰色拂晓中的小船，那些贩售象牙、龙涎香和铁矿的商铺，那栋如今终究陷入了哀悼的大宅，还有我下方那座芬芳馥郁的花园，我们全都被交付给了飘忽不定的命运。也只有那些拥有着什么的人，才会拥有安全的保障。于我，只有不安。我等待着，等待着一声叹息，等待着我的情感从心底涌起。现在，是时候了。

我，一个来自这国家中心腹地的人，潜意识里仍然流淌着水的呢喃，一种保存于我泪水和唾液里，于我静脉的血流里，于我

17

身体所有汁液中的对水的知悉。我，一个懂得如何运用我的水之存在来浇灭高烧侵袭的人，却发现自己在那个清晨的静谧中，为如此之多同时向我袭来的事物而不能自已地哭泣起来。太多了，我只想要哭尽、哭死这思绪的乱麻，而非为它寻得一个解释——一个解释，它无限接近于哀悼，但也是一种解脱感；是对未来的忧虑，却又是一份，在病房的压抑中度过一日又一日后，置身于清晨的纯净中所感受到的、朴素的喜悦。

我用长袍的一角，拭去眼角与脸颊上的泪水，然后向下爬回了那个花园。我得弄清这究竟是怎么回事。我走向海滩，又从那里——因为我朝海湾中那艘孤独的三角帆船的呼喊一直未得到回应——又从那里穿过一片无人打理的海港区，祈祷没有人会在如此重大的亡故所造成的忙乱与监管疏漏下，留意到我的缺席。不过，就算他们真的留意到了，我又有什么可担心的呢。我是悲伤得失魂落魄了，但悲伤之下，更多的是渴望。我不在意有谁发现了它。我的渴望是一颗小小的、坚硬的果核，它深埋在我的心底。我不在意如今有谁知道了它。如今，随着我恩人的故去，这份渴望已是我唯一的确定，也是它帮助我忘记了前途未卜的恐惧。轻浮吗？或许是吧，如果我是一个可以决定自身命运的女人。但是对于我这种从属阶级而言，这无疑是一次可以容许的逃离。愚蠢地爱上一个人，想要偷偷地藏起这幸福，却看见幸福就在一道裂隙背后，触手可及地等待着我，况且时机似乎也很有利。

所以现在我搜寻着那个让我坠入爱河的男人。我听见他在一道沉重的、有着繁复雕花的柚木门背后大声地笑着，在秘密商议

18

着什么，在与我无关的他的生活里。我看见他消失在一个转角的尽头。我可以闻到他的气息，闻到何处他可能有过停留，何处他可能尚未路过，因为他答应过会再次到来，他就一定会乘着波涛汹涌的海浪，站在灌满海风的大三角帆船的背风处，再次到来的。而我将跟随他，在我的想象中，随他的长袍下摆拂过泥土地，刷过一颗破裂蜜瓜的饱满果肉，拂过沙砾、鱼鳍以及鱼鳞。我将流连于他身侧，看他在那些摆摊妇女跟前停下脚步，用心观察最穷苦的穷人是如何生活的。成群的苍蝇从一堆堆的烤鱼、烤肉上一拥而出。它们落在他衣裳的蓝衬底上，组成各种各样的图案，它们爬过他的鼻子、眼睛以及额头，它们停在他湿润的嘴角，停在任何有湿气的地方。

一个老熟人拖着脚步慢悠悠地走来，头上顶着一个装满大蕉的扁平篮子。她呻吟着将篮子放下，在树荫底下的老地方坐了下来，伸展开腿脚。他上前与她攀谈，也与周围的其他人闲聊。他倾听那些回应他提问的无礼粗暴的回答，尴尬的回答，或同样尴尬的沉默，还有那些热切提供的信息和机智风趣的评论，这位显然不是来买东西的冒昧的先生，做着自己的推论。当他询问着螃蟹、蛤蜊、贻贝的价钱，肉类、鱼类、柴火的供应情况，以及是否可以交货等信息时，他是在用这些信息建立起自己的案例库，用此时获得的讯息，来批驳彼时出现的争议，并将这些信息与那些关于统治者和善良民众的泛泛之谈相对照。一个细心周到的人，一个好学好问的人，就这样渐渐使自己了解了最底层人民的日常，而这日常，比起一个生活在富裕大宅里的奴隶女孩的安逸存在，真是要复杂得多了，正如他常常向我指出的那样。

我这安逸、懒散的存在，是的，一个如今可能也走到了尽头的存在。

我此刻又是身在何处，这隐隐闷燃着的恐惧的气息，我为何如此熟悉？这是血水的恶臭。我从来不曾从这恐惧中逃脱，这如影随形的晕眩感，模糊了我的视线，使我忍不住用手擦拭眼睛，想要看得更清楚些，却又马上对这一举动感到懊悔，因为我身处的地方，我发现，就在我第二任主人有时会吩咐我去给奴隶们买些内脏的屠宰场附近。这气味我再熟悉不过了，还有这牛羊低沉、颤抖的哞哞、咩咩之音。湿滑的心、肝、肺、食管，被胡乱包裹在几片树叶中，因为极易滑落，我无法将其置于头顶，只好用手捧着，与身体间隔开一小段距离，就这样从这片满是粪便和污秽之地走开，从这个动物们屈着膝盖、悲伤的棕榈树身着长裙，干枯的树叶簌簌作响着，声嘶力竭着，终究还是无能为力地被禁锢着的地方走开，从这群说笑着的屠夫的戏弄、挑逗的话语和下流的动作旁走开，去烹煮要与众多张嘴巴分享的食物，去暗自盘算如何将肝脏单拎出来留给我和我的孩子，又要如何从主人和他妻子的饭食里偷偷捏出一小撮米饭——这对我来说还算方便——在杂乱无章的家务琐事里。

我们住在两个低矮的、屋顶都已经倒塌了的茅草屋里，所有的奴隶，不分性别。从黎明到深夜，我们为他，那个香料商人，辛勤地劳作着。工作就是区分我们的唯一事物：男人们在他位于码头的仓库里，女人们在他的宅院里。我们从四面八方来到这里，说着五花八门的语言，但在这里，我们把当地的语言重整、转变成了一种特殊的劳工用语，并以此相处。我们有些是二手购得的，有些是三手，甚至四手，大多仍然年轻、健康。女人们正值育龄、青春繁茂，夜里要在主人汗津津的皮毛地毯上，为他张开双腿。我们中有一些人乐于接受这件事，但不包括我。他笨拙又粗暴，我只羡慕那些被免于这项服务的奴隶，她们至少还享有某种程度的自由，至少，不必被人操控，我想。我不介意站在壁炉前生火。不介意在花园的酷热中劳作，采摘、锄草，保持芒果树和番薯藤周围的整洁。我也不介意在他那个悍妇妻子的眼皮底下清扫、收拾，不动声色地服从她的命令，将我的怨言留至夜晚睡觉的地方，但就算在那里也得万分小心，因为我们之间存在着告密者，而被发现，意味着你的舌头会被切掉。

我守口如瓶。我活得有多不安，便有多坚忍。我是个胆小鬼，什么也不拒绝。

我面无表情地躺在他的皮毛地毯上，聆听着大海的喧嚣。我变成了一枚牡蛎，虽然被从礁岩上撬起，但仍然保留着我意志的硬壳、我自尊的薄薄一层沉积物，就像我曾经被教导的那样，保持着自我。我没有放弃。我没有屈服。我让它发生。我可以等待。远远地，越过他的呻吟声，我聆听着海浪拍击的声音，它哄我入睡。我是属于水的。我是一道随遇而安、随形而形的水流。我可以保留他的种子，在我身体的汁液中将它孕育、使它结果。我可以跪在一波又一波的宫缩中，把脸贴近大地，与水连接的大地，将那果实从我身体里推送出去，用我滴着奶水的乳房喂养一个又一个嗷嗷待哺的孩子。我的眼睛笑了。我的嘴巴沉默。

永远沉默。一声怒吼中惶遽的老鼠，那就是我们，体系里的低卑下级，一目了然的温顺听话。我们的孩子，在还只是婴儿时，在我们的身体还仍然渴盼着他们时，就被从我们身边带走、卖掉。我们的过去是被无情虐待，或被以礼物讽刺的过去。我们的现在是看不到希望的现在。我们全都是同一个女人，可以互换，亦可以替换。所以我们安慰着彼此以及彼此的孩子，所以我们共同分担，所以我们为彼此在头皮上捉寻虱子，穿着彼此的衣裳，一起歌唱，一起闲聊，一起抱怨。看不到希望。一次，有某个人试图逃跑。她被抓住了，双脚也被砍掉了。第二次，又有某个人试图逃跑。她逃脱了。那些阉人也经常逃跑。

有传闻说，在远离城市的大沼泽深处，有一个逃亡者聚居的地方。在那里，那些成功逃脱的奴隶以捕猎为生，他们搭起茅草小屋，熬过难以忍受的高温与孤独，只为最终作为一个自由的人死在那里。传闻说，他们已经发展出了自己的管理体系，有一个头领和几个参谋；说他们感到安全，有蚊虫与水蛭泛滥成灾的无人可穿越的沼泽的庇护，且去往那里的秘密路径仅有先驱者们知晓；说他们知道当局对他们睁一只眼闭一只眼，因为清楚抓他们回来要耗费一大笔钱，清楚这些逃跑的人还会一直制造麻烦，会一直抱怨，一直反抗，清楚明智的做法就是惩罚这些叛逆的灵魂在荒野中被时间遗忘，清楚无论如何，总会有新的奴隶从内陆补给过来。传闻还说，那些阉人不允许女奴加入他们。

那天刮起了一场风暴，比我经历过的任何一场风暴都更加骇人。那感觉就像热浪要夺走我的身体，就像我的眼珠快要被吹出眼眶，一如螃蟹的眼睛，悬于眼柄之上。我用手掌紧紧按住眼窝，仿佛是有沙子和玻璃碴在磨锉我裸露在外的眼柄，仿佛是它们看见得太多，又太过纤弱，所以我要设法将它们重新按回我的头颅里去，然而它们在我脑袋里如此剧烈地跳动着，近乎是在我头颅里翻滚着，当我张开眼睑时，我什么也看不见了，只有热浪，将万物翻滚、掀举着的热浪。我也再听不见任何声音了，只感觉黑压压的空气向我猛扑过来，又席卷而去，开始肆意地推搡我，剧烈地拉扯我，让我东倒西歪，让我直面撕裂的闪电，它将万物推向华丽，又在顷刻间堕众生于黑暗，使我彻底惴惴错愕、晕头转向。我看见一棵凭空出现的苦橙树。我看见一片由凤头燕鸥组成的灰色云朵，然后是第二片由闪闪发光的沙丁鱼簇拥而成的云朵。我看见一场鱼群之雨，水母翻滚下坠，各种漂浮物宛如表演特技，看见一座小屋被吸入空气之漩直至爆破极限，然后突然崩裂，坍塌，然后突然，那一地碎屑重又旋转起来，逐渐远去。

在狂风将我和垃圾和一切脆弱的东西卷走之前，我逃走了，我歪斜着身子挣扎向前，几乎是爬着，从一个支撑物踉跄至下一个支撑物，树，柱子，门，房屋。我可能会被吹至天外吧，我，连同这些剥落之物，这些破碎之物，就这样涡旋上升，直至永恒。大海在拍击着。它在与它自己战斗着。它劈裂开去，又冲撞、揉攥在一起，它将自己高高抛向天空，又如雷鸣般重重拍落在高水位线上，它一波又一波地翻涌着，覆没了城市的棚户区和那里繁茂的树林，将那些为它而造、亦终将献身于它的三角帆船和小舟的残骸碎片猛掷下来，摔入富人花园里的棕榈树与蔷薇丛之间。还有风，它将船帆从树枝上撕扯下来——它们还妄图像鸟儿的幽灵般躲藏在那里——吹送至辽远而陌生的内陆。

海潮回落了，嘶嘶作响着，从它所摧毁的事物之上退去了，在最后一丝痛苦的、还泛着泡沫的喘息里，平息为一片阴郁的宁静。风亦平息了，留下如此稀薄的一片静寂，一声啜泣便可以彻底地击垮它。

这易碎的平静仅仅持续了一小会儿，空中便落下了啪嗒啪嗒的雨滴，又在顷刻之间，化作了倾盆大雨。密集的雨帘在大海之上飞驰，一片已全然忘记了方才那片刻宁静的大海，正掀举着，翻涌着，同时亦困惑着，因为浪要将它拖向一边，而风要将它推向另一边。倾盆之雨，滂沱之水；坚硬而笔直地，将路面戳满麻坑的雨滴，流淌、冲刷、洗净那狂风忘记刮走的东西，在哗啦啦的沟槽里奔逃乱窜的水流。一场彻底的、有目的的、沸腾癫狂的大雨。一场负有使命的暴风雨。

一定有人听见了我的呻吟。一定有人听见了我被压在一棵捻角羚果树[1]的树枝下发出的呜咽，一棵在暴风雨的号令下，想要将我献作祭品的树，因为我一直坚定地忽视着它的存在，从未试图寻求过其神灵的帮助，因为我忽视了所有神灵的存在，除却我心中的这一个。或许因为我并不知道有更好的神灵吧。或许。或许

---

1 学名 *Pseudolachnostylis maprouneifolia*，英文俗称 Kudu-berry tree（捻角羚果树），分布于非洲中部和南部，秋季一树红叶，极具美感，因此也是当地常见的一种城市遮阴树。

我只是固执地违抗着这个我孑然一身、两手空空来到的地方，还有那些在我看来空洞无物的当地仪式。我为宿在我内心的神灵创造了属于我自己的仪式，无知无觉地拾起了一枚白色贝壳和一枚黑色贝壳。让大地的神灵息怒吧，还有宅院的神灵，空气的神灵，献上赎罪的祭品，背诵押韵的祭词，呢喃祷告的套话，让这棵树的神灵息怒吧，他倾听着，他留意到了你献祭的姿态，他会照拂你的，只要你小心说话——不，那对我而言毫无意义。我对那些姿态一笑置之。我无动于衷地走过所有的捻角羚果树。毕竟，它们被种植在街头巷尾，不过是为了它们秋日里烈艳的色彩，它们又不是为了我才来到这里生长的。我走过它们，昂首挺胸，不献上任何祭品。不，我嘲笑那些在它们面前鞠躬行礼的妇人，嘲笑她们恭敬地用一棵发烧树[1]的硕大叶片盛起一小捧御谷粒[2]，将它放置在那棵沉默无言的树干旁，并对它喃喃自语着什么。我完全不祈祷，不为这世上任何一棵树的神灵。我的舌头是为我而生的，我的舌头，我的嘴巴，我的整个身体都是属于我自己的。我把耳朵紧贴于那棵捻角羚果树灰褐色的树干，全神贯注地聆听着，想听听它的神灵是否有话要说，然而我只听见树木缓慢生长的声音，缓慢地扩张着它年轮的编年史。我知道，有一天，关于一个女人曾将她的脑袋紧贴于他这回事，他没有什么好说的，就像关于那

些乞求他赐福的傻瓜们，他也没有什么故事可讲述一样。这是我深思熟虑后得出的结论，远在我自己被看作是一棵树的神灵很久，很久以前。

然后这棵捻角羚果树便惩罚了你，我的恩人笑道。是他在被告知家门口发生了一场事故后，派遣他的奴隶将我从那树枝底下救出的。他将我安置在奴隶们的住处，直至折磨着我的断骨痊愈为止。但还未等我能重新站立起来，他就已经成为了我的第三任主人。

所以他一定对我心生了喜爱。所以我一定给他带去了欢愉。一天晚上，他前来询问这个他偶然救助的病人的情况，当我笑话起人们对捻角羚果树的迷信时，他看上去有些惊讶，而后又引我说出了我浅短的历史，一如这城市大多数奴隶女孩的历史，无牵无绊，无趣无聊。一笔简单快速的交易，他买下了我，我也从此，怀着所有的谦卑，住进了这栋高处的大宅，有着从远方采石场运来的岩石建造的屋顶露台，可以俯瞰低处城市与大海的视野，以及整洁的外屋和精心打理的内庭院。我的恩人常常召唤我。我们说话。那个他与我共眠的夜晚也到来了。他觉得我很迷人。但比起床笫之欢，多数时候，他只是让我褪去衣裳，安静地与他说话，而他会一直看着我，就像一个人欣赏一场美丽的日落，或诸如此类的东西。他也会用同样的眼神看着他儿子豢养的薮猫。每当高烧来袭，只有我被允许留在他的身侧。我会坐在一旁，为他扇风。

我第二任主人手下的奴隶伙伴们，那些仍然在受苦受难的人——我没有机会为你们感到悲伤了。事情已经发生，那场风暴选中了我，而我也接受了降临在我身上的命运。我什么也不向往，什么也不伤怀，过去的任何事情都不能使我兴奋，事实上我不愿谈起过去。那是浪费时间。因为我已渐渐被自己迷住了。

而今，我第一次发现了美。我自己的美，还有那些花束，那些皂石雕像，那些玉钩扣，那些陶瓷的釉彩，靛蓝的蜡染，还有迷人的丝织品，轻柔如一缕气息的丝绸，或与金子交织在一起的沉重而笔挺的锦缎。我几乎重新学会了说话。我忙于各种精细的工作，比如繁复的刺绣——这是年长的女奴教会我的，还有为一屋子的宾客准备宴席的美食，以及宴席上得体优雅的服务。这最后一项，我表现得尤为出色。我学会了用一种截然不同的方式交谈，在话语的末尾附上一种带有金属质感的讽刺口吻。我学会了当谈话显得尖锐，太多急快的言论好似尖细的箭头齐齐发射时，让自己的声音变得甜美可人。我学会了纵情大笑。

最重要的是，我学会了在使自己看起来更有吸引力的过程中找到乐趣，以及，在权力中找到乐趣——人们显然认为我可以在我恩人的房间里为自己谋得好处。他赠给我一只象牙镯子，大小正好可以佩戴在我的左上臂，让我可以厚颜无耻地炫耀。在他心情不错的时候，我常常会别有用心地提及其他几个奴隶女孩最明显的缺点：瘦削的小腿，隆肿的肩膀，缺失的牙齿，不成比例的乳房，突出的下巴，黑猩猩般粗糙的手指；尽管他饶有兴致地不予否认，尽管他声称这些缺点不算什么，在"欢愉的长榻"上——他如此戏称他的睡席——几乎可以忽略，但我知道他听进了我说的话。然而我还是只从他那儿得到了一只镯子。

尽管如此。尽管如此。我的生命还是闪耀了。我轻轻地哼着歌，用椰子油涂抹着我的身体。后来我才知道，他有两种服侍的奴隶，一种为她们的外表，另一种，只因为她们乐意服侍。

那么，那些有时会向我袭来的忧郁的缘由是什么呢？当我从露台眺望波光粼粼的海湾，看三角帆船和小舟在其间闪烁，当我俯瞰城市的屋瓦，看它们延绵直至地平线的微茫，然后一切都逐渐混沌了，因为我心中那一份愚蠢的不安，直至一只海鸥的尖声鸣唳，将我惊醒。我的双手为何捂住了我的脸颊？我有什么好感到悲伤的呢？拥有我新任主人的喜爱，一个富甲一方的鳏夫，一位举足轻重的市民，他像清凉的苔藓，凉爽而柔软地将我保护，让我在他的照顾下感到安宁，不仅是感到安全，而是对生命新阶段可能到来的火花的憧憬，在这段相对宽松的关系里，我生活着，展露着我的才华，几乎无所限制——为什么我的眼中会涌出泪水，令城市都在折射的色彩中颤动不已？为什么我的脑袋会深埋在我的胸口？为什么在被召唤时，我会想要尽可能地让自己显得渺小，想要躲进一个黑暗的角落里，假装自己不在？

我坐着，渺小如一只甲虫，哀泣着。我浑身上下都涨满了被压抑的哀泣，已是随时都可能爆裂。我希望自己有一副动物的口鼻[1]，那样我便可以钻掘到地底下消失不见。或者我可以藏进一棵树的树皮里，无声无息地潜伏在那里，将自己压得扁平。

这是我最为熟悉的心情。我很久以前就熟悉它了。即使到了

---

1 此处特指猪那类可以拱地、刨坑的口鼻构造。

这里，我也依然很熟悉它，我向你坦白，忠实的猴面包树，我的知己，家，堡垒，水源，医药箱，蜂蜜罐子，我的避难所，我身不由己的漂泊前的最后一根救命稻草，我的中心，我强烈情感迸发时的守护者，残叶落尽、凝固起丰腴体态的冬日，生机勃勃、绿叶穿顶与花朵与清酸果实随风摇摆的夏日，那果实悬挂着——我将脸颊紧贴于它们之上（灰绿色的绒毛抚摸着我的肌肤），我破开它们的外壳，烘烤你的果肉，将其大口吞下——一如我从你那里获得的满足，直指着地面，等待着。你保护了我。我尊敬着你。这说的是，田鼠和我都居于你的腹中，但只有我尊敬着你，我想。只有我。

倘若我能够书写，我会拾起一支豪猪的棘刺，从上到下划满你巨大的腹部。我会向上攀爬至你的枝杈，在你的腋窝处刻下凹痕，逗你发笑。大写的字母。小写的字母。我会用一种满是钩垂和鬈曲的字体，以一种圆周书写的方式，环绕着你写上一圈又一圈，因为我有太多的话想告与你知，关于一趟去往全新的地平线的旅程，如何变成了一场去往一棵树的远征。此处是一个讲求韵律的停顿。哦，我已经从那些诗人那儿学到了太多，我已经深谙那些技法，精通抒情诗与叙事诗的拼凑。讲求韵律的停顿和流转的思绪，围绕着你的躯干一圈又一圈地铺呈开来了，那是一段疯狂的渴望造就的诗性历史，是我们最终能够抓住的所有，在载送我们前行的艰难航程中，逐渐剥离了一切物质的东西，逐渐使我们憔悴支离、筋疲力尽，这往昔的压舱石。

我就这样一行又一行地，用我们的幻觉装饰着你，使你能够消化、生长，将这些荒唐之事抚平，在你粗厚的皮肤里保留下这些无用的信息，直至你自燃焚毁的那一日。而我会心满意足地放下那支豪猪的棘刺，后退几步，双手叉腰，欣赏我的作品。你身上已满是我的伤痕了，猴面包树。我不知道我有如此之多的伤。

倘若我能够书写。就算那样，忧郁也仍将占据着我。我疲惫不堪地走向河流，在那方清凉里，用我姐妹的潺响将我的存在填满，让我在鸽子木[1]和小花土蜜树[2]的温和气味中恢复精力，让我的目光停落在那缠作一团的猴绳藤[3]，蕨草叶，还有那缓慢下坠的落叶上，让我寻得平静，整日、整夜的平静。

总有猿猴想要玷污我的避难所。当动物企图僭越其动物本分，而与我站在同一层面上对话时，我是多么的恼火啊。比方说，那些水莓树[4]顶上的长尾猴群。就好像他们被我轻视了似的，就好像我是一个巨大的威胁似的，就好像我并不属于这里，是必须以辱骂和严重的警告驱逐出去的东西似的，他们竟然无礼地瞪视我，竟然喝叱我，竟然不惧直面我以表达他们的不满。

我恩人豢养的那只灰色鹦鹉也是如此。那小小的眼睛里是冷冷的不满、嘲讽，还有奚落。如果他祝福你早上好，他真正的意

---

1 学名 *Trema orientalis*，英文俗称 Pigeonwood（鸽子木），分布于亚洲、非洲和澳大利亚，因会吸引来成群的鸽子栖息而得名。
2 学名 *Bridelia micrantha*，中文称小花土蜜树，英文俗称 Mitzeerie，分布于非洲南部、东部和西部的湿润地区，通常生长于河流或沼泽附近的森林里。
3 学名 *Cynanchum ellipticum*，英文俗称 Monkey rope（猴绳藤），分布于非洲南部，是原始森林中常见的一种藤本植物。
4 学名 *Syzygium cordatum*，英文俗称 Waterberry tree（水莓树），分布于非洲南部，因喜生长于河边而得名。

思是滚开，那双眼睛也会眯成细小的黑点。他把语言翻了个底朝天，语义都掉落不见了，那些话语便什么也不是了。他将他的鸟笼搅得污秽不堪。他用他的吵嚷声叫醒整座大宅。当你责令他安静些时，他会用一声清亮的、纯净到足以划破空气的口哨声向你挑衅，并且他，一只笼中囚鸟，会大获全胜的。他以他那微不足道的鸟类的智商能够学会如何大获全胜，而我还在蒙受抑郁的折磨，行事彷徨犹豫，把伤心写在脸上，以刻薄为自己辩护，在人后道闲言冷语，讥讽那两个儿子和那个至今仍然居住在那座大宅里的女儿，使我自己不受奴隶们喜爱。

我与大宅里那只被驯化的薮猫的关系则完全不同。多少次，我希望自己可以鼓起勇气，去若无其事地滑开那鹦鹉笼子门上的钩扣，这样他便可以飞出来了，那个白痴，这样那只薮猫便可以从某簇灌木丛里猛跳出来，于空中将他一掌拍昏，再将他擒住。然后他会把这只鹦鹉叼走，残虐地吃个精光，残虐地，直至全身尸骨只剩一根灰色和一根红色的羽毛。鹦鹉的终结。

楼下的庭院里，那只花斑猫漫步着。他用脸颊蹭了蹭一簇桂叶黄梅[1]，零星绯红、翡翠绿和黑色的花朵撒落在他身上，灰白的树皮的斑驳黏上了他的口鼻。他受到了惊吓，轻哼一声，小跑溜走了，抄近路穿过铺着石板的小径，心中显然揣着一个明确的，且肯定是最为重要的目标。他没有理会我的呼唤。我看见他用前

---

1 学名 *Ochna serrulata*，中文称桂叶黄梅，英文俗称 Small-leaved plane（小齿金莲木），原产非洲南部，是一种观赏性园林植物。

爪摁住了一只壁虎，正思索着下一步该怎么做；他先是抬头看了看我，然后用一种猫类特有的掩饰的神情看了看他的猎物。我盯着他。我可以长久地盯进他那双善变的眼睛里，想象我们拥有同一个灵魂。他深深地打了个哈欠，舌头向后卷起，打哈欠的样子残忍得可怖。即便只是错觉，这错觉也足以让我明白，我们不是玩伴，我们之间需要保持一段距离，而我会保持的，我答应了他，抚摸着他的皮毛，挠搔着他的耳背。黑鼻子的甜美小脸，你的独来独往、自得其乐把我给逗笑了。也许我们之间的共同点远比你想象的要多。

作为一只小猫，他被当作礼物赠给了我主人最小的儿子，而他，作为一个少年，显然把收集野生动物当作一项爱好。那个时期，幼子的兴趣主要集中在钓鱼上，家中几乎见不到他的身影，因为他从早到晚都待在他那艘极其昂贵的快速帆船上。但是只要他出现在这里，我总是喜欢他那无比健康的粗犷，他的少年稚气，也喜欢他所有的恶作剧。年轻、快活的人儿，最是迷人，而谈及他的爱好时，他又是那般的严肃，那般敏感得可笑。我是故意将其称作他的爱好的，因为我不相信他父亲会允许他选择钓鱼作为职业，除非，谁知道呢，除非它作为一项分支被纳入家族事业来打理，如此，那男孩便可以像一个富人的后代那样去做生意，而不是像一个贫穷而淳朴的渔民那样去拉渔网。

现在，我知道自己为何而忧郁了。我已经目睹过那行进的列队。好吧，我知道这是意料之中的事，我知道他们迟早会出现的，因此我在每一个感恩的日子里爬上屋顶守望，守望着我向自己允诺不会去看的东西。那可怕的列队，那折磨人心的缓慢行速。我从我的守望台上看着他们远远走来，便鬼使神差地着了迷。那支离破碎的形影撕裂了我，粉碎了我的意志，令我绝望地注视着他们，令我每一次都无可奈何地看见他们的命运，令我不得不压抑自己的怜悯，强迫自己去开他们的玩笑，如此才可以忘却，才可以忍受。我的目光追随着他们，看他们从破败零落的定居点夹缝间的灌木和芦苇中现身，穿过街道上刺目的阴影与阳光，有时会从我视野中消失不见，但我太清楚他们行进的路线了，会提前将自己不情愿的目光安放在他们必将经过的地点；领头的是几个服役的士兵，虽全副武装，却像是他们的人类猎物般在前面步行着。紧随其后的是一顶简陋的轿子，那个奴隶猎人正坐在上面休息，在两名被他房获的奴隶的肩膀上摇晃着。这个大头目如今不再昏昏欲睡了，一如他在他们一路走来的那条难以估量的荒野长路上所做的那样，如今他已经清醒地意识到那个时刻，那个最重要的时刻即将到来。然后是那些戴着镣铐的人，有些头顶上还驮负着一包包的豹皮、象牙、犀牛角还有粮草，个个面容扭曲，因为脖颈上的铁圈擦破了他们的皮肤。接着是年轻的女人和稚嫩的小女孩们，被用较轻的锁链捆绑在一起。他们就这样迫不得已地踏上了去往目的地的旅程。队列的末尾是更多全副武装的士兵组成的后防线。

我跟随着他们。我知道地点。我抄近路穿过街头巷尾，穿过开阔的、尚未修建的空地，在他们到达之前抵达了海滩附近的广场，躲在那些残破不堪、尘土飞扬的蓖麻树和那周围稀稀拉拉的矮树丛后面。新一批奴隶的运送一切顺利，不会引起任何人的注意。我是那唯一一双不情愿的眼睛。

铿锵，铿锵，我命运的同伴们到来了。那些未被触碰过的女孩，我的小妹妹们。那些正当年轻的阉人，不再是男子，不再是人类，是一次深入内陆的突袭的幸存者，是我的自己人，半人，也许不是人了，是被迫的屈从者，是可怜的强壮而健康的货物。他们静静地站立着。他们被允许坐下了。

轿子被放下了。那个奴隶猎人浑身僵硬地站起，伸了个懒腰，一个惬意的、悠长的懒腰。然后他走下轿子，向城里走去，去边谈生意，边喝一碗无花果酒，抽一烟斗大麻。他是一个老人了，我看得出来。他的下巴尖上有几撮灰白的胡子，但是他大步流星地前进着，仿佛是这海边的空气令他神清气爽，这如释重负的感觉使他精神焕发似的，因为这项艰巨的任务终于顺利地进展到了这片海岸。卫兵们仍然坚守在岗位上。我想知道他们此前是否来过这里。我想知道这次补给的奴隶人数是否充足，有多少人因为旅途的消耗而变得虚弱不堪，因为无用而遭到遗弃，又有多少人因为沼泽热[1]而丧命，有多少人因为反抗而被杀。那些残存下来的人如今无声地躺在地上。甚至有几个卫兵也坐了下来。

海滩上，一群顽童正朝一头死去的双髻鲨踢沙子。他们奔跑，喊叫，怒喝，假装自己是一群狗，嬉笑着，亢奋地在鲨鱼的尸身

---

1 沼泽热，即疟疾，又称瘴气，古时人们以为疟疾是由沼泽地的瘴气所引起的，因此得名。

上跳来跳去。他们是把快乐都放声大笑出来了。然后他们便对那具皮质的尸身失去了兴趣，转而到海滩上更远的地方去寻找乐趣了。他们沿海浪的泡沫线捡拾枝条，竞相追逐，在浅滩上溅起阵阵水花。短暂的快乐消逝在空气里。闷热的死寂重又围拢上来。

几天前，我就在海滩上看见那头双髻鲨了。它在痉挛中抽跳着，一旁的晒鱼架投射出网格状的阴影。它试图将自己的整个身体从沙地上举起，仿佛是要向上游入天空。有时这边眼睛被埋在沙子里，有时是另一边；一边看见了劫数，另一边窥视了希望，在悬而未决中这可怜的家伙挣扎着，间歇性地抽搐着，癫狂直至死亡，而眼睛直至死亡都将世界一分为二地割裂着。他是否仍然——即便已经死去——仍然要寻求这一半与那一半的和解，才能在那迷雾之中寻得他的出路？他扭动着脑袋，越来越深地，将自己拖向了死亡。向左，死亡垂落如一个灰白的幽灵，向右，死亡垂落如一个灰白的幽灵，他没有选择。但或许他只是捏造了自己的死亡，他只是选择了再看不见任何东西的、全然彻底的空无。这空无没有色彩，没有触感，亦没有实质。

我不能给这些新来者们提供茶点。我曾试图这么做过，但是被卫兵赶开了。尽管如此，我还是走近了些，用我劳工的用语温柔地欢迎了他们，向他们表达了我的同情；但看起来并没有人听见或听懂了我说的话。尽管如此，我还是同他们说话了，因为我不知道除此之外还有什么，尤其还有什么有用的，是我可以做的。

我告诉他们我所知晓的关于我出身的一切，我卑微地为他们奉上了一段贫瘠的历史。我的故事是由我偶然想起的一点一滴拼凑而成的，我的记忆是一段以恐惧为起点，也以恐惧为终点的旅程。我对恐惧了解颇深。我能在我的血管里感受到他，因为他已经住进了我的身体，我闻起来已经开始有他的气味了。我用他的眼睛看过了，看过森林与平原在毒素和扭曲中变得面目全非；我用他的耳朵听过了，总有一种低低的怒吼，甚至在万籁俱寂中也轰鸣不已，令我常常面露苦色。哦，恐惧绝不是事件的鉴赏家。他吞噬一切。他碾碎一切。他身后没有留下任何血迹，因为他只是静静地伫立着。从来都是万物涌向他，是万物被他吸引，而他深知这一点。

我不知道。我知道的是：我在我的梦中、我通过我的梦，减轻了恐惧和惊怖，从而使那些无名的、无形的，成为了无害的。但我还需要学习。这是苦难的后果。这是我仍然在做的事情。

我知道的是：我没有像这些人那样受罪，因为我抵达的那一天，我也是听别人说的，说我，作为唯一一个被俘的女孩，没有戴镣铐，从其他人身边走开了，一个人飞奔向了大海，拾起了一枚白色贝壳和一枚黑色贝壳。因为我是属于水的。我知道是什么把空气化作了水。然后天空下起雨来了，他们说。雨，毛毛细雨。

我转过身，不再看那些被诅咒的灵魂。我是这城市最富有之人手下最重要的奴隶女孩。我的权力比许多人的妻子还要大。我的生活是贪图安逸的。我可以慵懒地静观其他人的愚蠢，因为我的手臂上佩戴着我主人宠爱的象征，它对那些想要羞辱我的人而言，不亚于一声训斥。纵使忧郁极其频繁地向我袭来，极其频繁，我也咬紧了牙关：至少它不敢袭向我的上臂。我的存在是浮华和气派，是耀眼和兴奋，是覆没在一床鹅卵石上的闪闪发光的水波，是神秘的井水馈赠在唇上的佑福，是海水的恩泽与力量。

仿佛有个婴儿躺在它的腹部之上，在它试图扳直身子时，不断压弯它的脊椎，那头双髻鲨就这样一直挣扎着。

脚步匆促，目光呆滞，我走向那尸身，用我的双手将他埋葬在沙土里，跪在他那小小的坟冢前，哭得停不下来。没有一丝的宽慰。我停不下来。

我不记得来到猴面包树里生活后，我还有那样悲伤地哭过。出于愤怒，有的，经常。出于挫败，一开始有的，当我还在为点火而发愁，当我就是无法掌握摩擦取火的窍门，那火花就是不肯跳动起来，或者当我，一个不具备求生技能的愚蠢的文明生物，尝试跟随狒狒和疣猪的脚印去寻找块茎，却在胃痉挛带来的痛苦扭曲中悲哀地学到，它们是仅在特殊情况下才可适用于人类消化系统的食物。我吃蝗虫——跳蝻[1]。有一回，我偶然发现了一株豪猪和狒狒错过的豺食花[2]，在欣喜若狂中，我不顾鼻子的警告，大汗淋漓地将那果实挖出，只是我尚未来得及将那可怕的、棕褐色的、带着麝香味的绿头蝇的诱饵送入口中，就呕吐了。想起那味道我就恶心。窒闷的恶心。我将长草的茎秆从保护着它们的草叶中拔取出来，咀嚼它们白嫩多汁的底部。我尝试偷鸟蛋，但我实在是个太过笨拙的攀爬者，我甚至还未够到鸟窝就摔下来了。我

---

1 跳蝻，蝗虫的幼虫，没有翅，能够跳跃，因此得名。
2 学名 *Hydnora africana*，英文俗称 Jackal food flower（豺食花），分布于非洲南部，花朵像肉质，散发着恶臭，豺和狒狒等动物会不惧恶臭吃食其果实，因此得名。

也没有敏锐的视觉，无法辨识出隐藏在稀树草原地面上的窝巢。

随着时间的推移，我变得愈发消瘦、迟钝了。我的虚弱也影响了我的视力。植物，树木，树墩，岩石，蚁丘，都在我混沌的目光中化作了蒸腾的线条，自行排列成了惊心动魄的美丽图景，而我沉浮其间，任凭它们穿透了我的梦，因为如今我大部分时间都在睡梦里，我睡在汹涌起伏的色彩上，它们在不安中寻求着安息，我并不想要控制它们，它们爱抚般地漫过我的身体，体贴地将我卷起，我沐浴在它们之中，心满意足地叹了口气。

然后我醒了，彻底清醒了，在天堂般的繁盛里像一个傻子似的游荡着。这真是一个花园！让我熟悉一下吧，这满目无人理会的荆棘和野果。让我再检查一遍吧，那淘气地躲藏起来的浆果。我必须更好地学会这个游戏。一棵榄仁树奉上了它带翼的果实。但这是给我的吗？这是一棵榄仁树吗？让我在一波又一波的热浪里，在我目光所及的陌生的丰沛里，走得再远一些吧。每一棵树都鸣响不已。这让我晕眩。这喧沸。这蓬勃。这意气风发。这疯狂色彩碎片的碰撞与蹦跳。

我发现了一种藤蔓植物，它将自己攀缘在一棵树上，有着布满厚刺的橘红色果实。这果实在我看来是那么的可爱，那么的诱人，但我确信它们是有毒的，我确信它们不适合我。让我走过它们吧。然而，我转身了，走近了，摘下了一颗果实。或许我应该试一试。我不敢。这是一颗死亡的苦涩苹果，我警告你。但是这果实是如此美好地悬挂着。我从一根毛刺处将它剥开了。果肉是淡淡的绿色。我将舌头小心地贴在那果肉之上，尝到了一种美妙的滋味。我尝了更多。我把它吃光了。好几日，我等待着自己生病。然后我欣喜若狂地跑到那棵树下，那神赐的藤蔓植物生长的地方，摘下了所有的果实，将它们吃了个精光，包括那些被鸟儿啄啃过的。我想给这果实取个名字。但我想不出任何一个合适的。我叫它"冬日里装饰了骆驼蹄树[1]也点缀了那片高地的攀缘植物的红色刺果"。我太害怕了，不敢把蜂蜜从我家树顶的蜂巢里取出，好为过冬储存些食物。我构想了很多计划，哦，是的，我想得都要发疯了，但我还是很害怕。一边挨饿，一边明知食物就在那里，却无力得到它。

挨饿，就像城中那些乞丐一般，还有其他无家可归的人，比如那些被禁足在灌木丛中的麻风病人，那些被弃之城外的天花患者，还有那些跛足的和残缺的、试图倚靠一截木头的残根苟延残喘的人，那些眼珠翻白、由一个孩子带领着四处乞求施舍的瞎子。我什么也没给。我一无所有，什么也给不了。我厌恶地看向别处。带着绝望的怒火，他们追上前来，向我伸出手臂，急不可耐地逼视着我；他们是如此的刺目，如此的肮脏，且浑身是疮。我不是我的主人，更不是他的长子，他会随手扔一把十字币在泥地里，让那些乞丐如海鸥般贪婪地蜂拥而上，争抢、哄吵出一阵滑稽的骚动。由此，一场喧哗、脏乱而癫狂的为生存而起的搏斗，便会在城郊的街道上演。我不参与。那场面就像他们随时要撕咬向彼此，啄击向彼此，直至流血方可罢休。我只是一个不情愿的旁观

---

1 学名 *Piliostigma thonningii*，英文俗称 Camel's foot tree（骆驼蹄树），分布于撒哈拉沙漠以南的非洲大陆。

者。在我早年的艰难岁月里……不可否认，我仍是被照顾着的。我可以经常吃点东西，那是真的。我头顶有棕榈叶制成的通风的屋顶，虽然在雨季里漏水严重，从未被修葺过。我还有几件棉布衣裳，日子久了有些破旧，但足以遮挡我赤裸的身体。我可以活下去。不可否认。当然可以。尽管如此，我在沉闷枯燥中四处奔忙，我用苦工累活勉强维持着生计，我在单调乏味里任凭日子蹉跎。不可否认，那也是生活。我第二任主人手下的一个奴隶女孩与我成为了挚友，我们尽自己所能地帮助对方。她更愿意浣衣，我则是做饭，我们便不理会其他奴隶女孩，将工作分配成了适合我们的方式，尽管这样会遭到她们的谩骂，我们知道，就算她们向我们的主人抱怨也将一无所获，因为对他而言，我们全都是一样的劳动力。我们俩拿他开了许多有趣的玩笑。我们讨论他那些恶心的习惯，详尽到最小的细节，比如他如何拨弄他自己，或是在床事进行到一半时起身去外面解手。他大概是患上了尿失禁吧。说起他和他那个目中无人的妻子，我的挚友与我总会爆发出阵阵大笑。那个又老又枯的女人，那个又老又不育的女人。

我们的孩子在贫苦中生得圆胖而苗壮，我们也从不区分她的孩子和我的孩子。她将我的孩子背在背上，而我背着她的。她为我的孩子哺乳，而我哺乳她的。我是她的助产士，她亦是我的。一个孩子，对我们来说就是一个孩子，一个我们臂弯里温暖的小身子，一张寻觅着乳头的垂涎的小嘴，这一个胖乎乎的小脖子同另一个的小脖子一样可爱，这一个的长牙期同另一个的长牙期一样恼人。我们带回贝壳给他们嬉耍，编出一根芦苇绳让他们蹦跳。是那样一个温暖的小家庭啊，我们和那些幼童们。轮到我做饭时，我会偷取一些椰子汁带回给他们；而她会带他们去河边浣衣的石滩，让他们在那儿无所顾忌地调皮捣蛋。是那样一种令人心满意足的、美好的充实之感啊，如此巨大地弥补了我们那褴褛不堪的生活。

她比我年长几岁，经历过我所经历的一切。

她与我都经历了如下往事：

年幼时被掳，还未受割礼，也正因此才会被搜寻、被抓捕。在一群尖叫着的女人和老人之间，在一堆或反抗至死，或来不及逃跑的健壮男性的尸体之间，在着火的茅草屋、倒塌的部落栅栏、破碎的御谷罐子之间，在茂密却无法提供一处藏身之所的草丛里，在某个想要救你的人将你拉到一棵大树背后的徒劳尝试里。全都是徒劳。这是一声徒劳的惊恐尖叫。这是一片广袤森林里的一场小小骚动。它所引起的关注并不会多过一帮猿猴的喧哗。这短暂的干扰过后，鸟儿们会继续啁啾。犹豫的紫羚会踏入开阔的平地，谨慎地闻一闻那灰烬、废墟、血腥和惊恐汗水的气味，然后向后转身，悄无声息。下雨了。淤土和泥浆留了下来，腐烂的黑色池塘，是一段沉没的历史。暴风雨的叹息多么沉重。树林的摇摆多么盛大。然后太阳升起了。星宿移转了。

我的朋友告诉我：她是如何第一次看见了大海，她有多害怕那面蓝色的水墙，那片海浪席卷而来又轰然崩塌的海岸。

我告诉她：我也是在这儿第一次看见了大海，但我一点儿也不害怕。我径直跑向了它。

我的朋友告诉我：那个后来她随之生活的男人对她很友善。

41

他就像一个父亲。

我告诉她：我们遇见的是同一个人。他在市场上买下最年轻的女孩，破开她们，就像破开幼嫩的豆荚。他是体贴的，会允许你在他的屋檐下生下你的第一胎，然后他便会将你卖掉。

他买下最年轻的女孩。他破开那柔软的薄膜，就像破开一个水疱。而你是那个血流不止的人。你屏住呼吸，忍着疼痛，也忍着那无疑会令人迷醉的什么东西。

我告诉她：他向我允诺了一个礼物。他温柔地将我拉近，拉向他坐着的地方，直到我站到他两腿的中间。他亲自褪去了我的衣裳，让他的手在我的身体上轻柔地漫游着。然后他指了指他的枕头，上面绣着漂亮的长豆角，镶着珍珠母嵌花，他允诺只要我乖，他便送给我这样一个枕头。好的，我会乖的。他宅子里的那些女人已经教过我该如何行事、如何应答；我点了点头。他很着急，几乎喘不上气来。

我拿到了我的礼物；你呢？我问我的朋友。

拿到了，她说。

我们的枕头如今在哪儿呢？我们大笑起来。

我的那个对我来说太大了。我的脖子还太短。

我的也是，我说。

你想它吗？

不。

他还在买最年轻的女孩吗？

他死了。

不！什么时候？

很久以前——很久以前了。他的心脏停止了跳动。

真遗憾，他死了。他其实是个非常善良的人。

是的。

是的，他是。真的。有趣又善良。而且我们真的可以待在他身边，一直到第一次分娩后。

哦，我那时真是最甜美的小母亲，我记得。整整九个月，我抚弄着日渐隆起的腹部，勤勤恳恳地帮忙做着准备，虽笨手笨脚，却非常乐意，比如含下一枚罗望子的果核又将其吐出。一个做母亲的小孩，那就是我。从我稚嫩的口中，发出了那成阴结子的妇人才有的腐朽笑声。自那时起，我完全熟落了，自那时起，我知晓了一切。我怀着我自己。我已不堪重负，我已不再能够，我从内部开始了颤痛，我变得越来越……我是如何坐在那海滩上，迷失在我的幻梦中，玩弄着我的贝壳，我的黑色贝壳和白色贝壳……那些女人待我是多么的好啊。她们就像照料一件小饰品一样照料着我。我咳嗽得厉害的那段时间，她们中的一个专门去市井摆摊的妇人那里，幸运地为我买来灌木柳根[1]，喂我服下那汤药。如果我抱怨一句头疼，哪怕是最轻微的，她们也会逼我喝下一碗角荚叶汁[2]，说角荚叶对治疗胃疼有好处，说头疼就是由胃疼引起

---

1 学名 *Combretum erythrophyllum*，英文俗称 Bush willow（灌木柳），分布于非洲南部的河岸边，传统用于治疗咳嗽等疾病。

2 学名 *Diplorhynchus condylocarpon*，英文俗称 Horn-pod tree（角荚树），分布于非洲南部，传统用于治疗发烧、头痛等疾病。

的。我被很好地照顾着、围绕着、守护着，话语变得熟悉可辨了，我感到快乐，只是仍然太过笨拙……然后，我感到所有人都得从我眼前让开。

没有人能、也没有人会告诉我，当那孩子的脑袋从我的身体里露出来时，我在呼唤着谁。那是一声喊向我出生之地的尖声呼叫。它在那儿回荡着。它在那儿回荡着。

我的孩子是那么的贪婪。他只要咿呀一声，我便会喂他奶水。很快他就重得我几乎背不动了。对我的主人而言，我已然不存在了。已然有另一个小东西填补了我的位置。我没有和她说话。

在海边的小广场上，我被第二次出售了，而早在那时，那些残破不堪的蓖麻树就已经伫立在那儿了。我是二手的东西。我是一个已经损坏的玩物。我那襁褓中的婴孩与我被分别标价、分开出售。只是玩物而已。有用，当然。我的主人觉得他卖亏了。一个我不认识的人抢走了我的孩子。什么叫被宠坏了？另一个人检查了我的头部，我的口腔，我的骨盆，我的胳膊和腿。他很犹疑。什么地方歪斜了？一个商人遣派一个代理人来购买与一只手上的手指一般多的奴隶。它哪儿漏了？裂隙在哪儿？它怎么就粗制滥造了？太阳在我头顶炙烤。我就要晕眩了。女性的、男性的日常用品。一个接一个。只剩下我了。换这一只腿站着。换另一只腿站着。啃咬着我的指甲。什么东西不见了？什么东西被扭曲了？我再也看不见我的孩子了。我猛地转身，什么也没有看见。我的内心在惊声尖叫。但凡我可以切开我的肚子，扯出我的内脏。我寻找着一把刀。但凡我可以将我自己从这身体里啐出去。我的心

44

脏凝固了。谁在买下我?

可恨的人。你同我一样令人憎恶。来吧,在我体内点燃你的恶疾。我是邪恶,是危险。我是干涸的猿猴的乳房,是新鲜、湿滑的公牛的眼珠,是撕剥下来的人皮,是致命的、带着吸盘大口的海蛞蝓的毒液。我是仇恨和仇恨的伪装。我是畸形的。我的血液里匍匐着一条蛇。我饮下我自己的鲜血。我在昏厥中踢蹬。我挣扎。

男人们来了,像女孩们一样唱着歌,以驱除鬼魂,但那火焰就是不愿燃起。全城的廷比拉乐手都聚集于此了,他们围绕着我,犹如水声的叮当乐响围绕着我,仿佛一片水之星空,那星星滴落下来,悲凉的星辰的露水,使我感到清凉,它们抛洒下来,浇灭了我的叛乱。可若我不再是我的孩子,我又会是什么呢?一个受苦之人,又怎会感到忏悔?

最后,是戈拉弓琴乐手。轻叩那单根的弦,一连串沉思之音便会逐个从琴弦中流淌下来,那是一种连续不断的叩击声,每一声都在顷刻间坠落大地,化作沙尘,而后便一直埋葬在那沙土里,永不发芽。坠落,坠落,乐音就这般滑落下来,坠入深深的沙土里。是所有植物的主根都未曾触及的深处。

是蚯蚓的王国都未曾触及的深处。这就够了。它已被埋葬。它已然终结。我被挑中了,显然是为了一笔可笑的金额,被处理掉了。戈拉弓琴乐手停止了弹奏,把小木棍塞进皮带,将戈拉弓琴背在肩上,离去了。

那一日,我的新主人还买下了一只光彩照人的雄鸡,头顶和

45

喉咙有着明艳的黄色羽毛，脖颈是紫褐色的，背部醒目地点缀着黄褐色的斑点，而翅膀是华丽的墨绿，翅尖还泛着铜锈之彩，胸膛则是一抹闪闪发光的黑灰与金绿，一只神采奕奕、啼声响亮的雄鸡，和一个我。

那只雄鸡在院子里随心所欲地走动着，也随心所欲地侵扰着所有的母鸡。清晨他用鸣啼声将我们叫醒，但夜里他也用鸣啼声向我们预报好天气，然后天就下起了倾盆大雨。我们用锅盆威胁他。雄鸡，雄鸡，我们真想把你吃掉。雄鸡，雄鸡，飞上我们棚屋的屋脊，将白昼啼成血色吧。你的主人对他的鸡群真是吝啬。我说的是我们共同的主人。你和我们，雄鸡，雄鸡，你的鸣啼和粪便和我们的话语，我们的排泄物和分泌物，我们的孩子，我们的红木豆种子[1]和我们身上的衣裳，这座大宅和那座装满香料和老鼠的仓库，全都是他的。这些厨具，餐具，我们的虱子，那些蟑螂，那些墙壁缝隙里的蚂蚁，还有这座大宅周边的土地，全都是他的。我的劳作是他的。我的睡眠是他的。我的到来和我的离去。我的汗水。我的头发。我的脚底板。那些蚂蚁可以躲起来。那些蟑螂也可以。还有那些老鼠。但我不可以。我不知道我可以躲去哪儿。你和我，雄鸡，我们被困住了。

当我怀上我的第三胎时，我拜访了一位堕胎术士。我的朋友阻止了我。生活欺骗了我，生活是有毒的蜜糖，我疲惫地抱怨着。

---

1 学名 *Afzelia quanzensis*，英文俗称 Pod mahogany（红木豆），分布于非洲南部，是豆科的一种树，种子可做成项链或工艺品。

她扔掉了我买回的那份诱人的、散发着清香的紫罗兰树根。

你拿什么付的钱？她问。

我自己。

她训斥了我。婊子，她这样叫我，这却使我发笑。

如果我真是婊子，应该很有钱了。

走开！她训斥道。

是啊，我不耐烦地戏谑道：世界就是主人的眼睛看得见的地方。

有一天。哦，是的，有一天。走到主人的眼睛看得见的最远处了，但我还想走得更远一些。有一天。

我的下一任主人，我的恩人，显然拥有更为广阔的世界观，从莽林深处延伸直至大海的海平线。他与采金人、伐木工协商，沿海岸线运输货物，也通过与那迷人的异乡人的合作——说到那个异乡人，我，一个俗鄙的奴隶女孩，心甘情愿地为他所俘虏——将事业扩张到了海洋上。

已经很远了，但我还想走得更远一些。我对远方有了一种渴望。

今天，在我的猴面包树里，我仍然被四面八方的地平线所囚禁。一个人是否永远无法冲破一条地平线？生活如此阴险，好似有毒的蜜糖。我走了那么远的路，还想着或许我应该将所有经过我眼前的风景打包收好、围成一圈，它们必定会带来更为宽广的视野，想着或许我走得愈远，这视野就会愈加宽广。而今一切都萎缩进了一棵树所能界定的范畴。

这里有静滞。这里有虚空和手工艺品。这里有关怀——我犹豫着是否该称其为崇拜——来自那些不想被我发现的小矮人们。这里还有礼物，一些鹿肉、酸李子和食用菌菇。我那戳有一个干净小洞的鸵鸟蛋壳破裂了，便被替换了新的。我收藏的珠子数量也增加了。我还获得了一些衣物。系着我的皮毛围裙，披着我以跳兔[1]骨头为装饰的披风，戴着我亲手串起的黑色和绿色珠子，还有我长串的鸵鸟蛋壳碎片，我感觉很好，我感觉很体面。它们是代表了新生活的衣物，我穿着它们走遍了猴面包树的远近四方，从未敢真正走远，因为来时路上所遭遇之事，我只会遭遇一次，而去路不论何去何从，将要面临之事（我苦涩地意识到），都不是我以一己之身可以应对的。

我是一个抑郁之人，但我不会停止寻找——当长子向他提出那个邀约时，我那永远在航行、永远在旅途、永远迷人的异乡人这样回应道。我愿意去勘查。我愿意去探索。我对人性并无热情，但我不会停止尝试，亦不会停止寻找。

不，我不愿诅咒他。他应该知道除了跟随他，我别无选择，因为我不是一个追寻者，我只是被动地从一处境遇转移至另一处境遇的人，而不论是谁买下我，他都得照管我，且这一次，他也会照管我的。有时，当一个人的所有物也很愉悦，很有利，很轻松。我只是某个人身边的某个人。

---

1 跳兔，一种生活于非洲稀树草原上的啮齿动物，体形较大，后肢发达，跳跃能力极强，因此得名。

甚至在幼子亡故之前，长子就已经在酝酿这个异想天开的计划，并且已经开始为一次全新的探险做准备了。从未有人听说过这样的事。这城市的居民绝非无知之徒，各种各样来自海洋和内陆的消息经常传至他们耳中。作为精明的商贾，他们对任何空穴来风之事，任何无端猜测之事，任何在他们深思熟虑的观点看来不过是诗人的闲言碎语之事，总是抱持着怀疑的态度。未知的幻梦。异国的诱惑。知识的游戏。为满足如此这般的需求，这城市孕育着它的边缘人群，比如那些用词微妙的文字艺术家，那些让孩童们张大了嘴巴聆听的广场说书人——他们的娱乐价值，包括那些文字艺术家的，都随他们能否成功令听众和读者感到心潮澎湃或枯燥乏味而上升或下降着。是啊，他们，一群五彩斑斓的疯子。而如果一个富人的继承人想要实现一件愚蠢的浪漫之事，想要证明一条陆上通道应当存在，那便意味着人们有机会在他离开时角逐猎物，意味着他父亲如此小心谨慎地发起、维系的商贸往来，现如今可以被任何人随意地攫取、接管，只要那人足够狡猾、足够快。没有人指望次子会加入这场争夺，因为他早已在他那利润颇丰的妓院产业里安定下来了，而这背后，是他在他父亲逝世前几年就已经开始管理的黄金交易所发散出的光芒与显耀。

　　然后就发生了幼子的不幸事故，那一个无忧无虑的人儿。这座大宅承受了如此之多的灾难。他父亲刚一离世，长子与那个恶毒的未婚女儿就发生了争执。她怒气冲冲地离开了家。如今她那干瘪的灵魂是靠着复仇的心思滋养的。它们涨满了她的整个存在。从清晨到深夜，她密谋、策划着要如何让长子跪倒在地，就算那意味着她和她已婚的姐妹，还有她的两个兄弟全都要破产。她脸上有一种捕猎者的神色。她身上有一种癌变者的气息。不论她接触了什么，她都会用她的毒液和她呼吸里的狡诈将其污染。她已被怨憎腐蚀了。

我尽量避开她的气息，怀着柔软的心贴近了幼子——我已经被遗赠给他了。他很好，很友善，对奴隶阉人、奴隶女孩，还有其他一切他所继承的职责一点儿也不感兴趣，总是带着迷人的微笑和随意的问候，悠然自得地走过。

不，我不相信那个故事，不相信他会因为对爱情失望而去寻死。一个像他那般熟悉那片珊瑚礁的人，怎会轻易被绊倒——奴隶们，还有聚集在大宅里的哀悼者们，彼此间窃窃私语着。两场死亡，从新月到满月。一个人的生命有多长？从一次眨眼到一次闪电的眨眼。从一颗愈发饱满的水珠到一次滴落。一个人的生命就是这么长了。从移动棋子到将军。然后头被摇晃着，手被攥紧了。是的，生命就是这么长了。然后小树被砍倒了，航程很短，小船倾覆了，沉没了，哀悼者们虔诚地做完了所有这样的场合该做的无稽之事。

不，他不是那种会一意孤行地踩上石鱼[1]的人。或许是其中一个同伴呼喊了他的名字，要他看看珊瑚礁外那片紫色深海水域中的一群银鲛，他抬起头，在摇摆之间，踩到了锋利的珊瑚礁的顶部，从而失去了平衡。这是最有可能的解释。这也是他那些同伴

---

1 石鱼，少数几种有毒海生鱼类的统称，生活于岩礁、珊瑚或泥底。

们所说的。他们带回了他的尸身。他躺在担架上，在死亡之中也仍然修长、美丽，与清晨走出家门，去往那偏远海湾捕鱼时一般无二。而他们只能眼睁睁地看着，看着他被带回海滩后如何失控地倒在地上，踢蹬着双腿，看着泡沫如何从他的嘴角涌出，然后，看着他的身体如何变得僵硬，如何在那帮助他从生命过渡至死亡的短暂而疯狂的插曲过后，再度恢复往昔的光彩，再度，在死后也如同生前一般完美无瑕、完好如初。一个自得其乐的年轻人，我想，以他那独善其身的性格魅力，大概从未体验过赤诚相待的友情，或不共戴天的敌意。

我细数着我因他的殒命而失去的，还有得到的。无数次了，未来何去何从，悬于一念之间。我焦灼地等待着。因为我识得这份恐惧。他与我不是老朋友了吗？若有任何人曾真心待我，那个人便是他，或许因为他已经成为了我的一部分，伴随着我的心跳，伴随着我的呼吸，因为他就坐在我的眼白里，藏在我手指的颤抖中。我的同伴，在我被迫行进的路上，远道而来、与我结识，大大方方、无拘无束地陪伴在我身畔，将他那令人窒息的气息吹拂到我的脸上——此刻他又到来了。

我恩人离世后的第二天，浸泡在爱意与困惑中的我，起身去寻找我的异乡人了。那时恐惧也尾随着我，恐惧与渴望驱策着我前进；还有不确定性，而那个我唯一可以依靠的确定，引领着我走入了大街小巷，那里，霉菌令墙壁绽放出斑斓的伤疤，一扇扇大门歪斜而腐烂地悬挂着，然后我认出了一栋建筑，我认出了一些背着篮子进进出出的奴隶。那是我前任主人的香料仓库。我决定去拜访我的挚友，我，还有我华丽的丝绸长袍，我新学会的快速的说话方式，我做作的姿态。我就那样格格不入地站在那里，带着一丝尴尬，被拘禁在我自己的矫揉造作里。

她双腿交叉，坐在一个荒废的茅草屋前，用一根小木棍戳划着沙土。母鸡和小鸡与从前一样在院子里来回翻啄着，绕着茅草屋和大宅，绕着那些芒果树，树下的落果散发出阵阵酸腐的气味。她似乎不介意那一地的鸡屎与污秽。一个赤裸的婴儿在她身旁爬动着，上唇还黏着些鼻涕，正要把肮脏的沙土塞进嘴里。我问她那是不是她的孩子。她没有回答。她只是盯着我。我想要抱起那个孩子，但想想还是算了。我琢磨着我能给他些什么。我的朋友盯着我。我离去时，仍能感觉到那尖锐的盯着我的目光。有人扔了什么东西，砸中了我。我转过身，看见她捡起一把沙子正扔向我。我喊了她的名字。那个婴儿也被沙子砸到了，先是高兴地笑了，然后便开始大哭。我走开了，我做到了。留那个婴儿愤怒地大哭着。

回来的路上，我又经过了那个屠宰场，还有那附近高耸的、努力不去看任何东西的棕榈树。我走过了市场摆摊的妇人，那个奴隶广场，那些被拖上海滩的小船，它们的桅杆像滑稽的触须，向后弯折着。我看见了那唯一一艘在海浪中摇摆着的三角帆船，我冲它再一次喊出了我对那个异乡人的尖声询问，也再一次看见了那些回应着"没有"的手势。我转身，返回了那座高大、阴沉而安静的宅子，一束束的茉莉花排满了花园的围墙，为死者献祭着它们的花香。

我的恩人是如何得到他的财富的？我曾问过异乡人这个问

题，当宴席散去，只剩他与我两个人时。我抚摸着他额头上一个个豌豆状的疤痕。我的手指滑过它们。后来，我们变成了两个疯狂的拓荒者，而此刻，是两个相爱的人。

如何得到的？我又问了一次，在一只蕉鹃虐人的鸣叫间隙。我的手指滑过他的嘴唇，那是无花果一般的紫。他变得多么枯瘦啊，瘦得叫我吃惊。他的面颊是那般的凹陷。他闭着眼睛，躺在一个满是柔软而腐败的落叶的空洞里。

多管闲事，他想让我安静下来。我还在不停追问。

是你这样的人让他成为了城中最有权势的人，异乡人随后答道。事实上，你应该感到受宠若惊才对。你的恩人是一个无与伦比的鉴赏家，他鲜少购买品味低级的东西。就你的例子而言，他便是绝对正确的。看，他向我指出，你的身材比例有一种罕见的对称之美。

他想抚摸我。我抽回了我的手臂。

他是如何得到他的财富的？

再一次，异乡人用含糊其辞的解释避开了我的问题，说是美学意义上的考量引领着我的恩人，一个商人，去追求极致，追求一种美丽外表与内在本质之间的平衡，也是这些考量引领着他，让他将手下的奴隶看作一种艺术收藏，他会以投资的眼光精心采购他们，有时也通过教育使他们拥有良好修养后单独出售，以此获利，就像他对我所做的那样。他继而向我指出，我的恩人对我的品质表现出了非同寻常的欣赏，如此非同寻常，以至于他从未打算将我转手，甚至允许我在他临终前陪伴左右。

那不是他变得富有的方式，我反驳道。他一定是已经拥有了一大笔钱，才能负担得起这样一个爱好。这个男人是如何获得实现其爱好的财力的？

如果我说他是一个强盗呢？

那他就是一个强盗。

一个奴隶劫匪？

每个人都是某样东西的劫匪。我只认识劫匪。

我也是吗？

我如何知晓？

倘若我也是呢？

那你就是。

我劫掠钱财而非人，异乡人说。我在公海上打劫，在我被劫之前，在我变成其他人的战利品之前，先下手为强。

战利品，就像我，我说。

是的。

我的恩人也在内陆抓捕我们吗？

不，异乡人大笑起来，那不是一个人变得富有的方式。犯不上为那些麻烦、那点利润付出那么多。还不如做一个象牙猎人，因为你的商品是死的，运输起来更加方便。而人，恰恰相反，会大批死亡，需要被喂养，还会试图逃跑，你花费在卫兵、食物、武器上的开销将会是巨大的。人的损失就相当于资本的损失。不，只有特殊类型的人才会成为奴隶猎人，且这也意味着，你面临着反过来被杀害、被劫掠的危险。这才是你恩人事业的起点。他的密探和信使遍布各地，而他会埋伏在海岸线附近某个地方，伏击经过的奴隶猎人和他们押送的队伍，趁着他们所有人，无论俘虏或卫兵，都已经精疲力竭、无力反抗之时。那是他年轻时候的事了。他积攒了足够的钱财，建造起了他的宅邸，于是他便可以作为一位有名望的杰出市民，心平气和地生活在里面，彻底远离盗寇之事，专注于黄金、龙涎香和木材，专注于铜矿——城中的富人们赋予其比黄金更高的价值—— 还有专注于他的爱好。

语毕，异乡人闭上眼睛躺着，沉默着，仿佛是说话已经耗尽了他的力气。

我因屈辱而备感无助，但压抑着自己不哭出来，或者，只是不那么明显、清晰地哭出来。占有与爱意是相互诅咒的两个概念。我不想成为他或其他人，其他所有我生命中出现过的人，从我最渺远记忆里的茅草屋，母亲，那片氤氲而闷热的森林盆地给予我的安全感，到那个买下我、夺去我贞操的好色之徒，还有那个让我咬紧牙关、劳作煎熬的香料商人；我不想成为他们所有人眼中的我，他们所有人，包括那个带给我父亲般慈爱的恩人，还有眼前这个人，这个我以我全身心的力量去拥抱着，允许他一次又一次地进入我，好让我完完全全地被他占有，让我在完完全全、浑身颤栗的充实、饱和与满足之中，漂浮着，心醉神迷着，亦使他心满意足地成为我的一部分，只属于我的一部分的男人——就算是他，方才也那般头头是道地描述着我，将我看作是一个得到了豁免权的物品似的，就算是他，我也与他们所想的完全不同，与他们任何人所想的都完全不同，我拒绝所有的观点，所有的观察和所有我生命中出现过的女人的训斥，他们知道我是谁吗，他们又知道些什么呢。

我还记得那些诗人关于女人的嘲讽之词，但当时我并没有往心里去：说实话吧，我加入了那所谓精于世故的轻蔑之流，这种肤浅的色欲表现并不会击中我痛处，我不觉得它卑劣下流，因而也不必当场谴责。徒劳。徒劳而无谓地，我参与其中。穿着奢华的衣料——它好似温柔的爱抚将我包裹，踩着山羊革凉鞋，我很快就掌握了所有施展魅惑的小技艺，融入了那些谈话与欢笑。我能够感觉到，自己正如花朵般绽放着。我毫无保留地大笑。我将笑声向上、向外传送了出去，让它为我摘下一枝野生栗子花的淡紫色双星，插戴在我的头发上。

我的恩人微笑着。他觉得这场景很美。当我用手臂环抱他的时候，就像在保护一个孩子。真是疯狂，明明他才是我的所有者。但事实确是如此。他把头依偎在我的肩膀上，就像一个孩子，还带着一个孩童的纯真。然后，眨眼之间，他就变了个样，变得比我更加成熟睿智了。他训斥了我，接手开始了爱抚。当他与我交合时，他既是父亲又是儿子，而我，既是母亲又是一个值得信赖的女儿。我们在一起认识了世间万象，所有的一切的事物，我们再无所求了。直到后来，他变得如此羸弱，如此令人哀怜的消瘦、萎靡。随着高烧愈来愈频繁地袭来，他几乎不再出现在宴会厅里，只是一直躺在他房间凉爽的棕榈睡席上。午后室外的阵雨，傍晚携来的凉意，随之而来的夜晚捎来清亮而闪耀的繁星，仿佛额外的嘉奖，还有泼洒在他身上的白色月光——所有这些，都无法改变他的心境。这房间的每一个角落，都闪动着死亡之眼的微光。

有时，他会心不在焉地凝视着远方的大海，婉拒我们中的一个递上的，装在一个精致小瓷碗里的苦合欢豆荚[1]的萃取物。同样地，他也放弃了城中最好的医生开出的药方，他用沙哑的声音简单地致了谢，但没有使用它们。

在我完美的臂弯里，他死去了，躺在我完美的大腿之间，依偎着我完美的胸部，他与我，父亲，母亲，孩子，主人，有价值的艺术品，仆人，爱人。

这些事情已经过去了太久，我已不愿再去恨他。我已没有时间去憎恨任何人、筹划任何一种复仇。这片稀树草原威胁着我们。我回过头看着我的异乡人，在这漫漫无尽的、追寻一片红色沙漠中一座城市之幻影的旅途上，我也发现了他温柔的本性。从前我允许自己被他的机智所吸引，而在那段日子里，我学会了欣赏他的仁爱与好施。当时的环境自然不适合那些交织着轻松的论点与反驳的深入交谈，那些日子里，我们甚至很少在一起说话。我想是围拢着我们的寂静太过强大了，它迫使我们尊重它。不，这么想真是愚蠢，因为事实上，我们常常是疲累到无力开始一段谈话。我无法否认，我们的境况很不好。我们拖沓着脚步，一个接一个地穿过炎热的地域，用我们疲惫的目光丈量着去到下一个阴凉之地、下一个树荫之慰藉的距离，并且虽然明知我们负担不起，却还是在这样的树荫下，逗留了越来越长的时间。就像此刻。

---

1 学名 *Albizia amara*，中文称苦合欢，英文俗称 Bitter false-thorn（苦假刺），豆荚宽大，成熟后呈金黄色，分布于非洲东部、南部及印度等地，传统用于治疗疟疾、肺炎等多种疾病。

我们交换了一个致歉的眼神。我握住他的手，将他的手指压在我的嘴唇上。

　　我们得出发了。这样不好。我们得下定决心。我们想到了那座诱人的城市，以及所有在那里等待着我们的事物。我们在那些猎人提供的少量信息里填入我们的想象，我们愈是深入内陆，愈是远离家园，丛林就愈显荒无人烟，身体就愈发迟缓而勉强，我们也就愈加丰富地装扮起我们幻想出的画面。我们没有意识到，我们已经开始假装心中所愿一定存在了。当我们提起那座城市时，仿佛它已是一个既成事实，而我们很快就将抵达，只不过是一日又一日，只不过是几日又几日，然后我们就会看见它，卧伏于地平线上，在一片纯净的玫瑰色水晶筑成的群山脚下，平整，闪耀。

　　我梦见过那玫瑰色的水晶。我的梦都被玫瑰色的水晶给填满了。在那嶙峋突兀的碎块之间，我几乎无法移动。我梦境的地面是玫瑰色的水晶，还有我梦境的石柱和天花板。我从这玫瑰色的水晶之中向外凝望，望着世界的其他地方。我退回这玫瑰色的水晶之中，心满意足地打着瞌睡。

　　不过首先，我们得穿过沼泽，那些猎人是这么说的。

　　我越是强烈地渴望见到那座玫瑰色水晶山脚下的城市，就越想推迟见到那片阻隔在我们之间的沼泽。因为我不相信传闻所描述的，在那清澈如晨露的水面上，目光所及遍是白与绿交织的睡莲，金色芦苇上攀附着仅有一丁点儿大的红色和银色青蛙，而木舟压弯长草之时，会有蜘蛛从它们闪闪发光的蛛网里垂落下来。

　　在我们离开大海时，我已经见识过沼泽的样子。我能感觉到它扑在我脸上的闷热空气，它钻入我鼻孔的刺鼻气味。它那无尽的绿，一直延伸进围拢着我的雾霭里。我听见一声吸溜声和一声冒泡声，看见鳄鱼的口鼻躺在淤青似的泥巴里。我看见蚊子萦绕在水洼上的迷雾中。我看见弹涂鱼蠕动出半个身子，肆无忌惮地注视着我。而最可怕的是那种安静，我依稀能从过往的记忆里辨认出那种安静。那是埋伏在一段惊惶的旅途上等待我的压迫感。那段旅途已是如此渺远，我几乎无法陈述它。但是我认得这种安静。它是一种至高无上、辽远广袤的安静，它覆没了蛙群呱噪的鸣叫。这安静是有分量的，它会偃息你对生命的欲求，它会在一个漫长得好似永无止境的日子过后，试图将你按压进泥沼里，再在黑夜羽翼的扑闪下，将你掩埋。是这不可计量的无垠之感，令你的额头沁出了黄色的汗珠，扰乱了你的呼吸吗？我认得它。还有恐惧，一种黏腻的、令你喉咙紧锁的恐惧。我认得这种恐惧。我还能以何种方式再次体会到它呢？我认得嗜杀、孤立、愚昧、虐待，还有迷惘的恐惧。我认得他。

这恐惧是空气的一部分。它一路悬浮直至海岸，直至那座我几任主人生活过的城市，那座最初不过是一些简陋的棚屋和栅栏、一些无人照管的羊群和粪便满溢的沟渠的城市，那座我被掳往的繁忙的商贸城市。

我已经尝试想象过那种存在方式了，那种不作为任何人的所有物的存在方式，但这于我并不容易。倘若我可以在我的故土之上成长起来，我会是什么样子的呢？我会不会，比方说，换一种方式走路、坐下、站立？我会不会拥有其他类型的友情，接受全然不同的观点？我会不会信仰宗教？我会不会有一位丈夫，和一些只为他而生的孩子？一些，我可以抚养直至他们能够自食其力的孩子？突然我想到：我本可以当祖母的。我本可以坐在一院子驯化了的珍珠鸡之间，看孙辈们围簇着我玩耍嬉闹。

蓦然我意识到：在这里，在这座城市里，我永远不可能成为祖母了。在这里，在我的孩子长到与我的髋部一般高以前，我尚可以发挥母亲的功能，但那以后，我便失去了所有的发言权。他们从我的生活里消失了。对我而言，没有延续，没有过去与未来的连接。到来与结束，都只是一个定局，一如黑暗是永恒不变的。如果它是死亡，我还可以拥有某种确定。而现在，我不知道。

那些被我带入人世的孩子，现如今都在哪儿呢？倘若我在某个地方偶然撞见他们，我如何能够认出他们来呢？我能够认出他们来吗？有时，我会专注地凝视着一些年幼的面孔，在他们的容貌，他们的声音，他们的举止，他们的姿态中寻找我自己的影子——假设我的孩子们全都在这里，我痛苦地想着，而没有被卖去其他城市和国家服侍人。我想知道我是否可以凭借母亲的本能辨认出我自己的孩子，不论我们在何处，以何种方式相遇。我会知道那是他吗？我能否立即感受到一种穿透我身体的相遇的喜悦，渴望将他拥入怀中，小心谨慎的确认已变得毫无必要，因为我体内那一份甜蜜而心酸的知悉，一种比太阳更温暖的确定感的来源，就像是母亲本应拥有的那样？毕竟，母亲是深不可测的。

这样的事情尚未发生。我也从未听说过这样的先例。但我仍然继续观察着稚气的面孔，倾听着稚气的谈话。

在我恩人的大宅里，每当他已婚的女儿或他的次子携配偶和孩子们前来拜访时，我的职责之一，就是逗他的孙儿们开心。这样的拜访次数频繁，他们会随时在没有事先告知的情况下到来，而我也颇为欢喜。我喜欢看那些小人儿大口吞下甜点，我喜欢让他们在我身上不知疲倦地爬来爬去，我也喜欢给他们讲故事；但我和年长一些的男孩女孩们就相处得不太好了。与他们在一起时，我总会感到异常的尴尬，好像我会有意识地去感知他们的态度和喜好，好像我那欠佳的直觉会在我的行为举止中表现得尤为明显，好像我会暴露自己的困惑，甚至好像我会害怕他们在我身上察觉出某种缺陷，某种过度的友好与亲切都无法掩饰的缺陷。所以我与他们始终保持着距离。幸运的是，他们中的一些已经拥有了属于自己的奴隶阉人或奴隶女孩，会专门照顾他们的需求，而那些随同前来照顾小孩子们的奴隶女孩，就只想把她们的工作和麻烦留给我。我是乐在其中的。我乐于擦拭肮脏的小嘴，倾听糟糕的指控，为小小的受伤和大大的惊吓寻找安慰的言词。嘿！嘿！我叫喊着——不能把手指放进鹦鹉笼子里！哦，不！我搂住那小小的身体，直到他们开心地笑出来，笑得上气不接下气。

每每被我的恩人撞见我做这些事，我都会感到很不自在。他微笑着。这与我想要为他成为的自己全然不符，这也肯定无益于我在他卧房中展现出的自信。我总会突兀地停止嬉戏，等待着，低着头，等待他的离开。

总的来说，我无法抱怨这个地方，还有这座大宅给予我的空间。我认为自己是一个幸运的、享有特殊地位的人，虽然没有权利，但也并非全然没有选择。我可以用我自己的经历证明，不是所有奴隶都能像这座大宅里的奴隶一般，受到这么好的照顾。诚然，我们睡在一间外屋里，但它与主宅一样，是用石头砌造的。我们的地板上没有铺地毯。但我们睡在厚实的椰棕睡席上。我们的房间里没有精雕细刻的矮桌台与红铜水壶。但与我前任主人那两间奴隶棚屋的邋遢、窒闷相比，与那酸臭的泥巴地和被风撕破的屋顶大洞相比，我当然可以认为自己是幸运的。再加上我的特殊地位——这一点我很清楚应该如何维持——以及这座大宅的整洁、宽敞，我真的没有什么可抱怨的了。

感谢我拥有主人最宠爱之人的地位，可以不经允许地自由出入屋顶露台。闲暇时，我喜欢在那里度过日落时光。在那样的时刻里，我会远远望着从绚烂云层中铺洒下来的、笼罩着内陆的霞光——我就来自那里，而另一边，是渐渐晦暗下去的大海——它曾经召唤过我。我会站在明与暗交界的完美平衡里，在无可避免的转瞬即逝中，像一个幽灵般遁入疾速降临的黑暗。光线标记出了我平静、完整的轮廓。一只狗吠叫起来，我方才从我的沉思中醒来，深深地吸了一口气。咸风的空气，小龙虾的气味，大马士革玫瑰的气味，丁香和蚕豆的气味。我还能闻到初升星辰的气味。因为这个原因，我不能理解为何我不能留下我的孩子。因为这个原因，我不得不接受长大的孩子是我所不可得的。

因为这个原因，我感到宽慰，我尚未再次怀上一个孩子。

也感谢我没有被遗赠给长子，他的天性与他父亲迥然不同，那些虐待的传言都并非只是传言。我就亲眼见过他手下一些奴隶的肩膀上有开裂、红肿的鞭痕，还偷偷地为他们料理过伤口。长子似乎是将自己的怒火全都发泄在男人身上了——事实上他手下也没有女奴。倒不是说他在他父亲家里需要女奴，只是我仍然觉得很奇怪。我们这些奴隶女孩，对这个性格乖戾、手中永远持着藤鞭的年轻男人而言，几乎是不存在的。当他不得不与我们说话时，他总是采用一种生硬唐突的方式，比方说，在餐桌上，当他不得不让我们中的一个递一盘食物给他时，他从不说那些作家们常用的、男人对女人的逗趣客套话。他有些害羞地坐在那里，半倚在一个垫子上，细嚼慢咽着他的食物，唯一能真正令他活跃起来的，就是那些与其他国家的历史有关的谈话。那时，他的眼睛会在他眉毛的细线之下隐隐散发出光芒。他闭上眼睛。当他的面容如此出人意料地放松下来时，他那带有短而卷曲的睫毛的眼睑看上去也毫无防御能力了。就像一个孩子，他用小指掏了掏耳朵，晃了晃脑袋，然后睁开眼睛，目光炯炯。

幸运的是，我几乎无须与他打交道。在我看来，他似乎很笨拙，很封闭。幸运的是，我做梦也想不到，有一天我竟然会在他的陪伴下度过我生命中如此漫长的一段时日，而甚至在那之后，在他无耻地抛弃我们，带走所有剩余的东西之后，甚至在那之后，我也依然无法理解他。他有个习惯，会撞向奴隶，或是绊倒他们，当他们和一大包沉重的粮食一起摔倒时，他还会咧嘴一笑。他会狠毒地鞭打桑格牛，直到异乡人出手阻止，最后演变成两人挥拳扭打在一起。他令我不寒而栗。他未曾招惹我，是否因为奴隶女孩对他而言几乎是不存在的；他未敢侵犯我，是否因为当时我是异乡人的所有物。我不知道。直到现在我也不知道。在我的异乡人身边，我感到自己是被保护着的。

因意志消沉而心烦意乱的我，在幼子亡故后，异乡人第一次登门拜访时，上前与他搭话，并乞求他在我被送往奴隶市场拍卖前买下我。那正是我害怕会发生在我身上的事，我害怕自己不得不再一次去到那里，站上那个耻辱之地。我还记得我的动作是何等的歇斯底里，我的声音是何等的刺耳尖锐，后来又变得何等的胆怯颤栗；然后我沉默了。在未知的紧攥之下，我挣扎得太过悲恸欲绝，太过筋疲力尽了……是过分在意自己的冒失与鲁莽了。他回答前的短暂间隙里，饱涨着我的紧张情绪；在他的无言面前，我苦苦的哀求好似一种无礼的吵闹，我湿黏的、摇摆的手臂好似两根无助的触须；而我跪地的姿态，是一种太过明显的谄媚的伎俩。

当他向我保证我不会被拍卖掉时，我体内那一闪而过的情绪的过渡——从最初那份不可思议的解脱之感，到随之而来的领悟与平静——是多么的美好啊。我咬住自己的衣角，强忍着我那不得体却不受控的啜泣，用上我所有表面的平静，向他表达了我的感谢，同时压抑着我的情感和我想要疯狂地尖叫和雀跃的心情，就这样克制着自己，离开了他。

因为他又再次到来了，正如我所笃信的那样；但这一次，有一个我无法猜到的意图。我想都没想便以为，他是前来打理他的日常生意的，前来买入铁矿、铜矿，以交换一卷卷的丝绸、棉布，与往常一样，乘着商贸之风，站在由他所指挥的小小的三角帆船船队的最前端，穿过波浪起伏的蓝绿色，从笼罩在一层陌生薄雾中的其他海岸线上的其他商贸城市，远道而来——那就是我所以为的。我以为他和他的团队就是前来卸下一船货物，再载满另一船归去的。

我无法得知这一次，他会暂时卸下他对水手们的指挥权，将其交与一个下属，以便去履行一趟与那些山川、平原之上的金贝粉蝶的白色舞姿背道而行的旅途。没有人知道去往何处，没有人知道为何而行，也没有人知道他为何允许自己被说动。他没有给出理由。他只是去了。我与他同行，我是他最新购得的所有物。我成了一个庞大布局下的一部分，而这布局令他和长子终日忙碌着，令他们在油灯下做着各种计算直至深夜，令他们拆解开各种可行的、可能的、真实的和神秘的，将它们互相权衡掂量着，直至其中一方感到疲乏。可能的、不可能的，在天平之上跌落、上升、盘旋着。细节越堆越高了。一个想法堵死了，一些新的想法被寻获了，而最终那个问题——为什么——变得彻底不重要了。好奇心与利益的动机。孩子气的梦想。对遥远之地的渴望。繁复详尽的评估。叛逆的性格。或许是最后一个吧。

于是。出于这样的原因，我们向着精神的边境出发了。迁徙的无脊椎动物，那就是当时的我们。在沙滩上滑动的贝壳。仅凭一只触手在干燥的岩石上爬行的海葵。用鱼鳍行走的鱼。摇摇摆摆的盐鳞腔棘鱼[1]。悲声恸哭的儒艮[2]。

---

[1] 腔棘鱼，一种古老的鱼种，鳍棘中空，鳍呈肢状，可在海底爬行，是鱼类向两栖类进化的重要证据。
[2] 儒艮，一种海洋哺乳动物，行动缓慢，性情温顺，叫声持续，时高时低，好似哭泣。

我们一行人，脚夫、牛群、轿子，还有脚夫肩膀上的乘轿人，就这样蜿蜒如织地走入了内陆，走向了那片轰鸣在世界尽头的浩瀚大海。它不会太遥远的，正如长子和异乡人——理性地，在地图的帮助下——断定的那样。它不会花上一辈子的，他们计算过了。事实上，若将所有因素纳入考量，这条路应该是通往那片大陆的捷径。那些英勇的水手们不久前才到访过我们的城市，向我们吹嘘过他们在那方无垠而未知的海域上乘风破浪的艰辛。他们可以用船员中数不胜数的坏血病病例佐证，他们确是来自世界尽头的尽头。

在我们看来，他们仿佛是一夜之间凭空出现的，仿佛是缓慢潜行穿过那片箔纸般的大海来到这里的，哦，如此的缓慢，乘着一艘艘笨重的卡拉维尔帆船[1]，撑着一张张修补过的风帆，在那风帆的索具上，我们还能看见上下爬动的船员，带着猿猴似的敏捷。我们并没有为其折服。或者说，我们并没有表现出为其折服的样子。尽管如此，我们还是聚集到了海滩上，还是爬上了屋顶露台。如果你是富有之人，你会命人抬来一顶轿子；如果你是一个精力充沛的孩子，你会爬上一棵椰子树的树顶；如果你是一个木匠，你会放下你的工具，忘记你的工作，站起身来；如果你对新的商贸关系有所疑虑，你会锁上你的商行，带上几个抄写员作为随从，到外头闲逛，若无其事地闲聊，互致问候，假装很无聊地，或远

---

1 卡拉维尔帆船（Caravel），特指15世纪和16世纪被西班牙人和葡萄牙人广泛用于海上探险和远洋航行的一种帆船。

或近地，走向我们那暗藏危险的海湾，走向他们要抛锚停泊的地方。他们能拿出什么我们所没有的呢？这是当时这座城市给人的总体感觉，没有因为兴奋而沸腾，因为不愿表现得过于明显，新的到来者们受到了冷淡的欢迎，不至于引人怀疑，但仍然……不愿表现得过于明显。

长子是首个受邀登船的人。他请求异乡人陪他同去，因为他更了解航海相关的事。我仍然记得，异乡人身着一件绿色条纹长袍，搭配绿色头饰，看上去是何等的高贵，当他站在指挥官的甲板上时，他比那群蓄着胡须的新来者们高出了一大截。他和长子尝试用水手的语言同对方交流，带着大量的比划、摆头，上上下下，前前后后。而我们所有人都在等待着他们的报告。我们了解到地球圆盘另一端的一片大陆，了解到航海者们是一路沿着世界的边缘航行至此的，了解到气势磅礴的暴风雨，那是神明试图将他们逼至边界、使他们堕入虚无，了解到他们在风之哀嚎中听到的仿佛在警示他们即刻返航的话语，了解到他们在某块陆地靠岸取水时遭遇的怪物猛兽，了解到为修复破损的帆桁而不得不作出的一次次短暂的休整，了解到他们在海上竖立起的灯塔，了解到怀有敌意的落后的人类族群，然后他们指了指那些黄色风帆上的红色标记，于是我们了解到，这些矮状、多毛、穿着厚实的奇装异服的男人，扬帆远航，是为了他们的国王。

悄无声息地，如同一个波浪的诞生，一个想法也在日渐成形、日渐隆起，悄无声息地。城中最富有商人尚未娶妻的长子，一个只对遥远的地方感兴趣，因此被异乡人所吸引，总是缠着他询问各种问题的人，一个如今，在他父亲逝世后，继承了最重要的商贸利益，本应心无旁骛地管理它们，将自己纳入这座城市的整体利益，方能与他的地位及声誉相匹配的人，就是这个人，在出发前夕仓促地结了婚，随即便启程前往了那个在所有人看来都仅存在于他想象之中的目的地，且这件事已招致众人窃窃的嘲笑。

仅有一人不曾嘲笑，那就是异乡人。他已说服了自己，要将自己的命运封存。于是他中止了——只是暂时吧，人们以为——往返于公海上一片陆地与另一片陆地间的航行，中止了穿渡于一片已然习以为常的、虽苦于龙卷风之灾难却享有季风之恩惠的水域上的航行，转而要去试验一段充满未知的陆地上的旅程，仅仅仰仗着一个虚无缥缈的目的。那适应了不安的海水波澜的目光，而今不得不去适应森林与沼泽的青绿，去适应那好似藏匿于老者胡须下的峡谷与陡峭的悬崖，去适应平原、迟缓的河流和地平线上状如穹顶的山峦。繁星不再遍布于一片动荡不安的水域之上，而是遍布于一片坚固安稳的大地之上，在广阔无垠的夜晚里，它们看上去更加平静，也更加沉着了。大地上的星空看上去愈加静止。夜色愈加浓重。世间万物，看上去都愈加可靠了。

我想这就是冒险的精神吧。我不愿费心去思索，是什么使他踏上了如此愚蠢的旅程，最终落得一场置身于荒野中央的微不足道的死亡，而为之哀悼的，也仅剩下他最后的所有物：我。仅剩下我一人，在河岸上来回踱步，焦躁、哀伤、急切而万念俱灰地呼喊着，感受着在那河流上、树木间来回编织着空气的鱼鹰用它们刺耳的鸣唳向我丢出的讪笑，还有它们受巨型鳄鱼之命向我发出的警示：勿入禁地。

他的生命，就这样在一只爬行动物的腹中走到了尽头。我有时实在忍不住想笑。毕竟，这实在是一场极其可笑的死亡。人们如此地习惯将地球上的其他居民看作食物，将它们看作毋庸置疑的食物的来源，将一切可以吃的都交付给了消化系统，又佐以五花八门的调味品，饰以精美雅致的餐具，将对食物的摄入提升成为一门艺术，更将一顿饭小题大做，发展出许许多多围绕着它的礼仪习俗，使之僵化成为一项仪式，从进食这一完全自然的身体功能，演化出了一整套繁琐冗长的作业——人们对此是如此地习以为常，以至于当一个本应摄取食物的人被当作食物吃掉时，那场面真是可笑至极。那不可触及的、至高无上的力量，到头来不过是食物而已，一条瞄准目标的尾巴，一次挥甩，他就被撞翻落水了——事实上甚至没有瞄准，事实上只是无意间的完美一击，他就被溺毙、被吞咽了。

他的灵魂有可能从那气泡中逃脱吗？是我的同伴，我的水之神灵渐生了嫉妒之心，才要求将他收去，成为她的人吗？

由此，我开始害怕深究我的想法。我，一个属于水的人，从未希望这样的事降临于他，无论有多么荒唐，他都已不复存在于这人世间，无论作为鳄鱼的粪便灰飞烟灭有多么可笑，就像被埋葬、被蚯蚓噬尽会不那么可笑似的。他都已寂灭。他都已不在。

自那以后，我便小心揣度着他死亡的本质。我是将它当作一件平常事来想起的，我对自己掩饰了真相，我向自己隐瞒了详情，然后我告诉了我自己一个全然不同的故事。即使在我深陷孤独，极尽尖酸地诅咒着他和他的高贵，或者像我所决定的那样，诅咒着他固执的正直的时候，我也使用了一种修辞手法，我那伟大神灵的名字因此从未出现过。诅咒那饮下他鲜血的土地吧，我更愿意这样说，试图将我的怨憎排遣到大地上，或者将其附着在鬣狗和秃鹫身上。我给河马那黑漆漆的池塘献上了我的祭品，那是众鳄鱼之首领的居所。我郑重其事地将我的象牙镯子抛入了水中。它无声无息地沉没了，几乎没有泛起一丝涟漪。世界重归敦睦。风起，四野阒然，只有鱼鹰的鸣唳，守护着这一潭池水。

但愿我能够知晓，我是否也会有一场命中注定的水之死亡！我渴求着它。或许我必须明白，水终将是他的宿命，因为他没有忠于他赖以生存的伟大的水之神灵。

我发誓我会忠于你的。每一次，我将我的鸵鸟蛋壳放入那潺潺的溪流中时，我都轻声地低语着：

潺水，是的，潺水

你居于芦苇的河床之上

还有猴面包树的空心之中

潺水，你从空气中落下

潺水，你自大地上涌起

你覆没了大地

这大地之下、之上皆为你居所

你的神灵在一滴水里

与在大洪水，在暴风雨中同样伟大

渴切地，我捧起你，饮下你

潺水，你在我之中了

　　这溪流中的潺水清甜可口，我很庆幸我在异乡人消失后游荡到了这里。我谦卑地感谢了我的水之神灵，感谢它对我的指引，感谢那一场场将猴面包树冲刷得舒适、干净的雷阵雨，一场场催促着他萌芽，然后在一夜之间将他所有绿叶全部破出，在他枝桠之上挂满一朵接一朵硕大花朵的雷阵雨。雪白、褶皱，将要接受蝙蝠授粉的花朵，雪白、褶皱，散发着恶臭的花朵。

　　猴面包树开花之时，我就不会感到忧郁了。那时我会将这趟旅程看作一场我不得不经历的困惑，那时我就不会试图解开它、求索它的意义了。我会大声说出这棵树的名字，水的名字，空气的，火的，风的，大地的，月亮的，太阳的，它们全都意味着我所喊出的名字。我大声说出了我自己的名字，我的名字毫无意义。但我仍然是我。

　　有一次我从树上奔逃了出来，漫无目的地跑入了那片稀树草原，试图躲在一块高大的圆石背后，以逃离它的视线，然后我张大了我的嘴巴，发出了一声，一定是一声属于人类的声音，因为我是一个人类，不是一只喷着鼻息的角马，不是一只用翅膀发出嗯哨之音的角蝗，不是一只瓮声瓮气鸣叫着的鸵鸟，而是一个说话的人类，这个人类发出了一声声响，抛出了一声控诉，将它用力猛掷在了黄昏的空气里。一声血淋淋的呼喊，暴露在空气中了，我想要用它来震慑周遭的一切，用这一道彻长的、原始的声音，去成为万物的主宰。

夜里，我能听见狮子的咆哮。时不时地，我会起身往火堆里添柴。有时，我会在火光之中瞥见闪动着绿光的眼睛。清晨，我在火堆的余烬中烘烤那些小矮人带给我的块茎。我用一根小木棍撬开猴橙[1]坚硬的外壳，再用这根小木棍把果肉舀进嘴里。喝一大口水，吞一大口烤熟的块茎，我又准备好继续与时间抗争了。我们在一个无穷无尽、循环往复的圆中争斗不休。我没法将他分解开来，分割成块，好让他形成一个图案，并以此控制住他，尽管我在那些珠子面前极具创造力。我有时会陷入困惑，忘记自己何时将何物与何物连结在了一起。绿色的、黑色的，依据我的心情全都混杂在一起了。我没法甩掉时间了。他一直蹲坐在我的树前。所有我生命中出现过的事物都永远与我同在，并且所有事件都拒绝好好地、一个接一个地站成一排。它们相互钩扯、移动、散落，将它们自己强加于我，或试图从我的记忆里滑落出去。在我的记忆之链面前，我困难重重。我根本不是一个无忧无虑的放牧时间的牧童。白昼、黑夜过去了。然后是夏季、冬季。又一个夏季，又一个冬季。这很简单。但这不是使我成为今天这一个我的时间，也不是宿在我心中、正以另一种节律流转着的时间。

有时，当我在河水中清洗身体的时候，我会以挑剔的目光审视那片平静水面上的倒影，尝试判断我又变老了多少。这并不容

---

1 学名 *Strychnos cocculoides*，英文俗称 Monkey orange（猴橙），分布于非洲南部，果实有着光滑、坚硬的外壳，成熟后为黄色，味甜美。

易，因为无论我和水面保持得多么静止，我的形影之上，总会有反反复复细微的皱褶和扭曲，一种奉承似的替代了我可能出现的岁月痕迹的波纹。我把一颗小石头扔进了我自己。我诡谲地上下摇荡着，揉碎成了一团混沌。无法安宁的我。然后我将自己从那水中分身上抽离了出来。我的灵魂是何等的挣扎啊。我在太阳底下把自己烤干，穿上衣裳，然后走上了那条返回我居所的小径。很快那些大象就会来了。太阳已经低悬在猴面包树的臂弯上。

有时，就只是忧郁。

我听不懂那些小矮人咔哒咔哒的语言。它在我听来，就像壁虎开始说话一样。总之，我怎么可能学会呢？在那初次诡异的近距离碰面后，他们就极少在我能听见的范围内说话了。有一天，我看见他们合力打死了一只长颈鹿。在他们剥下那动物的皮毛，将它开膛破肚之时，他们兴奋得喋喋不休，甚至是争执不休，至少在我听来是这样。我全神贯注地聆听，但是我什么也没有学会。这是一种为壁虎和红毛窃蠹而生的语言。

出于尊重，我站在猴面包树入口的位置，这样他们就看不见我了。自从那次，我强迫他们看到我，却发现我的举动极大地冒犯了他们之后，我就再也不将自己的意愿强加于他们之上了。我只是怀着感恩与欣喜之心，接受他们献上的每一粒食物和每一件有用之物。

以及每一件无用之物。就像那一把小金钉。它们是何等的闪耀，何等的迷人啊。我已经拥有了珠子，陶器碎片，一个鸵鸟蛋壳，衣物，以及，奇迹中的奇迹，一个完整的陶罐，虽因年深岁久而陶体发黑，但使用起来仍然非常完美，它也是那些小矮人发现并带给我的，我把它顶在头上搬运溪水。现在又有了这些可爱的小玩意儿。

我放任自己的思绪去漫游，去想象最为精彩的历史，想象一座有着臃肿的垣壁和参差的石砌块的城镇，想象一道呼啸于这片稀树草原上传递着神谕的神圣回音。一座城镇，多少与我们沿途所见的、那些女人正在建造的有些相似。事实上，我们已经途经了不少这样的石砌小镇。一些已被遗弃，满目疮痍，一些只修建了一半，就那样被扔下、被荒废了，还有一些仍在修建之中。而那些支撑起露台的石墙，那些支撑起屋宅、庙宇或谷仓的石墙，全都是由女人们搭建起来的。目光所及，无一男性，这在我看来实在是一件很不寻常的事。

或许男人们只是外出捕猎去了。他们是外出捕猎去了吗？我回过头去，询问异乡人。

我想是的，他回答。

这些女人总是自己修建房屋吗？她们总是自己搬运石料，自己捆扎打包，自己起草规划？

奇怪，奇怪，异乡人回应道。

从我们乘坐的左右摇摆的轿子上，我们好奇地打量着这些干劲十足的女工们。我将一片大树叶举在眼睛上方，好遮挡住阳光。像一位真正的夫人，我端坐着，观看着人群在烈日底下劳作，不时还会怀抱着轻松、满足的心情，发表一些评论和观感。我感觉如此的好。生活从未如此愉悦过。

或许男人们是外出征战去了。或许他们正计划袭击我们，异乡人开玩笑地说。

　　我们的领队有说什么吗？我问。

　　哦，他总在发脾气。他太紧张了。

　　是的。

　　我感觉自己是一个高高在上的、不可触摸的、永远不会停下脚步的临时观众，这个观众在她的座位上又想出了一则言简意赅的妙语。或许她们是……我想说，女奴。我把这个词咽了下去。

　　或许她们之中，还有几个我不知道的、留在了内陆的家人。或许我就来自这里，或来自这附近的某个地方。还是不要问任何问题，让事情就此过去比较明智。或者，男人们是在一次抓捕奴隶的突袭中被掳走了？所以这些女人才不得不承担起男人的工作？这些女人腰部以上全部赤裸着，戴着蜗牛壳和五颜六色的护身符，脖颈上佩有珠饰，脚踝上套着铜丝环。而我乘坐在轿子上，在恰到好处的优越感里，在被偏爱的安全感里，在这趟远行借予我的特殊地位里——我有幸被挑选为其中一位领队的女仆，不，不是女仆，完全不是——而是女主人。我拥有将自己置身于陌生之地，置身于一个我本可以无限宠溺的男人、一群仆役和一个性格乖戾但也不常被我想起的领队之间的自由。没有逃离的可能。难道要将自己丢弃在这荒凉之境，寄希望于它也有怜悯之心吗？那真是太愚蠢了。愚蠢，甚至想要同这些女人接触，在全然不知她们是否会欢迎我、是否会提供帮助的情况下。就这样，在摇摆之间，我姿态傲慢，但目光热切地经过了那些绿草丛中的褐色石墙。没有直角，只有柔和的弧度，与大地的曲线连为一体的弧度。这便是女人们的建造。

我已经留心一阵子了，我前面的脚夫头发里藏有什么东西。现在我看清了，他在那儿藏着十字币。偷来的钱，因此。今晚我会警告他将它们藏好一些，因为我们会经常更换脚夫，以便更好地分摊重负。不久之后他就会被换去抬长子的轿子了，而后者是否会让如此明显的罪行逃过惩罚，我很怀疑。可怜的恶魔。有一天他会想要逃跑吗？他会想要在某个夜晚悄悄溜走，在途经的村子里购买食物吗？他会想要逃之夭夭，让他的脑袋似金属般沉重，他的心因欢欣而轻盈，他的内脏被恐惧给掏空吗？

事实上，他确是我们的第一个损失。但显然，他是自己设法消失的。我们的第二个损失则是一个更为沉重的打击。那些漂亮又温顺的桑格牛一夜之间消失无踪了，仿佛是大地之神打开了一个巨洞，一个接一个地，它们全都走了进去，如今正站在大地的肚子里哞哞叫唤着，长长的牛角相互碰撞着，伤心地来回踩踏着。

我们发现那天晚上我们没有安排守夜的哨兵，因为我们从未守过夜。我们还发现我们没有可以胜任的追捕之人，而我们自己在被大雨冲刷得干干净净的稀树草原上，什么也没有发现，只有属于我们自己的泥泞的脚印、轻浮的痕迹、无知的证据，跋涉在这辽远、宽广的天地间。

这是一次严重的损失。那些桑格牛不仅驮负着最为沉重的包裹，当饥饿凝视着我们的脸庞之时，它们还是我们的最后一线生机。此外，如果有必要，我们还有意用它们与那些内陆部落交换食物、消息，或者在需要时寻求他们的保护。这便是一开始的计划。

远征领队间的第一次争吵，引致了一场不安的沉默。一次怨愤的短暂爆发，一番尖锐的相互指责，然后两人都从这场冲突中撤了出来，烦躁，忧心，大阔步地来回走动着。他们的头顶上仿佛长出了戴冕鹤那光彩熠熠、愤愤不平的冠羽，而他们僵硬的脸庞则流露着不愿和解的神色。固执，傲慢，不会一直相安无事的。一个水手会永远站立着，永远奔忙着。大海，他的道路，永不会停息的。它会推促你，拉扯你，将你倾搅得天翻地覆，将你抛掷上码头，抛掷上帆船的右舷，它泼溅在你的身上，横扫过你的身体，它随心所欲地变幻着姿态，它化作山巅，高高翻涌而来，它化作漩涡，将你卷入那深海之蓝的轴心，它舒展开来，将你囚禁于它安详的绿色氛围里，它变幻着，但在变幻之中亦保持着不变，最终使变幻成为了一种永恒，使它的不可预测成为了它唯一的可以预测。它并非变幻无常，它只是一向如此。所以，他更愿意走路，异乡人解释道，戏谑着他自己。简单来说，他不曾有过休憩，也不曾有过安宁。简单来说，他走路，是为了让奴隶们减轻些负担。

我也是的，有些日子里，通常是在清晨。露水在我的衣裳上画下了一缕湿痕。天边已浮现出一道破晓的微光。我试图用越来越大的步伐，追赶上我那长长的影子，试图踩着我自己的脑袋前行。可我从未追上过我自己，我欣慰地叹息着。鸟儿们从草地上呼呼飞起。我看见：一只小羚羊轻快地跳跃着，一晃而过，不见了踪影；一群马鹿面无表情地反刍着；一只白犀牛，稳如磐石；一只红犸，焦躁不安；还有一只鬃毛粘结，任凭苍蝇在它口鼻四周打转的狮子，打着那吃饱喝足的人才有的哈欠，滑稽地滚来滚去。直至太阳归巢，栖落于我身后，直至那时，我才示意那些脚夫走近些。

很久以前，我就放弃与他们对话了。我的要求是在沉默中达成的。没有回应。没有提问。这感觉就像你在试图与一帮还魂尸[1]沟通。比起当初在城里，我不得不与这类人一起工作时的感受，在这里，在这原始荒蛮的大自然里，我为他们的行为举止是如此的非人而感到震惊。无论是不情不愿，或是表面上的热情恭顺，他们的行为举止，我突然想到，都与托科洛希[2]之流一般无二。他们的瞳孔是一种古怪的空洞，他们的动作是机械的运转，仿佛是在遵从某种内置的命令似的。

我们之中有人被施了魔法，我对异乡人耳语道。

你此前从未发现吗？

我惊讶地看着他。我们坐在一条涨水河边一棵漂亮的黄瓜木[3]下，正在正午的灼热里休息。长子散步去了，和往常一样，没有同我们打招呼，也没有告诉我们他要去哪儿；他回来时，大概也

---

1 英文中zombie一词事实上起源于非洲，特指非洲原始宗教中被巫师施以毒咒致死，再通过巫术复活，失去自由意志，任凭主人奴役支配的还魂尸。当代研究认为土著巫师是利用了他们掌握的某种强效麻醉剂和致幻剂来达到还魂尸的效果的。
2 托科洛希，非洲南部民间传说中的一种水中精灵，似人形，会被心术不正之人召唤，给他带去麻烦。
3 学名 *Thilachium africanum*，英文俗称Cucumber bush（黄瓜木），分布于非洲东部和南部，是一种景观遮阴树。

什么都不会提及。而我们俩，只要有对方的陪伴便已足够幸福了，幸福到没工夫搭理他那病态的缄默。我们俩是自给自足的人，我们都唯恐失去分秒地渴求着对方的关注。让那个讨人嫌的家伙走他的路去吧。

我们刚刚吃完奴隶们为我们准备的食物。若不是他们中的一个前天夜里捉来一把飞蚁，将它们做成勉强可以忍受的酱汁，我们还得生生强咽下那些粗稠的御谷粥。我们已经那样强咽了好几日了。因为，随着桑格牛的消失（又或是被盗？）以及那些包裹的重新分配，我们不得不丢弃一些物品，因而在阴错阳差之下，不得不承担一个后果：大米、干虾、芒果酸辣酱、干无花果蛋糕、椰子、大枣，还有许许多多其他的东西，都被丢下了。没有人指责任何人疏忽大意，但不和之心仍在隐隐闷燃着。一个领队带人组成了先头部队，另一个领队与我组成了后防线，我们被不信任感与一长队的奴隶给分隔开了。

食蜜鸟攥紧了绽放在我们头顶的紫红色花丛。四周传来鸽子懒洋洋的柔声低语。一种毫不虚妄的万物静滞。水面在羽毛似的芦苇丛间波光潋滟。一阵爱抚的微风。我在听着，我说。说吧。

夜里，我召唤来所有我知悉的神灵，异乡人压低了声音，装作很神秘。你还没听见鬣狗的鼻息声吗？一如你深深的睡梦。你还没听见远方狒狒的吠叫声吗？

你还没看见土豚隆起的背部吗，它在月光下清晰可见，还有他那长长的口鼻，他用它来嗅探尸体的所在。我们沿途所经村落的居民多么可怜，他们不知是什么袭击了他们。他们不知巫师会

79

时而出现在这里、时而出现在那里，遣使自己的亲信去侵扰他们的坟墓。你还没看见黑夜里闪闪发光的眼睛吗，火一般猩红的眼睛，细眯着的眼睛，觑视着的眼睛？你还没听见低沉的怒吼，摸寻的抓挠声，拖行的脚步声，还有骨头迸裂的噼啪声吗？我遣使我的亲信闯入那些栅栏守护的村落，来到那些酋长的坟墓跟前。牛群太过惊恐，以至忘记了哞叫。它们只是躲在一旁。第二日，母牛诞下双头的牛犊，那片我的亲信和他们中了魔法的骑手们策马疾驰的金红色御谷地亦被夷为平地，颗粒无收，一场大饥荒在我们沿途所经的所有地域蔓延开来。储粮的筐篓空空如也。牲畜死亡。人类用火一般猩红的眼睛，细眯着的眼睛，觑视着的眼睛看向彼此，继而群起扑向那些弱者，将他们吃得精光。他们切下他们的嘴唇和指尖，任他们在一锅锅的水中流血至死，然后把他们煮熟、吃净，最美味的部位留给最强壮的人，下水和肉汁留给尚在人世的孩子。

异乡人走过去，平躺在大地上，透过树枝筑起的格栅和树叶墨绿的镶嵌，凝视着支离破碎的蓝天。

相当好的故事，他说，用手支撑起头部。我也曾试图活下去，他说，没有宗教信仰，没有其他此一类的迷信，没有任何一种逃避现实的方式，而如今我发现自己置身于我一生最大的幻觉之中。如今我在短视中寻求着慰藉，如今我目光之长远，远不过每一天的黑夜。

接下来是一阵呢喃的沉思，我无法完全理解。我想我听见了他请求我的原谅。然后他停止了喃喃自语。他坐起身来，凝视着我。

我应当把这个故事活到最后，他决定。所有故事都有结局。有一阵子他静止了，他的注意力被一大群环绕着这棵黄瓜木飞行了一圈又一圈的椋鸟吸引住了。

我只知道我想要，他突然开口，仿佛在回应一个我未曾问出口的问题。我想要。接着他又补充了一句，嘴角的皱褶之中、眯起的眼缝之内，流露出一丝极其轻微的微笑：我想一个人也可以荒唐得有尊严，或尽力如此。

有什么东西从我们左边的矮树丛中钻了出来。拍打着，挥舞着，惊惧地大喊大叫着——长子就这样朝我们飞奔了过来，像一个小丑似的跌跌撞撞，滑倒在草丛上。他衣裳的下摆钩住了一株喃喃木[1]，又将他拽了回去；他拼命甩动、拉扯，用他的藤鞭将那树丛打得扁平，气急败坏地试图从那荆棘的利爪中挣脱，但只是让自己被缠得更紧了，最终不得不将衣服撕扯下来，方得以脱身。而在所有这些进行的当下，他还在声嘶力竭地命令我们和所有的奴隶趴下，藏好，蜷缩起来，或悄悄溜走，躲开他所看见的东西。

非但没有躲开，我们全都站直了身体，目瞪口呆地注视着眼前的这一幕。伴随着一声低沉的诅咒，他挣脱了那株喃喃木，费力地踩踩向我们，解释说有一支军队正朝我们行进而来，就在这条河上。

---

1 学名 *Carissa macrocarpa*，中文称大花假虎刺，英文俗称Num-num bush（喃喃木），原产南非，是夹竹桃科的一种带刺灌木。

趴下！趴下！他气喘吁吁地催促着我们。他一定是在这烈日底下奔跑了相当长的一段路。

他自己随即跪伏在茂密的芦苇荡背后，像在进行祈祷般安静了下来。我考虑是否要效法他。异乡人与我交换了一个被逗乐的表情，虽然不再完全是焕发着自信和大胆的笑脸了，而当其中一个奴隶无声地指出他看见了什么东西时，我们也的确全都在原先站立着的地方趴了下来，鼻尖紧贴着大地。

我小心翼翼地把头转向一边，凝望着河流，但尚未发现任何动静。芦苇平静地低垂着。水鸟还未令自己陷入惊慌。我能看见野鸭浮游在浅滩上，一只巨鹭将他一动不动的脑袋和脖颈从芦苇荡中探伸出来。当我将脸庞稍稍抬高一些时，我看见了一只正以下潜之姿紧张地悬停、颤栗于水面上的蓝色翠鸟，还能看见远处的堤岸上长满了枝繁叶茂的野生无花果树，好似一堵壁垒，将稀树草原远远地隔离在外。

我的耳朵帮助了我。我听见船桨拍击的砰然之声，我全神贯注、万分仔细地聆听着。我以为我能够分辨出人类说话的声音。话语的碎片传至我们像野兽般安静地卧伏着、等待危险过去的所在了。不久，透过芦苇荡那锯齿般的缝隙，我看见了几根被挖空的树干，正以两两一对、从左至右排成一列的队形航行经过，且每一根树干上都有一队桨手，正奋力向上游划去。船桨滴水而起，铿锵下落。他们行进得非常缓慢。又或者是这里的水流速度对他们很不利吧。大约在队形中间的位置，有一根比其他树干都更加粗大的空心树干正独自滑行着，上面的船员——他们上臂都缠绕着一簇动物尾巴——人数在我看来也更多些，船尾处似乎还有某种类似王座的座椅，其上端坐着一个男人，肩上披着一件银灰色的猿猴皮斗篷，身旁还站有一人，举着一把由棕榈叶或草叶或二者共同编成的像是伞一样的物件，保护他不受太阳的炙烤。

我听见的并非话语的碎片，我意识到。那是桨手使劲时发出的呻吟声。

那只巨鹭竖起脑袋。他迈开一步，又一步，以确保他的倒影不再落于水面之上，然后他凝固了。那群野鸭则不然，依旧是无动于衷地漂浮着，嘎嘎叫着，摇摇晃晃着，摆动着他们的尾羽。那只翠鸟已然消失。在野生无花果树苍绿色的背景映衬下，只有那一支树干舰队鲜明可见，正以令人痛苦的缓慢行速向前移动着。

我开始抽筋了，因为我趴得那般纹丝不动，一心希望那些战士，如果他们是战士的话，可以加快速度。我还想打喷嚏。我怀疑相距如此之远，隔着一河之水，他们是否还能听见，但为了安全起见，我还是忍住了。倘若他们真是战士，倘若他们对我们怀有敌意，那么一切就都结束了。在我被抓走之前，我对自己发过誓的，在我被抓走之前，我定会夺下异乡人佩带在腰带上的匕首，杀死我自己。无论战士与否，这阵仗看上去都像某种经过我们、行向上游的武力炫耀。但从何处来？又往何处去？我们已经有很长一段时间没有见到任何一个村落，一处废墟，一方有男孩们坐在高台上大声呼叫、吓跑成群的红喙雀的耕地，一群有牧童尾随其后的桑格牛，或是前来取水，坐在扁平的石块上洗澡，用石头擦洗脚底，大声说笑，纵情嬉闹的女人们了。

我们早已偏离了黄金和奴隶运输的老路，转而踏上了一条由那些水手的故事，亦由我们的野心——渴望成为第一个发现一条更近、更便捷的去往他人之城的路线，以此开辟更多商贸可能性的野心——所抉择的道路。第一个发现者。成为第一个。站在革新的最前沿。做第一个带回一份令人瞩目的报告的人。而我们会出售些什么呢？奴隶？象牙？玳瑁？黄金？成为第一个，抢在所有人之前，所有竞争者之前，发现这些人需要什么样的商品，以及他们可以提供什么作为交换，并且要当机立断，如此你说的话才具有权威性，你才可以第一个庆贺自己成为轻松赚得巨利的赢家。这就是扮演一个发现者所意味着的。

我想他们俩都低估了这场游戏，并且在我看来，他们也都意识到了这一点，只是坚决不肯承认罢了。如今这只是一件要硬着头皮去推进、去完成的事情。遥远的某个地方，坐落着一些已经存在商业活动的城市，这是一个事实。大地终归是被海水环绕着的，这我们也已知晓。有一天，有一天，突如其来地，毫无防备地，我们眼前会隐隐耸现一片蓝，我们越是接近它，它便越是与天空的混沌之蓝区隔开来，直至彻底宣布自己是一个独立的存在，是由水组成的，就是水，是运动中的水，有波澜，有泡沫，有飞溅的白色浪花，是永恒边缘的水之苍穹。然后我们会听见一声轰鸣，也许还有海鸟的鸣叫。然后，在距离终点仅有一步之遥时，我们全都会狂奔起来。

啊，冥想未来之事。去听，去看，去闻，去感觉未来之事，多么令人愉悦。去想象经历。

我们的食物储备越来越少了，着实令人担忧。我们也越来越依赖奴隶们的技能，以及他们在孩提时期所掌握的野外知识来补给食物。比方说，他们会挑选出一种圆形的橙色水果，里面满是硕大的果核，但有一层薄薄的可口又清甜的果肉。他们还能分辨出可食用的虫子：他们会把它们从树叶上捉下来，把脑袋捏掉，烤食剩余的部分，只是在烫手的灰烬里，这剩余的部分可真不多。

我鲁莽上前，笨拙而唠叨地恭维了他们一番。我大胆直视着他们的眼睛，建立起一种熟悉的关系。然后我捧起双手，获得了一份他们的果子、浆果、幼虫和根茎。我带着我的馈赠走到一旁，坐在他们和异乡人和长子的中间。不多时，异乡人便会坐到我身边来，而我会分给他一些我的东西。然后他会把他那一丁点东西再分给长子一些。一个复杂的系统。但情况尚不算危急。

还有一些有趣的事件，像是有一次，长子捉住了一只淡水龟，想连壳将它烤熟，谁承想它散发出的恶臭叫人如此难以忍受，我们全都退得远远的，没人愿意让它通过自己的唇齿，包括那位捉捕者和烧烤者。

那只貂羚被闪电击中的事件就不那么有趣了。事实上，回想起这件事我还会苦笑出来。我仍然能够看见异乡人取出他那把精美的、手柄上镶嵌着珠宝的小匕首——绿宝石和玛瑙被擦拭得闪闪发光——试图割穿貂羚腹部的皮肤。他一定是从那里开始切割的，因为他认为腹股沟处的皮肤会薄一些。

远远地，奴隶们表情严峻地伫立着，观望着，一致决定不去触碰这对我们来说好似一份慷慨大礼的东西。叛乱的第一个征兆？或许吧。我不知道。长子也做出了他的贡献，牢牢地抓住了貂羚的角。这动物反正也不剩什么气力了。异乡人放弃了切割。没有人想到去我们一路携带的物品里找找屠宰用的工具。一把斧头，一柄长矛，或是其他这一类的东西。

当我围着那只貂羚打转时，他那双呆滞的眼睛一直凝视着我，我害怕地想着。或许闪电只是将他击昏了。不，他是真的死了。是我们把那群白颈鸦从他身上赶跑的，只是这些东西仍然不肯消失，仍然在这里晃晃悠悠、自以为是地徘徊着。等待着。等待着。等待这几个无聊的人类的离开。我抬头看时，注意到一棵树的树顶上还停有一只秃鹫。而当我走近他，询问为什么不在我们带来的物品里找工具时，异乡人发出了一声冷笑。

他和长子从一开始就把他们的武器全都塞进了其中一个包裹里，因为将它们一直放在身边实在太过麻烦，它们就是有些碍手碍脚的。是什么阻止了奴隶们奋起反抗，把他们除掉，然后逃离这一切呢？他们当时已是如此怯懦了吗？我想我在奴隶们的眼神里察觉到了一闪而过的幽光。他们注视着，一如那群乌鸦。

从异乡人用匕首在貂羚腹部切割出的小小狭缝里，缓慢地渗涌出了一股暗色的液体，浸染在了白色的皮毛上。雨后的空气格外清新。我真希望我们能离开这儿。你能看见一道彩虹。在那儿，在很远的地方，而闪电就沉睡在它的脚边。我真希望有一道闪电能够让这只貂羚一跃而起，如暴风雨般猛袭向我们。

夏日已经开始变得饱满、醇熟。我们上一次看见大海还是在冬季。模糊、咸湿的记忆。转眼已是如此习惯这样的生活。

经过一整晚的协商，两位领队决定，我们应该穿过那条我们已经沿其河岸行走了有一段时日的大河，为了能够一直朝着远方的夕阳前进。他们对那空心树干上的王子或指挥官以及他的臣民或军队的共同恐惧缓和了他们之间的不和，但是当异乡人挑逗似的询问长子，他是否可以挑选出一棵嘶嘶树[1]建造一艘小船时，这不和几乎又要燃烧起来。

你可以吗？长子愠怒地反问道。然后他们一同尴尬地大笑起来。在这里，在距离家园、距离大海如此之遥远的地方，他们感受到了自身相对而言的无力，也非常清楚地认识到他们并非总能掌控全局。长子用他的藤鞭抽打着他的小牛犊，没精打采地，仿佛是承认着自己的无能。我从他们的眼睛里看到了他们的不知所措。男人看上去真是好笑，就像失望的孩童，当他们对某件事情失去掌控却又不敢坦然承认时。而我只有以一只寄生虫的特殊身份热切地祈盼着，祈盼他们能够寻得一个解决方案，让我们尽快抵达那些城市，抵达我们宣称的目标。每一个清晨，我以我最美丽的姿态绽放开来，好让他们欣赏我兰花般绚烂的天性。我对自己外貌的关心程度丝毫不亚于在城里的时候，而我内心的痛苦也在逐日增长。我完完全全地依赖于他了，他与我在一起是因为一场交易，亦是（我希望）因为爱情。但我完完全全地依赖于他了，就像一只寄生虫。

---

1 学名 *Parinari curatellifolia*，英文俗称 Hissing tree（嘶嘶树），分布于非洲中部和南部，因用斧头砍树时，树皮会发出一种嘶嘶声而得名。

时间流转，穿渡大河的计划却没有任何进展。两个人都没有足够的内在力量站起来，召集起奴隶们，找到一棵嘶嘶树，开始工作。在死气沉沉的寂静里，我们就这么徘徊、蹉跎在河的左岸。食物的供给如今锐减到了危急的地步，鞭策着奴隶们用葡萄干木[1]设置起一个个陷阱，在某个节庆般的日子里给我们烧了一只鸨。

　　我所不能理解的是，领队们显然已经缺乏决断，奴隶们却没有动过离开我们的念头。每一晚，他们都温顺地允许长子将他们用铁链拴在一起，这是在那个把钱币藏在头发里的奴隶逃跑后所采取的措施。每一晚，他们在睡梦中翻身时，我都能听见他们的铁链发出的哐当声。清晨，铁链会被解开，只是不会再被整齐地卷起、存放起来了。不，它们只是被随意地扔成一堆。我们好似全都变成了睡梦中的存在，身处一方我们全然不知要去往何处的过渡之中。日复一日，周而复始。

　　这条大河仍然令人赏心悦目。我们所在之处正是萨夫柳[2]生长的地方，而长子，又或者是异乡人吧，记得如果一个人想要涉水渡河的话，遇见萨夫柳就预示着脚下的坚稳。只是要完成这件事，我们必定得在此等到冬季，甚至是冬末了。之所以这么说，是因为我们曾吩咐其中一个奴隶下河去试探水深。他没精打采地踏入河流，直至河水没过他的腋下，才开始游动起来，但那之后不久，

1　学名 *Grewia occidentalis*，中文称水莲木，英文俗称 Climbing raisinwood（攀援葡萄干木），分布于非洲中部和南部，土著人会利用其木材和茎皮纤维来制作捕捉小动物的陷阱。
2　学名 *Salix mucronata*，英文俗称 Saf-saf willow（萨夫柳），是一种沿南非河岸生长的常绿柳树。

我们便听到了他的哭喊声，眼见着急流携裹着他远去。他的几个奴隶伙伴紧追着他向下游跑去，大声疾呼着让他朝岸边奋力划水。我看着他的脑袋在水面之上沉沉浮浮、愈行愈远，且距离愈远，他看上去愈像是在惬意地漂浮着。后来，他的奴隶伙伴也回来了。他具体是在何处溺毙的，他们也无法断言。

观察食蜂鸟追逐飞虫时掠过水面的样子很有趣。水面本身是一种略带棕褐的绿，且肌肉强健，轻轻拍打着河岸边参差错落的石块或树墩。柳树只露出树梢的顶部，绵软无力的枝条，半溺于水中地垂挂着。我感觉自己也像这柳树，任凭时间流过了我。丛鹦只闻其鸣啼，不见其踪影，也很有趣。我们也渐渐习惯了蝉鸣。

长子和异乡人用庄严的语调向彼此朗诵诗歌，或猜答谜语。我也会参与其中。有一回，长子以一种极其深沉、情感充沛的嗓音念诵了一首诗，异乡人怀着由衷的钦佩想要拍拍他的肩膀，但他像是不愿被人触碰似的，猛地将肩膀扭开了。他诉说着他对他那位新娘的思念。他一遍又一遍地呼唤着她的名字，就像一个人把一颗宝石从一只手扔到另一只手上一样。

异乡人说：就算此刻天空哗啦一声坍塌下来，我们也几乎不会在草地上留下一块凹痕。

在他坐着的地方，他拔下一小把葱郁的青草，咀嚼着它们，闭上了眼睛。他是开始做梦了。我搂住了他。我已不再会为长子可能看见我们的爱抚而感到不安了。河水的轻拍抚慰着我，仿佛诗歌的叠句。我摩挲着我的象牙镯子。我的幸运之物。我亲吻了它。我的脚后跟非常肿痛，且蚊虫无时无刻不在四处叮咬。那位被留在城里的孤独的新娘，在毫无音讯的情况下，是如何度日的呢？那座城市里的人们如今又在忙些什么呢？除却那位新娘，还有任何一个人记得我们是怎样离开的吗？

而我们也真的抵达了河的对岸，且过程非常容易。在逆流而上行进了一整天后，我们在一片芦苇荡与小雀巢间拖出了一条做工简陋的木筏，同时还发现这地方有一座河中岛将大河分隔成了两条河道，水流都不似此前那般湍急、致命。就这样，我们没有损失任何人员和物品便抵达了河中岛，继而由河中岛顺利抵达了河对岸。在岸上，我们又花了一天时间把所有物品整理妥当，逐个检查、确认了一遍。其中一个奴隶打死了一只侏羚——他朝它投掷了一根圆头棒[1]，这是他在我们停滞不前时，用一根灌木柳的淡黄色树干为他自己打造的。有了这么一份可喜的食物补给，远征的队伍又一次向前挺进了。

我们加快了脚步。两位领队身上弥漫着一种明显的紧迫感，一种久违了的机警敏锐，仿佛是那些猎人带来的关于那座红色沙漠之城的零星消息，使他们经历了一场性格的大变似的。现在两人都走在队伍的最前方，步子一个比一个跨得更大，一人比一人迈得更精神；你甚至能听见他们的笑声。他们的好心情带动了我们所有人，奴隶们也受到了鼓舞，变得勤快起来。在一种齐心协力而非监督管理的气氛下，他们轻而易举地分配了工作，丝毫不落后于他们的主人。我们共同感受到了那座玫瑰色水晶山脚下的

---

1 圆头棒，即一根顶端呈球状的短棒，是南非土著人的传统武器。

应许之城的召唤。

尽管如此，我还是忍不住留意到我们看上去有多邋遢。从这个高度，从我的轿辇之上，从这队伍的最末端，我被我们的不修边幅给惊呆了。无可掩饰，我们看上去肮脏、疲惫、衣衫褴褛、灰头土脸，衣服上满是油脂的污渍。其中一个奴隶的头顶上甚至连一个包裹也没有了。这是怎么回事？他以为他在这里做什么？另一个在他的脚踝上捆绑了一串摇摇晃晃的黄色种子，它们在他行走时不断发出簌簌飒飒的声响。还有一个逐渐显露出了他模仿鸟类语言的天赋，于是有时，在犹豫片刻过后，鸟儿们也会以鸣叫回应他的呼唤。听他说话很有趣。

我想知道我在其他人眼中又是什么样子。可怜兮兮，但至少是充满活力的？

在高莽、蓬乱的长草之间，我们这一小队人类的线条是多么的渺不足道，在成群奔腾的斑马、角马、马鹿以及那永远令人惊叹的鸵鸟之间，全然是难以觉察的存在。我们进入了高地，空气愈发清新了，而风无休止地吹拂着长草、灌木和树林的顶梢，在草地上翻腾汹涌，在灌木丛中抽搐颠簸，终于在树林里得到了缓慢庄重的回应。藤蔓植物那松散垂挂的枝条彷徨无助地飘荡着，紫红色小喇叭似的花朵从上到下开满了整棵寄生的主树，颤巍却不失狡黠地窥视着。在这些较为开阔的平原上，云朵总是彼此独立地飘浮于湛蓝之中，只在偶尔才聚拢到一起，仿佛得到召唤似的，生成雷鸣闪电，后又在暴风雨中解散。我们躲在树下，等待它们的散去。这里更冷了。我们继续前进，仿佛一幕不断移动的群像画，在那些日子里。

　　远方的那座城市之后，一定就是我们计划前往的城市，它一定能够满足我们所有的祈盼，在它身上我们寄托了我们的希望，为了它我们竭尽全力，倾注所有，重新整顿了我们自己，我们一定会在那里寻得一处栖身之所，遇见各色人等、熙熙攘攘的街道、建筑、市场、广场、挤满微笑的女人们的窗口、孩童嬉耍的花园。

　　那座城市——那些猎人是这么说的，也是那些猎人建议我们使用他们用树干和灯芯草为自己打造的木筏，他们将它留在了芦苇荡里，就在大河被河中岛分隔成两段的地方——那座城市就坐落在一片红色的沙漠之中，大风飞扬，红色城墙被太阳晒得干裂，而它背后的地平线上，耸立着崎岖不平、参差交错的玫瑰色山峰。

　　那它们的背后呢？异乡人追问道。

　　它们的背后就是大海。

　　啊……大海。

　　一个奴隶首先发现了那些猎人。我们为自己能够提供给他们的食物和饮水如此之少而感到难堪，但事实上，正如我们很快注意到的那样，他们的境况比我们要好得多，也比我们更加有组织、有条理。他们正要将他们的战利品，象牙，运送回他们的村落，且显得很着急，因为他们已经比预计返回的时间晚了很多。夏日正在流逝。那些大象，他们解释道，比以往迁徙得更远了，因此他们花了很长时间才找到它们，好在所有的耐心和坚忍都得到了回报，他们心满意足地指了指那一捆捆的长牙。这种原始的象牙形态在我看来相当丑陋，尤其是从血肉之躯上砍下来的粗钝的那一端，这些长牙的质地也全然不似我手臂上佩戴的东西。然而，据说这一带出产的象牙质量比大海彼端，我们城市附近捕获的象牙要好得多。我怎会知道呢？

　　那些猎人很是讶异，居然能在此遇上一个女人。其中一个笑得把所有牙根都露了出来，令我非常恼火，兀自退到了一旁。相反的是，我们的两位领队兴致勃勃地与他们攀谈起来。我理解他们想要获取尽可能多的信息，但我总能不自觉地感受到那些猎人偷瞄向我的目光。没过一会儿我便离开了，躲到了一株灌木丛的背后。我听见长子试图安排一场交易，试图向他们购入一些食物。我听见他从他那饰有长而柔软的流苏穗子的压花皮袋里掏出一把十字币，让钱币在他手指间叮当作响，然后又落回他的皮袋里；但那些猎人对这样的交易并不感兴趣，因为，他们解释道，他们的肉食也仅够自己充饥而已。长子不得不又收起他那一大笔现金，什么也没有得到。

　　异乡人对我们应该前往的确切方向更感兴趣。那座城市坐落于夕阳之下，这是他得到的信息。仍然有漫漫的平原要走，然后植被会愈加稀疏，然后草丛间的土地会变为沙砾，然后是愈来愈多的沙砾，而草丛会零星散落，颤动着银光，然后沙砾会变成沙丘，它们会赫然耸立，此起彼伏，形成完美的驼峰，其间是完美的死寂，然后，在疲乏不堪地攀爬过一个又一个、一个又一个的驼峰过后，那座城市便会出现在那里。

　　但首先是渡河，其中一个猎人说道。是的，另一个肯定道，首先是渡河，那浩瀚的波光，那满目的花海，满目的阴影，满目

93

的诡计，那倒影看似真切，却会有虎鱼从其间凶残地扑跃而出，而响蜜䴕会无休无止地呼唤着，日暮时分，捻角羚会步出莫帕尼[1]之森林，秃鹳会如幽灵般飞起，用它们的羽翼遮蔽住月光。

口信已被传递给猎人们，当他们回到村落，会再经由他们传递给那些从城里前来购买象牙的象牙商人，由此，异乡人和长子试图与城里恢复联系。而我无话可说。其他奴隶们也沉默不语。我们仅存在于自身所处的这一刻，而他们，异乡人和长子，存在于从那座沿海城市一直延伸至这里，还将一直延伸至那座沙漠之城和其他令他们心驰神往的城市的地域之上，他们甚至存在于比那些城市更加遥远的地方，存在于陆地之间的汪洋上，同时亦存在于那些陆地上。但我是毫无牵连的。我只是孤身一人的我。

猎人们才刚从视野中消失，长子和异乡人便迅速投入了工作，他们的满腔热情也感染了奴隶们，眨眼间，万事俱备，我们又可以继续前进了，在那么多个浑浑噩噩的，好似被妖术蛊惑了的日子过后，在那些我们仿佛梦游者一般，各自被编织进一个欢愉而恍惚的茧里的日子过后。那些水之神灵迷惑了我们，束缚了我们的思想的日子。

那些猎人已经离去，我暗自松了口气，因为他们那好色的目光好似要紧紧黏附在我身上似的，我感觉我在努力将那令人腻烦的气息从我身上甩掉，从我的乳房、乳头上，从我的小腹之上甩

1 学名 *Colophospermum mopane*，英文俗称 Mopani tree（莫帕尼树），中文俗称可乐豆，分布于非洲南部。

掉；但最为糟糕的是他们在我身上唤起的情欲。

夏日就这样流逝着。那条大河已经被远远地抛在身后，那座憧憬的城市仍然在极其迢遥的远方。

一天下午，我们在一座有圆石作飞檐的小山丘前停下了脚步。迄今为止，我们已经遇见过不少这样顶部耸立着巨石的山丘了。在沿海地区，我们还从未见过这样的地质构造，于是总忍不住要评论一番，就像在讨论一些艺术作品似的。我们称赞它们的比例和绝妙的平衡，仿佛是某种将它们摆放至此的工艺和巧思使它们看上去好似会滚落下来，会轰隆隆地碾压过稀树草原，直至它们发现一个可以停留的小小凹陷，而那里的烈日会将它们晒至迸裂，又或者，直至它们与另一块它们的同类相撞，粉碎，同归于尽。

我们想要更近距离地观察这些岩石，于是便一起爬上了那座小山丘——长子、异乡人和我；奴隶们则在无人监管的情况下准备晚餐，为我们铺好就寝的垫褥。那个不再驮负任何包裹的人正是那个发号施令的人，我注意到。奇怪，他是如此的不显眼，身材瘦小，相貌平平，在我看来从来都不是一个潜在的领导者，虽然我也必须承认，直到这一刻为止，我都从未想过他们中间会出现可能的领导者。他们就只是奴隶而已，一些没有选择地做着繁重的工作、没有应答地服从着远征领队的命令的阉人。他可能拥有王室的血统吗？一个人很容易在自己的猜测中变得想入非非。或许他只是他们之中最聪明的一个：从他的组织能力上推断，这是最有可能的解释。他的脖子上佩戴着一颗硕大的白色蜗牛壳。总之，他还是值得密切关注的，我想。但我不确定是否该向异乡

95

人或长子说出我的疑心。

　　有一回，我看见这个奴隶领袖打开了一个包裹，从中取出了一些工具，锛子、半圆凿、锥子，等等，大概是为了在必要时挖空树干才带来的吧，只是这个问题已经被那些猎人的木筏解决了。我看着他如何像一个手艺人般爱惜这些工具，看着他如何沉浸于将它们根据目的、尺寸分类摆好，又看着他如何将所有工具重新包捆起来，很灵活，很熟练。然后他将这个包裹重新放回了其他包裹之间。

　　山丘的顶端给了我们一个惊叹。不，两个惊叹。第一个是一些人类遗迹，数量不多，但存在着，且那些石墙与我们沿途多次所见的残迹风格一致，只是被损毁得更加严重了，又或是被废弃了更长时间吧。总之，更加残破不堪。没有一段完整的墙体，只有风化了的、及膝高的颓垣断壁，荆棘丛生；尽管如此，你还是可以从这一块接一块的石砌块中推想出建造者的意图。在午后的阳光下，山顶的岩石与这些彼此倚靠、叠加、堆积在一起的石砌块闪烁着同样的蜂蜜般的光泽。如果你能停留得更久一些，或许还会有其他的发现。曾经的居民们都去哪儿了？我们寻思着，猜测着。他们的骸骨是否就蹲坐于我们四周这片平原的大地之下，正犹豫着要不要站起，要不要勇敢地踏上一条去往先辈故土的危险旅途，或者，他们是否会觉得自己被后人抛弃了？无一人留下，为他们奠酒。有的只是冷风和鬣狗的笑声。这里，有某些东西彻底地泯灭了。这里除了悲伤，除了无意义，除了破碎的昔日荣耀的痕迹，便什么也没有了。一缕轻烟从下方升起，飘入天空，证实了我们这完全多余的存在。唉，我叹息一声，我们的旅途又还有多长呢？

山顶的第二个惊叹，令我更加悲伤了。是异乡人最早发现了东边的洞穴，但却是我最先留意到岩壁上那些稀奇古怪的图画的。它们看上去似乎是人，又像是一些条状的爬虫，画得漫无目的，有时成群出现，有时形单影只，有时一个在另一个之上，呈铁褐色和白色。很是暗淡了。谁会以万物之造物主的名义来到这里，又以这样一种未完成的方式使自己获得不朽呢？这太奇怪了。肯定不会是那座石墙之城里的居民。异乡人和长子也是同样的困惑不解。异乡人抱怨这些笨拙的尝试欠缺完成度，亦明显地欠缺艺术规范。显然是一个落后社会的一群落后画师。完全是业余水平。是业已成年的孩童的画作。但又不完全是。我们想不出任何一种解释。这些小小的图形游离于所有的联系之外，被放逐在这荒野的中心。这里有太多的疑问，和没有答案的阒寂。这里的人们来了又走，一次次地，来了又走，唯有阒寂，直至永生永世。

这里，长子说，这一个看起来像一只雄鹿。

异乡人饶有兴致地讲起他在异国旅行时遇见的、绘在羊皮纸和丝绸之上的画作，那丰富而敏锐的色彩运用以及树、鸟、人之间的微妙平衡——清晰可辨的树、鸟、人，他强调道——它们均是出自训练有素的艺术家之手，被分门别类，归入不同的流派和风格，还能成为极有价值的收藏品。他用匕首的利刃刮划着这些荒唐可笑的画作中的一幅。某个人消磨时间的方式罢了，他认定道。与艺术毫无关系。它们没有记录任何事物，也无意传递任何讯息，或达到某种审美上的满足。它们是无用的。异乡人说得越多，他对这些岩壁画就越感愤怒，事实上他已经开始试图将它们刮掉了。

这儿有个东西，看上去像是个女人，长子说道。它有乳房。这儿是一条蛇，我觉得。看这儿！一头大象，背部是扇形的！

他忍不住爆发出一阵大笑。

我背对着他们，站在洞穴的入口处，越过暮色苍茫的稀树草原，望向微光闪烁的黄昏之星。远远地，我能听见奴隶们的声音，但永远为风声所裹挟着，而这风声听上去，时而啸唳，时而轻柔，恍如呼吸。我感到如此的绝望。我感到我的喉咙就要哽塞，我感到那些我无法理解的事物就要勒住我的脖子，令我不得不在风中用力猛掷出一声哭喊，而它也会在风中顷刻便化为乌有的。

全都没有意义，我想着，独自一人离开，走下了山丘。我一直走到一块突起的岩石上，当我伫立在那里时，我听见自己开口说了些什么。不是说。是喃喃自语。是支支吾吾。我听见那些话语从我口中断断续续地滚落下来，跌入悬崖，被灌满山风的寂静吞没，说着一只尾巴着火的豺狼会在空气中穿梭奔跑，终将所有空气全部点燃的话语，就这样，一只豺狼从我的口中一跃而出。我听见自己狂热地预言着尚在沉睡的语言，预言着终有一日，诡谲的树木会列队出征般穿过河谷，越过山岭，铺满山坡。我预言人类将会在地球内部四处游荡。我预言巨大的灰色防波堤将会被抛向大海，预言船只将会潜于水下，预言生命将会经受一次又一次的迁徙和一遍又一遍的灭绝。当所有这些话语从我身体里滚落出来，当所有纤维似的声音从我舌头上消失之际，我感到仿佛有某种东西一直在啃噬着我，仿佛我早已被啃噬得千疮百孔，再不能够抵御风，也再不会有任何阻力了；为这样的自己感到害怕，我以最快的速度爬下最后一段山路，匆匆奔向那群奴隶，奔向那片火光的欢愉。

一到那里，我便询问他们有没有在无意间听到我说话，而他们只是一脸麻木地盯着我，然后便继续他们的差事去了。那个不再干活的人，那个所谓的领袖，甚至连看都没有看我一眼，也不屑回答我的提问。而异乡人和长子，从我小心翼翼的旁敲侧击中推断，似乎也没有听到我说话。我感到烦躁，也极其疲累，心头困扰重重，无可消解。

事情就这样发生了。异乡人与我和其他人隔开了一小段距离，睡在属于我们俩的摇曳的篝火旁，而长子虽然睡得稍远一些，却更靠近那些脚夫和那堆更大的篝火。那些桑格牛失踪后，我们一度每晚都会安排几人守夜，然而这一实用的措施却在我们被水之神灵蛊惑的日子里被逐渐废弃、遗忘了。抵达此岸后，那些日子的怠惰无疑已经被热情和勤勉所取代，而勤勉是既不需要鞭策，也不需要监督的。就连那些锁链都被丢弃在了河的对岸，奴隶们如今也同我们一样自由地入睡。说实在的，他们已经可以主动地轮流看守入睡之人、看守日渐减少的物品，也可以越来越独立地作出决定了——当然，是他们的领袖。

事情就这样发生了。异乡人与我从未察觉到长子与奴隶之间有任何阴谋的迹象，然而一天清晨，当我们揉搓着双眼从睡梦中醒来时，他，那一大群奴隶，连同所有的物品，全都不知去向了。人间蒸发。无影无踪。异乡人爬上一个白蚁冢，环顾四周。一无所获。稀树草原，就只是稀树草原而已，带着稀树草原的种种声响——窸窸窣窣，喊喊喳喳，叽叽啾啾。

我们尝试追踪他们，我们鼓励着彼此，但结果仍是失望。我们在火堆附近发现了被踩踏过的草丛和一些脚印，这就是全部了。我们想当然地以为，如果长子和奴隶们决意抛下我们继续这场远征，他们势必会朝着日落的方向行进，但是沿着那个方向我们也没有发现任何看上去像是人类脚步留下的痕迹。坚硬的土地上没有留下痕迹，只有遍地歪斜的草秆。我们四处游荡，就这样荒废了一整日，因为心底仍暗暗祈盼着他们的归来。他们没有归来。夜幕降临之际，一个庞大、骇人的念头方才向我们袭来。我们在沉默中睡去，第二日清晨亦在沉默中起身，然后便以平稳的步速继续前进了。我必须补充一点，我的轿子，也是从城里带来的三顶轿子中唯一还在使用的一顶，被我们丢下了。没有工具，我们便不能将其劈成柴火，这件无用的东西于是至今仍停留在我们拣来枯树枝的骸骨生起的小小篝火的灰烬旁，停留在死一般的寂静里。

我们根据太阳找到了方向，但河流的流向又迫使我们偏离了它。没有奴隶驮负我们渡过河水，我们一筹莫展。我们没有水袋。我们依靠稀树草原上的食物为生，我也是因为一直留意着那些脚夫，才会在无意间学会如何挑拣它们的。这是个苦力活。我尽力了，但我们的收获也仅够我们勉强果腹而已。尽管如此，在这一片荒凉之境，在这一段经受试炼的日子里，我们仍然能够感受到彼此的善意与温存。只是夜晚那令人生畏的恢弘万象，总叫我们心灰意冷。

一天，我们看见了几只秃鹫，于是便蹒跚着朝它们盘旋的地点走去。一股令人作呕的恶臭向我们袭来。我知道，我们在想着同一件事，但这恶臭实在令人难以忍受，何况那些秃鹫也不肯让位于我们。它们围绕着这几根肋骨——大概是角马的吧——一瘸一拐地转来转去，啄击着彼此。它们贪婪地啄食着，好似我们，就站在它们圈子之外的我们，根本不存在似的。

我们走了很多天。稀树草原并无变化。有时我们也说话。我表达了我对长子的惊讶。

他们会杀了他，拿走他的钱财，到那座沙漠之城里去追寻他们的自由——这是异乡人的看法。

时至今日，我都无法理解长子的所作所为。这个沿海城市最成功商人的第一继承人，这个因为他父亲的影响与权势，自幼年起便只享有最好的，只享有文明所能给予的最优质东西的人，却长成了一个性情古怪、脾气暴躁、会将他的坏脾气发泄在手无寸铁的人身上但也同样会慷慨地分发施舍的追梦人和空想家。上一次我看见他这么做还是在城市的郊外，在我们离开的那一日。他从他的皮袋里掏出一把钱币，从高高的轿子上猛地抛下，扔向那个蹲坐在路边的麻风病乞丐，连看也没看那家伙一眼。有几块钱币砸到了那个人绷紧的脸上。他除了弯下身子，趴在那些钱币后面爬行之外别无他法，因为他的双脚已经僵硬得不能行动，他的双手已经变形成了枯干的莫帕尼虫[1]，也与之一般棕褐，一般灰暗了。他试着捡起钱币，或者说，想方设法地将它们夹起。

我左右摇晃着，消失在了路的转角。那个无家可归之人就是我见到的最后一个城里人了，我想。那些可怜虫，为何不溺死自己呢？他们只会一直腐烂下去，直至回归大地。这真叫我恶心。我们在小树林里就遇到过自戕之人，不止一次。我们能看见一些双脚，有些赤裸着，有些还穿着粗糙的凉鞋，有些与我们视线齐平地晃悠着，有些只是一动不动地悬挂着。我们还能在那些树影间瞥见几张扭曲的老妇的脸孔，看上去仿佛在厉声辱骂着我们。也是些无家可归之人。无儿无女的妇人，或被指控行使巫术而遭致众人厌弃的女子，只因她们无法证明她们没有造成牛群的神秘死亡、引致土地的连年歉收。

当然，我也常常想要知道，一个人究竟可以坚持到什么时候。在某个地方，一定存在着一道分界线，一道在你眼中会变得越来越清晰的分界线，而走向它，然后抵达它，仿佛是走入睡眠的苍茫，再经由那苍茫，遁入梦境的冥晦，而置身于那冥晦，恍如置身于一场略小的死亡，你会遇见善与恶，这形影不离的一双人，这蔑视死亡的孪生子。

我的睡梦填满了我，也帮助我吞食着时间。我仍然无法巧妙

---

1 莫帕尼虫，一种非洲南部独有的帝王蛾的幼虫，也是当地有名的食物，主要以莫帕尼树的树叶为食，因常见于莫帕尼树上而得名。

地部署时间、存储时间，或最好是遗忘时间，但这些于我已经不再重要了，因为如今我明白了，梦与醒并非相互诅咒的两码事，而是相互延伸、相互渗透、相互丰富、相互补充，使彼此都成为可以忍受之事的存在，且我的猴面包树即是一个梦境成真的所在，当我看见那些小矮人时，我知道他们是我梦中的人，他们是真的外出狩猎，真的为我提供了食物，也真的看见了我，却又没有看见我，因为我亦存在于他们的梦中，他们通过照顾我来喂养他们的梦。我们遇见了彼此，又对彼此一无所知。我们各行其道，又相互依赖，他们依赖着我因为我是这样的我，我依赖着他们因为他们做着这样的事。

如今我满怀懊恼地嘲笑着我那些间歇性的尝试——企图用捡来的黑色珠子和绿色珠子去衡量那荒谬到无法衡量亦无法记录的东西。我将其归咎于我所受的教育，尽管散漫，但仍然是教育，而分配、计算、归类在其间扮演着如此重要的角色，它们激励着人们踏上一段旅途，一段理应可以促成这个那个，收获这些那些，因此为了这般那般的原因，应当采取这种方式而非那种，选择这个季节而非那个，朝往这个方向而非那个，带上这项装备而非那项的旅途——每一样因素都被纳入考量了，只是当我们启程的日子与夏末的慵懒一同到来之时，当白昼滑落进黑夜的王国而我们遗忘了我们的睡意与哈欠之时，当最后一次，纯粹只是出于习惯地，我们望向大海，看见三角帆船和小舟摇曳起伏，捻角羚果树间的天空开始燃烧起火焰的颜色之时，无一人留意到我们正在走入一场梦。睡梦之旅，山高水险。

我很清楚，饮尽那些小矮人赠予我的最后一份礼物，我便可以进入一个全新的梦了。我不知道这汤药是什么，但我无需知道便可以确定，鳄鱼脑髓是它的主要成分。或许这正是我长久以来企盼的东西。会有一阵阴暗而混沌的风前来把我接住吗？

我该如何处理我的所有物，那些小金钉和那些珠子，那个近乎是黑色的水罐和那个鸵鸟蛋壳呢？但愿时间可以收回它们。那些钉子是最无用的礼物。我不知能拿它们做些什么，如何为它们表达谢意于我也仍旧是一个谜。现在，它们就像种子似的躺在我的手掌心里，仿佛可以茁壮地发芽。

我所做的每一件事情都被小心翼翼地注视着，甚至我的最后一个动作，将那鸵鸟蛋壳举到我的唇边，也将被观望着，然后（但愿吧，大概吧，可能吧）将得到他们的认可。我会恭敬地饮下它，缓慢而庄重地，以这最后一次徒劳的努力，去满足那些我不明所以的需求。

若不是他们，我早就饿死了。我们相遇之时，我已是日暮途穷。

初冬烈日炎炎，但我还在那棵大树的腹中昏睡着。我因饥饿而精疲力竭，而长睡不醒，就那样神志不清、一点一滴地枯萎着，再无力气去更换居所，迁移到更好的草场上，只为自己有一处宽敞的藏身之所而心怀感激，这光秃赤裸，树叶落尽，住起来并不舒适，还向外探伸着手指的庞然大物。我半梦半醒地昏躺着，不确定我所听见的是真实发生在外面的，还是只是我脑中的幻觉，因为我意识到有人在说话，但就像在睡梦中一样，有人在说话，

104

然而你什么也听不懂。这些幻影围绕着这棵大树忙个不停，我好奇他们是否会闯入我的梦之现实，是否会俯身贴近于我。然后我闻到了某种气味。我闻到了烟味。它让我害怕。我不敢相信我会被焚灭于自己的谵妄之火中。透过一道裂隙，我看见漂浮的身影往来穿梭，我用一只手肘支撑着自己坐起。烟雾。人类的声音。那些幻影搬来一些剥光了树皮的长树枝，将它们以一种粗糙的方式捆扎在一起，组合成类似梯子的模样。我对所发生的一切一无所知。而所有的一切仍然围绕我的居所上演着。我看见了脸孔。透过烟雾的迷蒙和我的茫然，我看见那把梯子被倚靠在光滑的树干上，男人们攀爬向上，带着燃烧如花束的枝条，我听见欢快的叫喊声，我看见众人如幽灵般起舞，男人、女人、孩子们，我看见他们狼吞虎咽、舔舐着他们的嘴唇，我听见他们大声欢笑，然后我走出了我的猴面包树，那虚弱不堪的我的残躯，从洞口的阴影里走了出来，走入了令人眩目的冬日的光线，穿着一件丝绸长袍的褴褛碎片，我的眼睛圆睁，我的嘴唇微张，我的双手在无助中向前伸去。我说话了。

直到第二日，他们中才有一两个人返回这里。一定是他们了，因为当我从饮水的溪流那儿回来时，发现在裂隙的入口处有一颗干燥的、挖空了的猴橙外壳正等待着我，里面装满了蜂蜜。深褐的，近乎是黑色的蜂蜜，还掺杂着蜜蜂的幼虫，透着一股原始的粗糙。

该如何表达我的感谢呢？我捧起那颗猴橙，伸直手臂，站在距离树干不远的地方，好让自己能更容易地被看见。我就那样站了一会儿。蜜蜂在我上方那个躁动不安的蜂巢里嗡鸣着、忙碌着，像是要修补寒冷的侵袭所造成的损坏似的。在光与影的流转之间，它们看上去仿佛在往来游动、上下沉浮一般。如此，我向蜜蜂和它们的同党致上了我的敬意。

每一天都会有某些东西在等待着我。我去饮水的时候，他们便会带着他们的礼物到来，将其搁放在入口的位置。出于好奇，有一日我悄悄窥视过他们。我假装走进了河边的矮树丛，但并没有立即下到水中，而是躲在灌木丛里，暗中观察着猴面包树周围的动静。我看见两个男人穿过长草走了过来。他们的个头很矮，且长草使他们看上去更显矮小了。他们有着较浅的肤色和宛如苔藓般覆盖着头顶的短发。他们的衣服和武器都很粗拙。他们先是看了看那棵树，然后迅速地走过去，放下某样东西，又迅速地跑开了。长草吞没了他们。

一只地犀鸟出现了，踱着步。我看见他正朝猴面包树的入口踱去。我可以清晰地从他那淡蓝色的瞳孔里捕捉到他精于算计的神色，这神色就娇媚地粉饰在他僵硬的睫毛之下。我顿时火冒三丈，在他有机会接近我的礼物之前，便猛冲出我的藏身之处，将他驱逐了。第二日，他们什么也没有带给我。直到第三日。就这样，我学会了遵照未知的规律行事，尽管强烈的好奇心灼烧着我，尽管我愿意付出一切去了解更多。

我尤其喜欢他们送给我的那些耐穿的兽皮衣物。眼看着冬季就要到来了，且这一个冬季会比我以往过惯了的冬季要严酷得多。严酷得多，干燥得多，也枯黄得多。大地崩裂，碎成粉末。落叶树的枝干在愈加明亮的天空映衬下，显现出错杂纷乱的轮廓。羊蹄甲的花朵凋零腐烂，化作疯狂迸裂的荚果。世间万物，在我看来都好似被遗弃了一般。鹮鸟的群落也显得黯淡、邋遢。甚至连大象看上去都很惆怅。

我也受到了影响。又一次，忧郁覆没了我。狐獴的顽皮捣蛋、水獭的水中嬉戏都无法令我开怀。摇头摆脑的岩蜥蜴也没能转移我的注意力。我只是垂头丧气、漫无目的地游荡着。

被一只狒狒哨兵的恫吓伎俩驱赶到某个地方的我，捡起了我的第一颗珠子，在某个岩石的缝隙变成了裂隙的地方，在某个尘土之中缠绕着枯死的草梗、草穗、花萼、花瓣、根茎的地方，在不久之前的某个地方。

人类的物件。人类曾到过这里。在我与留下珠子和陶器碎片的人之间隔着的，是不可估量的距离、无法挽回的时间和难以逾越的鸿沟。无可消解了，因这小小的发现而愈益强烈的我的孤独。永无绝期了，这孤身一人的岁月延绵。我在这里，在那些与我隔绝之人的围簇之中，我为他们而存在着，但也只是作为一个幽灵。

作为一个幽灵，我日渐康复了，并且通过吃食菌类、腐肉花茎、蟒蛇肉、马鲁拉果[1]、长寿果[2]和水羚的肝脏而再一次变得圆润、丰满起来。但凡冬季和夏季可以奉予那些小矮人的眼睛、采集袋

---

[1] 学名 *Sclerocarya birrea*，英文俗称 Marula（马鲁拉），分布于非洲南部，被誉为当地人的生命之树，其果实也是当地主要的水果之一。
[2] 学名 *Lannea discolor*，英文俗称 Live-long berry（长寿果），分布于非洲南部，果实成熟后为紫红色，与葡萄相似。

和弓箭的，我也都可以美餐一顿。不再有匮乏的困境了，倒是有点儿慵懒的过剩。

该感谢谁呢，我有时也这样问我自己。我的水之神灵沉默着。于是我感谢了那些蜜蜂。我感谢了这棵为蜜蜂提供了安身之所的大树。我感谢了这片给予这棵大树立足之处的土地——这极其困难，因为它是颠倒着生长的[1]。我感谢了那些恰好降至这棵大树树根的雨水，如此它才得以喝饱水分，长出绿叶和花朵。但我的水之神灵沉默着。猴面包树，白日里，环绕着你，蜜蜂翩然起舞；夜幕下，环绕着你，敏感的花朵如月亮般绽放，如此之多的蝙蝠振翅齐飞，在你的枝杈上，大雨为我倾倒下雨水，对你，我的水之神灵亦沉默不语。有一回，我发现一只受伤的蝙蝠，就躺在日光满溢的裂隙边上。起初我以为它是一只滑稽的爪蟾，正在那儿向后挪动着。然后我注意到它有毛皮。然后我看见了耳朵。我向溪流走去。当我回来时它已经不见了。

我寻找着我第一次捡到那些珠子的地方。我反反复复、纠缠不休地寻找着。

那只蝙蝠已经不见了。一串鸵鸟蛋壳碎片制成的项链，一如野梨花的白，和一小把野欧楂[2]在等待着我。

不久后的一个下午，我在一处杂草蔓生的岩石缝隙中发现了岩榕苍白的盘根。我性急地攀爬上那块岩石的背脊，拖拽着松垮

---

1 此处形容的是猴面包树的独特外形，树冠巨大，分枝繁多，酷似倒立的树根。
2 学名 *Vangueria infausta*，英文俗称 Wild medlar（野欧楂），分布于非洲东部和南部，果实口感与苹果相似。

而垂悬的根须，抵达了一处小小的高地。我爬上来的这一面陡坡，与日出、日落都成一定角度，还可以俯瞰一片绵长的、几乎是空无一物的山坡，只有几簇树丛点缀其间。几只长颈鹿，几团角马和斑马扬起的混杂着鼻息和低吼的尘土。除此之外，当时我便再没留意到什么了。一群飞鸟，是的，那也是有的，倏忽间便消隐于远方天际。而风无处不在。它持续不断地发出飒飒的声响，仿佛它是寂静的同伴。这便是我在彻底侦查过那片高地后所发现的全部了：风，以及风的背景，寂静。我幻想着这就是那个将一切摧毁抹去的守护者，而谁在四处探寻，谁就必将蒙难。为何要划破、挖出、揭露、思索还有推测呢？随它去吧，且随它去吧。这里曾经有过，也许。

一座城市，也许，有着统治者和他的臣民。我不知道他们到这里来追寻什么，是什么使他们在所有地方中偏偏选中了这里建造起他们的房屋，目之所及，渺无边际。他们是否知道那环绕着、轻舔着地平线的浩瀚大海，是否想象过属于他们的各种各样的、居于众星之上或万物之中的神明；或者，他们是否目睹了为他们而举行的祭仪，他们从那里启程离开，眼神因信仰而晶莹，心中满怀善意；以及，他们是否事先知晓，自己注定难逃一死，还是死亡对他们而言只是一场碰运气的游戏，有时因疾病而变得棘手，有时不过一场溘然，但无论如何，它才是生命真正的起始，没有肉体的烦扰，因而也没有对时间的需求，而如果死亡就是生命，他们便仍然活着。在这里。就在这里。

风逐渐平息了。在令人难以置信的空寂中，一块巨石从悬崖侧壁上滚落下来，颠簸着，弹跳着，仿佛在表演一场魔术，奇妙而无声地，在我身下某处获得了安息。这般的万籁俱寂，叫我毛骨悚然。现在，我再听不见任何声响了。霎时我意识到，如果此刻我开口说话，某些奇伟磅礴之事便会发生。已死之人将会复生，或不是复生，而是在我眼前显现，时间将会翻滚，大地将会歪斜、倾覆，朝向无垠的黑暗颠倒、悬置，而我的水之神灵将会航入永恒的空境，永远地消失不见。

然后我感到有什么东西正在我耳朵里爬动。它抓挠、刺痒着我，我甩了甩脑袋。一只蚂蚁。一个活物。一只爬虫。我用手指碾死了它。我仿佛刚刚从一场昏厥中醒来，此时才留意到天空已是乌云密布，随时可能落下雨来。我被恐惧攫住了，匆匆离去，决意在闪电劈裂天空之前回到猴面包树，但最重要的是，决意及时回到属于我的时间中去，因为当我奔跑着，有时也被绊倒着的时候，我感到我身后有另一个世界正在生长壮大，我感到那已然存在的什么东西正在以越来越快的速度扩张它的领域，我感到很快，就在我奔跑的这一个动作里，我便会进入另一种全然不同的时间之中。

抵达猴面包树时，我的心脏狂跳，脾脏的一阵刺痛使我弯下腰来，当我蹲坐在裂隙的入口处时，我看见第一颗雨滴坠落在尘土上形成的玫瑰花的图案。

所以，我屈服于我周遭的力量了，或者，说得不那么沮丧些，我学会了与它们共处，就像我学会了与这片稀树草原，与那些动物、昆虫共处一般，我学会了在现实与我的梦境中选择道路，学会了与那些同我保持距离的人生活在一起。这是一种奇妙的体验，你们分享生命，却没有任何接触。我常常问自己，他们是在予我施舍，还是在向我进贡。我尽量表现得合乎身份。但我也向自己承认，我其实什么都不用做，只需接受自己作为一个饭来张口的俘虏的命运，然后相应地表达我的感恩之情即可。仿佛是他人的出现加剧了我的孤独似的，仿佛是我与他人之间的距离如今愈发遥远了，才令他们全都存在于有形的咫尺之间似的。我看见他们在远处走动，我看见女孩们在玩一颗猴橙，将它互相抛来抛去，看见女人们翘着臀部，背着婴儿，看见男人们肚子满是皱褶，双腿瘦如木棍，而所有人的肤色都好似乌龟的腹部一般黝黄，我只有用手捂住嘴巴，才能阻止自己呼唤近处的某个人。我听见他们发出的咔哒咔哒的声响，我也对自己呢喃起一些话语，听上去很像我孩提时代的语言。遗失的词语重又以朦胧的形影出现了。母亲，我看见了母亲，父亲，兄弟，姐妹。我看见了茅草屋和高大的树木，那树干布满褶裥，好似翻涌的裙摆，枝叶绿意葱茏。母亲，我又一次看见了母亲。温暖，柔软，一个纤瘦的身影，有着长垂的乳房和结实的乳头。我隐约听见了一些说话声，还有其他嘈杂的声响，切剁声，噼啪声。一瞬之间，我记起了从不吠叫的狗，吵闹聒噪的猿，还有那种欢快的氛围，我记起来了，那是当肉被分发给每一个人时的欢快的氛围，哪怕是猿的肉，是的，我还有过一个用树皮纤维做成的娃娃，娃娃的脖子上戴着一小串珠子，脑袋是一根小木棍，而当时我也带着我的娃娃，当所有人奔逃出他们的茅草屋，躲藏进茂密的灌木丛，当我的母亲使劲地拉住我的胳膊的时候，然而她被杀死了，她的脑袋被劈开了，我被从她的怀里猛拽出来，和其他女人一起被赶入了一小群人里。还有一大批的男丁俘虏。我紧紧地抓着我的娃娃。我将它抱在我的怀里。我们一直走、一直走，一直走到一个村子。男丁俘虏们被聚拢到一起，有人对他们做了些什么。然后我们再次动身了。这一次，我们走得更远、更远了，我们来到了一座城市，它坐落于一片极其浩大、无限宽广的水域之上，而蓝，从这一端一直漫延至遥远的另一端。

现在，我知晓了所有事物的名字：奴隶、阉割、商贸、沿海城市、大海、仆役。是的，现在我知晓了所有。

我知晓了所有的名字，却无一人聆听我说话。我拿这些名字毫无用处了。它们不过是一些叮叮当当的声响。

从远方吹来的风，带来了小矮人们的音乐声。那乐声于我，好似甲虫在火焰上跳跃。我还能听见他们唱歌、拍手的声音。

现在，我要迫使他们面对我了。

下一次他们到这里来采摘猴面包树的果子，将那酸甜白嫩的果肉从果核上吮咂下来之时，我发誓，就在那时。那时我将赤身裸体地面对他们。那时我将脱去衣物。我将把我的皮毛围裙、我那饰有跳兔骨头的皮毛披风，还有那串鸵鸟蛋壳碎片制成的项链放到一旁，我将面对他们、挑战他们，尽管我的挑战会被我已成习惯的优雅所缓和，羞涩然而高贵，诱惑但却冷漠；我会直直看进他们的眼睛，亦迫使他们直直看回我的眼睛，迫使他们承认，我是一个人类，且仅仅是一个人类。那就是我的全部。

我做到了。他们彼此交谈着走近了，我猜他们是来摘果子的，就像他们几天前做的那样。我脱去衣物，取下项链，松开我脚上的凉鞋，把它们踢落在地上，在怀疑和犹豫将我压倒之前，我走了出去，伫立在了猴面包树的入口处。他们从我身旁走过，其中一人爬上了那把他们为够到蜂巢而靠在树干上的自制梯子。他摘下果子，将它们扔向地面上的同伴，而同伴们也身手敏捷地接住了它们。接着，若无其事地，那摘果子的人爬了下来，将梯子搬到大树的另一端，并在那里又一次地收获了。然后所有人都离开了，每个人背上都背着一个采集袋，装满了这棵树的果实。

我被刻意地视而不见了。

在这个我被迫活下去的梦里，我更加经常地求助于那座玫瑰色水晶之城的庇护了。因为这个原因，我已经自行改写了那些猎人的故事。闪烁着玫瑰色莹光的不只是那座山，还有那座城，那座我在其他许许多多与我相似之人的陪伴下漫步其中的城市。我们无需彼此交谈，我们生来就能相互理解。我也在那里留意到了我的异乡人，但是发觉我已不再需要他的陪伴了，因为我是一种自给自足的结晶，我已化作至纯至净的喜乐。我既是一个整体，又是分裂之物，我存在于每一件事物，我存在于每一处角落。

奇怪，我的水之神灵会将我送至沙漠之境，但我也可以理解，因为，你看，水本身也化作了水晶，世间万物，岩石，水，人类，都拥有水晶的恒定，还有灿烂，还有即便支离破碎也仍旧保持着灿烂的壮丽认知。然后，当我醒来的时候，无论身处黑夜、白天，我只觉浑身皱皱、僵硬。

不被允许为人的侮辱，我已经克服。还有所有丑陋的幻象，那些长满毛发的茅草屋，那些歪斜的、试图诱我入内并将我锁起的大门，全都是虚假的答案，全都是错误的出口；因为我自己决定外表与实相。我统治一切。我在天地间做着梦，带着早已察觉这一切都只是表象的人才有的自信，我对自己微笑着，我沿自己选择的道路努力前行着，我将饮下这离别毒药的馈赠，怀着一份滋养着我的认知：梦境通往梦境。

没有其他的终点。我承认。我已被用尽了。对我自己而言也是如此。但这一点无论是否会构成他们斟酌审议的一部分，都几乎是无关紧要的。他们为何要在悲痛时还为一个令他们失望的人的感情腾出空间呢，一个本应提供一条出路的人，却如此可悲地辜负了他们。

举头三尺有神明，异乡人曾这样说。他们知道自己看到了什么。

那正是我所不知道的。和我想要加入的。我这样想着。

异乡人讲过许多神明和宗教的故事，许多他在贸易航行的旅途中接触过的城里的祭司、狂热的信徒和先知的奇怪习俗，还有他们彼此间的敌意，他们为争取群众的盲目服从而相互角逐，他们为赢得统治者的偏袒而相互竞争，因为这意味着他们将得到统治者的资助，从而为其所属的传教阶层获得权势，而所有这一切，所有这一切仅仅是因为人们惧怕死亡，所有这一切仅仅是为了驱除这些惧怕。轮回的允诺，复活的允诺，死后天堂的允诺，友爱的先人群体的允诺，通过斋戒也通过投资和捐赠而得到救赎的允诺；且每一种宗教都在毫无廉耻地招纳新人的同时，毫无廉耻地排斥着其他每一种宗教。

而死亡不过是家常便饭！异乡人语毕，陷入了沉默，等待着某个人的反驳。是吓唬孩子的故事，这是他的结论。顶多是个无聊的故事，有时算得上有趣，就像冒险故事那样。我们还是给彼此讲讲寓言故事吧，就不要在宗教问题上争执不休了。谁相信有一个地方，人们会骑在大象的身上？谁相信有一个地方，人们会骑在长有两块隆肉的动物身上？谁相信有一个地方，人们会用套轭的水牛来耕犁土地，相信有一个地方，人们会用牛奶来美白？然而你们却相信，你们这些哲学家和操纵者们，天堂？

异乡人轻蔑地大笑起来。

生命中已有足够多迷人的事物，令我好奇不已了。我总是贪得无厌、急不可耐地想要了解更多。看！

他取下脖子上的一条项链，那是一条金色的链子，上面挂着一颗硕大的鸡血石吊坠，好似一只甲虫，被精心雕琢成了一只瓢虫的模样，只是更冷酷，体型也更大。

你们有谁相信这宝石是从一个尚在人世的死人[1]脖子上偷来的呢？他问。

我仍然能够记起那些吃惊的叫喊，那些厌恶的手势，那些不满的牢骚，还有那几位最有名望的市民脸上挤出的勉强的笑容，这些人不能表现出无知的样子，因此不得不将它掩饰在轻松的机

---

1 或指前文中提到的还魂尸。

智下。

我希望，异乡人叹了口气，我可以游历到世界的最外面。我是如此的贪心。

我还记得长子也出席了那次宴会，记得他是如何专注地聆听着，如何用藤鞭轻轻拍打着他的小腿，但与往常一样，一言不发。我的恩人，也与往常一样，极少参与这类谈话。他病得太重了，被高烧折磨得太迷糊了。我的心与他同在，也与异乡人同在。当我的恩人缓慢地把一勺豆子送到自己唇边时，他的手都在微微地颤抖着。他，这个真正触碰到了死亡的人，对所有那些关于死亡的喋喋不休，又是怎么想的呢？他的眼睛，深陷在其眼窝之中，什么也没有透露。

在所有那些晚宴后进行的谈话里，我最不感兴趣的就是与战争有关的话题。我坦言，每当战争被提及，我便找到了装盘上菜或是收拾餐桌或是打理其他某件家务事的理由。他们谈论海上的战争，谈论陆地上的战争，谈论武器军备，海盗活动，谈论著名的胜仗和战利品的分赃，谈论赎金，勒索，空袭，征伐，以及其他诸如此类的事情，为此人们争执不下，企图令对方叹服，为此人们可以提出大相径庭的论点，并对对方的论述极尽尖酸刻薄之词。最高级别的利益游戏，这是异乡人对战争的说法，而他至少是这餐桌上少数几个能凭经验说话的人之一。

由他所指挥的小小的三角帆船舰队，曾进攻过他人，也曾遭到过海盗的袭击。与那些城里人不同，他已经同真正的战士进行过激烈的战斗了。他杀过人，也受过伤。当他提及一场血腥的屠杀时，他知道自己所言为何物，因为对他来说，记忆往往攀附于这样的事件，每一场战斗对他而言都意味着更多的经验，意味着对现实认知的不断累积，也正因如此，虽与他的个人意愿相违背，他所讲述的均是内行经历，而非虚构杜撰。不仅仅是英雄主义的故事。他见过伤者从甲板上摔落水中，见过被砍断的残肢漂浮于海面，见过水中的鲜血与骚动吸引来远近四方的鲨鱼，听过凄惨的溺水之人试图用咆哮来抵御那海怪的狂乱撕咬。全都是徒劳。尽管他坐在那儿讲述时是那么的平静、优雅，他使用的语言却是如此的野蛮、赤裸。砍，刺，切，踢，跟踪。

而那些站在历史的边缘上，生于不安的和平中，因繁华靡丽而日渐发胖的城里人只是喋喋不休地谈论着防御，谈论着建造要塞与壁垒，只是喋喋不休地谈论着而什么也没有行动起来，出于懒散，出于忌妒，出于缺乏相互信任以及最重要的，出于吝啬，我怀疑，也因为他们根本不觉得有任何威胁。他们与那些往来穿梭于海上的载满货物的三角帆船保持着极好的关系。他们自己的小船会将货物运输至较小的沿海城镇，用以交换满船的豹皮、象牙、龙涎香、玳瑁和犀牛角，再将其运回这座沿海城市，交与它的批发商们；这样互惠互利的合作已经持续了如此之久，他们不会相信任何一个可能预见到一场阴谋，一场破坏他们繁荣贸易之阴谋的人说的话。毕竟，谁会这般愚蠢呢？现在这样对每一个人都有利。毫无疑问，这些奇怪的卡拉维尔帆船——人们后来开始这样称呼它们——不会构成任何威胁。况且我们与这些新来者们也迅速建立起了联系。毫无疑问，他们不会有能力扼杀一段长期稳固的商贸关系。不，不会是这些要向我们乞讨水、新鲜的肉类和水果的傻子。

对每一个人而言，包括我自己在内，异乡人的报告听上去都很浪漫，而非富有教益或见地。我拿起一把心形的棕扇，为自己扇风。我点头，微笑，传递了一盘食物，想出了一句俏皮话，先说与一个客人听，然后又说与另一个客人听，试图将讨论引入一种轻松的氛围。我挑逗地调情、大笑，无可挑剔地践行着我的使命。我的恩人看上去也颇为满意。没药[1]的芳香，佳肴美馔的芳香，数不清的茉莉花的芳香，我洗浴身体的清水的芳香，我涂抹全身的精油的芳香，无比庞杂而复合的文明的芳香，这就是我们在此所呼吐着的。这就是这座湿热撩人的城市所奉予我们的。

这就是我对战争的了解所能延伸到的最远处。

人们说，女人天生就对暴行有一种本能的处理方式。这是一个谎言。虽然我曾经把死亡紧紧地搂在怀里，虽然我曾经亲手捧起一个被脐带勒死的死婴，将它用破旧的布料像一个包袱似的裹起，然后将它带离我们奴隶生产所用的茅草屋，虽然我曾经听过病人神志失常的谵语，也听过奴隶被惩处时的呜咽，但所有这些对我，都没有任何的帮助。

我藏在猴面包树最深、最暗、最远的角落里。这些惊声尖叫，这些战争的厮杀呐喊，这漆黑一片、覆没了我头顶的恐惧的洪水；

---

1 没药，橄榄科植物地丁树或哈地丁树的干燥树脂，古时被广泛用于制作香料和药膏。

这是穿透了我的恐惧，这是野兽般的临终哀鸣。我已是走投无路了；像一只岩兔，我在死亡的恐惧中颤栗着。

有好几日我都不敢出去。然后，是腐烂的恶臭将我熏了出来。

鬣狗在夜晚狂欢。我太害怕了，害怕到不敢为自己生起篝火，唯恐它成为那些前来屠村之人的一座灯塔。我蜷缩在猴面包树的腹中，理解了我那选择了黑暗而非生命之光亮的孩子，理解了他那明灭闪动的思绪的脉络。那是一种从未存在的狂喜。那是唯一的真正的胜利：死亡与生命都没有意义。它是平衡。它是不存在的圆满。

臭气将我熏了出来。这场战役的怒火几近肆虐到了猴面包树的脚下，我现在可以看清了；因为当我躲藏起来的时候，所有声响，不论远近，听上去都一模一样，四面八方传来的都是一模一样的声响，我根本分辨不出袭击者是从哪一个方向到来的。

屠杀开始前，我瞥见了袭击者的模样。我刚要从溪流边往回走，正摇摇晃晃地顶着那个发黑的陶罐，一手拿着我的勺子，我的鸵鸟蛋壳——也就是说，我觉得我看见了一个人，或不止一个人，正注视着我。我一边敛声屏气地走着，一边在恐惧中意识到，那是来自陌生人的凝视，而非那些小矮人的偷窥，如果我可以这样形容其行为的话，因为那是无与伦比的微妙，事实上我几乎从未察觉过。然而这些……太明显了，我知道有人正注视着我，太明显了，我看见有黑色的身影消失在长草中。他们一定是探子。然后，就在那个晚上。然后，它持续着。如此之久。而我只是极其偶然地有一棵可以藏身的树才得以逃过一劫。他们一定是没有找到或是留意到这棵树，因为当我发觉那尖锐的凝视着我的目光时，我距离这棵树尚有相当远的距离。那条我亲自踩出的小径看上去也漫长得令人恼火。我一只眼睛盯着我的树，就这样一直将它藏在我的视线里，然而我与它之间的距离却并没有缩短，虽然我的步子迈得已是如此之大。这里有探子。这里有其他人。

其他人覆灭了我们。这些其他人是什么人？又从哪里来？

再次幸免于难，多么令人沮丧。

我终于鼓起勇气去一探究竟的那天，我在那些被啃咬过的尸体中辨认出了属于那些小矮人的残骸。其他人的更高大些。我不知道应该如何排遣恐惧。

那些食腐动物一定已经美美地饱餐一顿了。太多了，它们根本吃不完。这一份献祭是如此的庞大。

最惊人的场景是一棵树上的一个其他人，身体铺摊在树枝上，眼睛的浆果已被啄食干净，嘴巴和舌头的果肉犹如碎石瓦砾。而腐烂之处几乎已成流液了。

蚂蚁们全都疯了，成千上万，数不胜数。但它们永远不可能分解完所有的东西，将其一小粒一小粒地运回它们的储藏之地，何况那地方也无论如何不可能有足够的空间。蚂蚁们四处疾走着。

丽蝇成群结队、欢欣鼓舞地萦绕在一摊摊乱七八糟的内脏上，形成一块块绿色的圆斑，好似危险的花朵。这些闪闪发光的花朵会愈长愈大，直至那些圆斑突然迸裂成不计其数的飘零的碎屑，直至这些碎屑重又停落、凝结成一朵朵全新的花儿。它们无处不在。

那些尸身已被豺狼、鬣狗和秃鹫撕咬成了碎片，被拖拽得到处都是，还被依照他们的喜好重新排列组合过；但到处都是一拥而上的丽蝇。

我无法判断谁是这场屠杀的赢家。我可以挑选出所有我想要的武器，在我的猴面包树里建立一个军火库。我可以用铁器塞满它，用铁将它喂饱，用铁加固它的内部，再在入口处装上木柱似的长矛。

我同样无法判断，这散落各处的袭击者的尸骸是否比小矮人的要多。这里太安静了。只有一如既往的鸟的鸣叫、风的呼吸，以及向晚时分大象的到来——与往常一样，没有受到任何打扰。它们娴熟地将鼻子排成一列，浸入水中，悠闲地沐浴、抛洒沙子，然后，在做完了所有它们想做的事情之后，在年纪最长的母象带领下，恬静安详地撤离。我向它们致上了问候。

我首先给自己拾来了一堆树枝。因为现在我要为自己生起一堆巨大的篝火。因为我一点儿也不在乎自己会被谁看见。因为就算长草会再次带来同样多的袭击者，我也不在乎。因为就让死亡到来吧，就让死亡降临吧。因为一切都不再重要了。因为这就是终结了。

头顶一捆长树枝，走在回程的路上，我听见了一声呜咽，或者我以为我听见了。还是，并不是我以为？我专注地聆听着，却再没有听见任何声响。我聚精会神、屏息静气地转过头，避开风的方向，以便更好地捕捉声音，却再没有听见任何声响。我伫立良久，然后继续朝猴面包树走去，在入口前放下那捆树枝，而心

121

里是清楚的，清楚我必须再度返回，去追踪那呜咽之声。我必须找到它。

这一份确信驱使着我。我仔细检查了所有的遗骸，并且强迫自己有系统地去做这件事，去有条不紊地搜寻，去谨慎入微地观察哪怕最为细弱的生命的迹象。我寻找着，寻找着，寻找着。我忘记了尸臭、丽蝇，还有那些伫立于树顶旁观着这一幕的秃鹫，以及人类残躯的可怖形貌。我围绕着猴面包树寻找了一遍又一遍，任何看起来像是人类的身形、人类的残余的东西，我都会上前查探一二，就这样来到了一处蚁丘跟前，就这样再一次听见了一声呜咽。我更加心急火燎地搜寻起来，来来回回，反反复复。这一带还能听见蕉鹃的叹息，但我知道，但我确信，我所听见的是一声属于人类的呜咽。那声音极其微弱，只是勉强能够被听见，只是勉强。要是我能够再听见一次该有多好。距离是有欺骗性的。

我回到猴面包树，从那一捆树枝中抽出一根，用它继续在蚁丘周围搜寻着，戳捅着缠绕在一起的杂草和茂密的地被植物；但我到底在做什么呢？我的空间感难道已经彻底紊乱，以致于我脑海中所搜寻之物已经萎缩成了侏儒那般大小，萎缩成了胎儿那般大小——那是我要搜寻的东西吗？为何我会拿着一根树枝在这里翻来搅去？我在寻找一声呜咽，一声没有形体的呜咽。一声消失于此的呜咽。那就是我要搜寻的东西。一声吁叹在空气里的呜咽，而我想要得到它。

我大笑起来。一半啜泣、一半嗤笑，从我的喉咙里滚落出来，从我的身体里滚落出来，有如呻吟。一个接一个地，我将它们像泥土块似的驱逐了出来，当它们终于被倾倒干净时，我感觉就像一个刚刚呕吐过的人。拿着我的树枝，我回到了我的猴面包树。

我生起篝火。火星。火焰。火。它熊熊燃烧起来，因为我往里面扔进了越来越多的柴火；我还想去拾来更多的柴火，燃起一堆光焰冲天的大火，用它那令人愉悦的草木灰的气味，熏走这人类之死灭的气息。我还想用这堆大火宣告我沦为孤儿的存在。让这样的我被看见吧。让啄木鸟和红毛窃蠹看见它吧，让那些猎豹远离我吧，让捻角羚和小羚羊嗅到这火光的气息，躲得远远的吧，让残存下来的人类看见它，并下定他们的决心吧。尽管来吧，我将如你们所愿。怀着虔敬与无力之感，我走过你们的尸体，一无所获。我，一个在一棵树的庇护下躲过厄运降临的人，一个并不来自这里，并不属于这里，亦并不愿意留在这里的人。我听见了你们战斗的呐喊、你们孩子的呻吟、你们最后的声息，而我只是一声不吭地躲藏着，待到一切过去，才走出了我的猴面包树。有谁看见我了吗？

有谁看见我为我所见之事而颤栗不已了吗？

如果这里还有更多的你们，无论矮小高大，无论肤色深浅，尽管来吧。

渐渐地，我又熬过来了。又是冬天了。挨过一个夏天，一个冬天，又一个夏天，现在，又是一个冬天了。这是一个艰难的冬天。又一次，我不得不依靠自己活下去，唯有风，现在还有这些幽灵，与我作伴。树的周围，白骨累累。猴面包树抓挠、紧攥着天空。长草犹立，苍白而僵硬。一株芦荟吸饱了大地的鲜血，将其化作一簇艳俗的红花，佩戴在头上，光鲜亮丽地映衬着清透的蓝天，对食蜜鸟来说，实在是一份太过诱人的存在了。树的周围，白骨累累。风吹来的尘埃，一点一滴，填满了头颅与骨盆的空洞。

我不得不开辟一些新的小径，因为这些骷髅用它们的肋骨挡住了我的去路。没有鬣狗和秃鹫的陪伴我也可以做到。

渐渐地，熬过来了。

我已有许久未曾留意到狒狒了。尾巴直立的疣猪倒是常见。

事实上，我的行动愈来愈迟缓了，仿佛要陷入停滞一般。我的领地也随我力量的衰弱而缩减着。一种无法照顾好自己的耻辱。虽然我知道自己可以吃些什么，我却不知道应该如何寻得，或去何处寻得它们，我又像初来乍到时那般四处游荡了；只是这一次，是听天由命了。毕竟，为何要歇斯底里呢？那般猛烈的情绪的浓度，目的何在呢？顺其自然吧。有些天我找到了一些吃的，有些天我一无所获。都无所谓。

藤蔓植物的盘根错节背后，永远有小溪流水的芳香慰藉、它淙淙潺潺的疗愈、它所营造的清凉氛围，还总有一群长尾猴用它们滑稽的喝斥对我的入侵表示着不满。尽管如此，这里仍然有一些我所熟悉的东西。事情就这样发生了。

这喊喊喳喳的溪水之后会安静地、胆怯地汇入河流，而那条河流会奔流向太阳和月亮升起的地方，奔流向我开始我的旅程的地方，奔流向那一座城市的那一片大海——我们从那里启程，要去寻找世界另一端的另一座海上城市。

我不再渴望任何东西了。

有一次，迄今为止仅有一次，我又一次经历了期待的痛苦，当我远远地看见一点火光蔓延成为一片草原大火，在地平线上蜿蜒曲折、扬帆航行，逐渐将地平线吞噬殆尽的时候。火之蛇，我真诚地企盼着，你也可以航行向我，将我吞没。它在遥远的地方继续燃烧着，在火焰熄灭了很久以后，那烟雾仍然像一块枢衣般久久蒙罩着空气。我闻到了它的气味，我留意到了树皮上的烟灰斑点。

造成这场毁灭的人，不论是谁，他是否看见了我夜里的篝火？

我的答案是，有一天，我在我惯常的取水之旅后发现的、一份为我而备的毒药。现在，有人知道我的身份了。有人一直都知道我的身份。但会是谁呢？在此，我可以用我的小金钉玩一个简单的小游戏。我可以将它们数一个遍，然后单纯地接受它们的说法。为什么不呢？我按照韵律数着它们。终归还是有用的，小小的钉子，将对我而言久远的往事与神秘的事物连接在了一起，是正在消失的意义的珍贵的、小小的迹象。现在，在你们的帮助之下，我最后的时光也变得好笑了些。

很好。我已经将它们数了个遍，我看着它们，那结果是我没有被遗忘，而这也是我一直以来的想法。我的猜测与偶然相一致，为此我将心存感激。我不再拖延了。我将钉子肆无忌惮地抛洒在空气里。让它们降落在它们想要栖身的地方，躺在那里，永不生锈吧。我真的是一位女主人、一位母亲和一位女神。足以令你们发笑了。

我站在裂隙的入口处，伸长手臂，举起这最后一份馈赠，好让自己能够被看见。然后我便隐入了幽暗的裂隙之中。

猴面包树，慈悲之树。我的猴面包树。

我饮尽了我的生命。快些吧，水之神灵。让你的使者快速地完成他的使命吧。

好的。

像鸟儿离开树枝。果子坠落。一只蝙蝠。像一只蝙蝠，漆黑的，求索着。

我潜入黑暗的水中，用我的翅膀向遥远的另一端划去，在缓缓而降的阒寂之中，渐渐失去控制，失去听觉，愈飞愈远。我将在颠倒的悬置里寻得安息。我合上了我的翅膀。

The Expedition to the
Baobab Tree

Wilma Stockenström

Translated from Afrikaans
by J.M. Coetzee

With bitterness, then. But that I have forbidden myself. With ridicule, then, which is more affable, which keeps itself transparent and could not care less; and like a bird into a nest I can slip back into a tree trunk and laugh to myself. And keep quiet too, perhaps just keep quiet so as to dream outward, for the seventh sense is sleep.

In the past time often caused trouble when I still wanted to have more than day and night and was obsessed with counting and uncertain whether the times during the day when I dozed should be reckoned as night, where night was the eventless and day the busy. Sleep as night. How I sometimes stretched out my nights, curling myself up into the smallest possible bundle in the darkest hollow, forehead pressed against knees to kill the gnawing within myself, entangled in confused thoughts, and fixed on a colour to which I held myself so that I could later say, my sleep was blue, or living red like blood, or a grey transitional shade. I woke up crumbled, sat up lightheaded, unsteady, and set a dusty foot down in the great assegai blade of sunlight that bores all day with a steady murderous twist into my dwelling.

That was the time before the beads. The time after the beads can be handled more easily. If I treat myself to sleep so often, it is no longer by chance and for a long while has not been an escape. Then only do I live, I tell myself.

With the beads began my determined effort at dating. I picked them up some days ago, and only later got the idea. I added the new find to the heap of potsherds that curiosity had led me to collect on my trips of varying distances from the tree, hesitant, bored, frustrated trips away from the path to the water that I had by then almost recognizably tramped.

Like the wild animals I make my paths. This conclusion came later. Like the redbuck, no, not like the redbuck and the zebra, not like the buffalo or herd animals of whatever kind that supplement each other's senses and confront crises together and survive what alone they would be too weak for, and that yet fall prey as individuals, and yet die alone, each in his time. I tread my own track, so clearly purposeful that I know I have already dwelt a long time in these parts, or rather there has never been any question of dwelling. Rather I should say: I too survive here, but I rely on myself, and even on the days when it feels as if everywhere under the earth there are snake eggs lying, even then

I have to fend for myself and try not to tread on them.

My path to the stream, made by me who tread so lightly, thin, faintly winding, weaving past bush and tree trunk and through flat grass plains where the winter is beginning to lie red – my path runs down a final sudden slope to sun-irradiated water wide as my outstretched arms between the trunks of two young matumi trees guarding my drinking place. Further downstream I wash. Higher up, where this tributary debouches into the main stream, is the elephants' ford.

The time when I nearly landed under the feet of the herd, I thought of a riddle that we young girls used to ask each other: What carries its life in its stomach? It must have been all the rumbling bellies that made me giggle anxiously for a moment and then left my throat quite dry in my meagre hiding place, with a stone ridge and reeds between them and me. The horde of feet trod springily past me into the pool, the water splashed, they bathed calmly. I shrank into myself. No one grows up under such close protection as a slave girl. I can also add, no one grows up as ignorant as a slave girl, and even I, the shining exception, seem to be stupid when it comes to wild animals and their habits, with my knowledge restricted to items of information about the ivory trade. Every other season an elephant swallows a pebble down, and the pebbles rattle around in their tremendous bellies all their lives, rattle and rattle. Whatever is incomprehensibly huge I reduced to the ridiculous to be able to assimilate it and prove my power over it, while I knelt comically curled up behind stone and reed, a slug without a shell, a soft-shelled beetle as big as the top of my little finger, anxiously in sham death, waiting for the long drawn-out gambols to come to an end so that I could again stand up like a human being and look around. A last trumpeting from the far bank, then I came stiffly erect and brushed the damp sand from me and shivered in the breeze that bent the reeds.

Now I live in friendship with the herd whose ford and bathing place I accidentally trespassed on. Friendship a condescending misnomer, however. I live. They live. Thus. Sometimes from my higher ground I see the bent backs milling in the faraway glint of the water, I hear the trumpeting, see pairs of tusks raised momentarily, and still I struggle to make the spectacle cohere with the smooth bracelet that once I could wear. There are connections that evade me.

If I cannot even know everything on the short walk from the entrance to the baobab to the heap of potsherds and other finds, so many steps there, so many back, what of my journey, which sometimes feels as if it took a lifetime and still lasts, still goes on, even if now I am travelling in circles around one place?

So many steps there, with feet already tiring. What did I think I was collecting when I carried it all here . . .? What did I think I was going to achieve with rubbish . . .? Time becomes beads and thus rubbish.

On the many paths of my memory there arise threatening figures that block every backward glance. I know these figures. I cannot name them. They loom up before me in the form of something human or sometimes like the corner of a hairy wall or a rolling hut opening that tries to swallow me and drag me off, an opening that storms down in a rage, storms down at a tremendous speed, and then a yard from me suddenly swerves away and saunters and entices me; sometimes too a quiet misshapenness of expectation followed by a noticeable dejection when the multitude of sharp pincers that grip me turn into the slack tendrils of a thicket, when the whole business disappears without further ado leaving an unfathomable grey behind. There are more tracks crisscrossing in my memory than I ever actually saw in a lifetime. What would I not have been able to track down if it had been granted to me and if my detective talent were not so frequently thwarted and the trail petered out inside me?

All kinds of paths leading nowhere radiate from my dwelling. They were not laid on. They came like that. Certainly when I arrived here I used the animal tracks because there was nothing else available except the paths to nowhere, but I soon had to conclude that my way of thinking did not slot in with that of other beings here. And I searched and opened a way and found.

Found, I say. Terrifying.

The most important item, water, I did not have to search for. There is plenty of it. It is visible and audible. I scoop the rippling of the stream up in my gift shell of ostrich egg. I hold the shell in the clear bow of water that leaps over a rough stone so as to catch the light and the sound. Again and again I scoop like this, and pour the water spirit's flickering and murmuring into my gift clay pot. Then I lift the full pot slowly with both hands onto my head, stoop from the knees to pick up my scoop shell, and walk back along the water path to the baobab.

Found: all kinds of veld foods; and found too that I was plucking, digging, picking them up in competition with animals, that trees did not bud and blossom and bear fruit for me to still my hunger, that tubers and roots did not swell underground for me, that not to please me did the greenheart tree drip its nectar, and not to refresh me did the flat crown stand at strategic points in the middle of a patch of shade, and not to give me pleasure did the flecked orchids display themselves, not for me did the violet tree put up tents of scent in early summer.

After the warthogs have grazed, a novice combs the patch of veld where experts have rooted, she kneels like them, tries to pierce the hard ground with a stick where she lacks tusks, tries using her eyesight to search out where she is not endowed with a sense of smell attuned to edible bulbs and roots, and dejectedly comes away with no more than a handful. After the baboons have grazed, the same procedure, except that she makes quite sure that they are out of the way before she ventures onto their terrain.

I fear the baboon's grimace more than the tusks of warthog and bushpig. He is too much like me. I fear my recognizable self in his ugly face. I am reminded of my inferior position here, my lesser knowledge. I feel taunted by the mirroring of my moods and desires in his monstrousness, and feel ridicule of my refinement, a demonstration that it is superfluous, in this vulgar hands-and-knees caricature. I despise him, his strength, his cunning, his self-evident mastery of this world. I despise the baboons one and all. The gluttons with the fat cheeks, they revolt me. Their unsightly public coupling and the self-abasing begging of the females, the ducking of the females under the hard hands of the males and the raucous scolding, and the eyes close together as you find them in brutes, and I think it is a sign of greed as well. I know too much about them for my taste. In a cage I would be able to laugh at them. As for what they know about me, they reveal nothing in those sidelong glances. I suppose I am no more than a nuisance to them. An outsider, far outside their realm of activity.

Only when I am asleep do I know fully who I am, for I reign over my dreamtime and occupy my dreams contentedly. At such times I am necessary to myself.

It was in hurried flight from the sentry of a troop of sickle tails that I came upon a flattened patch – it looked flattened to me – and stumbled and sprawled and gasped for breath. I turned around. My heart beat down to my fingertips. The puffs of breath from my nostrils blew against quivering blades of dry grass.

Thus I lay for a long while with the resignation of a food scavenger to whom hunger is something familiar that can wait to be stilled. Then I saw something shining, little beads of light between my eyelashes shone green and black, the light turned to solid beads when with the tip of my finger I burrowed between the grass blades and touched them. Then I sat up and scratched the beads out of the dust and the dry roots. They lay on my palm, two black and one green. I carried the useless discovery to the tree.

They were as small as pollen. I examined them. I arranged them in the limited number of patterns that their number and colours allowed. I recognized them. The next day I wanted to return to the place where I found them, but the direction escaped me and aimlessly I searched, hoping that I would recognize a tree or a rock slope, for it was near a koppie, that I remembered, and I remembered the white stepladder of roots that a mountain fig had woven up against a rockface; but I found nothing. I roamed about in the veld as if I had not yet forced any system upon it, just like at the beginning when I arrived here.

Right at the beginning was no time, for there was no time to devote to sequence and there were no categories, since the scrabble to survive wiped these differences out. Now I can permit myself the luxury of classification, as well as a judicious application of old and newly acquired knowledge. I can even reflect on what I am doing. I can let my thoughts run consecutively and regularly, without waves or ripples, I can form my thinking round as a clay pot and set it down cool and precise as water, I can make the mouth of the clay pot stand out like a spout against the uncertainty of blue and of black air that penetrates me and fills me completely if I am not careful. And I fill my thoughts with all sorts of objects, endless row upon row, not to be counted, I thank providence, I can think of enough objects to obliterate everything, and in addition I can make up objects if the remembered ones run out. I have good remedies against being empty.

Here now, the little beads that do not require imagining and of a kind that I used to see hanging around the necks and wrists of men and women. Once they used to be accepted in exchange for things, just as I was accepted in exchange for something. Of course I have no idea what my value must have been or what it ever was. A piece of ring money. Countless pieces. Another area of which I have little knowledge is the expenditure of money. It was the privilege of a slave girl to have everything given to her. The roof over my head. The cloth around my body. The food – in my case, plenty of it. How happy I was.

The beads are so tiny that they are barely visible on the knot in the tree where I keep them; but with my eyes shut I would be able to pick them up. I know the interior of my tree as a blind man knows his home, I know its flat surfaces and grooves and swellings and edges, its smell, its darknesses, its great crack of light as I never knew the huts and rooms where I was ordered to sleep, as I can only know something that is mine and mine only, my dwelling place into which no one ever penetrates. I can say: this is mine. I can say: this is I. These are my footprints. These are the ashes of my fireplace. These are my grinding stones. These are my beads. My sherds.

A supreme being I am in my grey tree skin. When I appear in the opening I stand proudly. Afterwards I suspect that I pose in the easily cultivated attitude of apparently relaxed expectation that I learned to adopt before my owners, mindful of the advantage of making an impression and at the same time beneath the surface brimming with conceit because I held this tiny scrap of power.

But imperiously I stand now and gaze out over the veld, and every time I step outside the world belongs to me. Every time I step out from the protecting interior of the tree I am once again a human being and powerful, and I gaze far out over the landscape with all its flourishes of vegetal growth and troops of animals and the purple patches of hills that try to hedge it in on the horizon. Reborn every time from the belly of a baobab, I stand full of myself. The sun defines my shadow. The wind clothes me. I point to the air and say: air make me live. And when the scrub warbler calls, he calls in my name. I am all there is, he calls.

Not everything is I. No. If there are still people here. Not everything.

How trifling the beads I have discovered compared with those I wore earlier, great oval red and yellow glass beads that hung like ripe berries around neck and wrists, complementing the ivory of a bracelet around my upper arm and my silk gown printed in shades of yellow. I was radiant. I laughed whitely. I was an object to be shown off, gloriously young as I first was. My marklessness, my smoothness, my one-time wholeness of skin. I was the envied uncircumcised one. I was the desired. I was too young to care in the slightest, to say nothing of understanding. I was a child. Such a child, such a child. I was still a child when I carried a child inside me.

Thankfully I remember the women who with their soothing gestures broke me in. Only here and there did I catch a reference, an intonation or an emphasis, for they spoke a language that poured down around me like a waterfall, it fell and fell from their mouths. Who were these women who adopted me and mothered me and taught me the game with men? I was overloaded with gifts to make me attractive. At the time I thought them gifts. I clamped myself fast to the women and tried to be good. Sometimes they scolded me. Then their lips opened and there was a creaking and crackling. But my tears were kissed away, they gave a clatter of friendly laughter, picked me up on their laps, pressed me to them, and I loved them like a child who once again feels safe; I climbed from lap to lap and jingled their bracelets. Thus, playing with me, they taught me, so that eventually I would remember the rapture and the torment, but inwardly remain untouched, remain whole, remain myself. I call you up in my memory. I cannot remember your faces but that does not matter. I remember your wonderful affection. I wonder whether you are now old and sad, and whether you still live in that house that was your destination, and whether you remember me, one of the multitude entrusted to your special soft playful care, and whether you ever tried to find out what happened to all of us. Whether you minded.

I never forgot your lessons, and even now I could laugh lewdly if I had to, and even now I could, like a cat, snuggle up lithely or wriggle free, and temper or increase my intensity as the situation demanded; but that has all become superfluous.

Now I live in a hollow with sleep the dense solution. I live in time measured by myself, initially with three beads, later with more and more till I chose the best of the green ones for my arrangement. So, to begin with, there passed in cycle a green day and two black days, later just a string of green days. Later I grew tired of green days and varied them with black in any conceivable pattern and number, as determined by mood and chance. My days became grouped. It was already a method to counter the vagueness of time hiding behind the course of nature. Time threatened me. It wanted to annihilate me. I thought I cheated it by changing my system every so often. Never did time know what I was going to try next, where even in the morning when light and chirruping awoke me I did not know what I was going to try with time, where I looked for firewood as and when necessary, fetched water when my supply was up, searched for food when I had to, and ate when I felt hungry, slept when drowsiness made my limbs heavy. And I dreamed and nodded through rose quartz.

I was reaching a stage of forgetting my counting toys, which then numbered only three and were gradually beginning to bore me, on the knot on the inner wall of the tree, when one day I picked up in various places more potsherds and beads as well as copper wire, and brought all this back. I added the rest, sherd and bead, to the heap, these leavings of inhabitants whom I wished ill because they could leave no more than this, potsherds that would not fit together and become a whole roundness, pitiful decorations that I irritably strung on stalks and carried around my neck, rusty copper wire rings, thick and heavy as shackles, with which I could do nothing, and nothing more in my vicinity. Nothing more – or was I roaming over graves? Nothing more – or was I roaming over walls submerged in dust and overgrown with plants? Was I perhaps roaming over courtyards and squares, fortifications, terraces, conduits, halls and shanties, settlements and streets crumbled into insignificance, taken over by the winters and the summers? Was I roaming over the place that we aimlessly came looking for, purposefulness long ago relinquished in the pitiless sun? Place of strips of underbrush and prickly grass, of a river off to one side hidden behind ripine trees and creepers, of hills with flattened crests on which gigantic round rocks piled in fantastic shapes, place of my towering baobab? Tableaus through which we roamed dazed, frightened? Place of predator and prey?

I imagine bloody wars of extermination. Droughts. An epidemic. I think of unflagging zeal, followed by collapse and despair. And then nothing, just a tiny residue that does not help me however much I make believe I have found a way of warding off the danger of timelessness through order. Because I resisted becoming a mere yawn in the lazy passage of the days, a mere transitory draught of air, a subordinate beat in the rhythm, a phantom within a rupture in eternity.

Too scantily endowed to fashion something myself, I used the artefacts of forgotten people to while away time, to coagulate time, with the bitter realization that it was changing nothing in the nothingness. But it made me feel good to handle the things and to wonder and to give my imagination rein, supplemented by memories of a different kind of earlier time.

For it was endowed with nothing but memories that I landed here, a famished, tattered being, struggling through plains and valleys, fevered with privation, stumbling on towards a steadily receding horizon, always day stages away, always the same, to be swallowed in by a tree, merciful harbourage, merciful cool shelter that reminds one roughly of a building with walls and spout-shaped rising ceiling and earth for a floor, a giant hut crowned with branches and leaves.

Curse the will-o'-the-wisp that led me here, that traveller through my life and the lives of others on whose lips I hung and whom I slavishly obeyed, blind with obsession, disordered, out of my senses. Curse him who made a spectacle of our sacrifice and wanted to give the attractiveness of understanding to hardship, the attractive useless self-knowledge that killed him, oh the talk, the talk, the omniscience, the all-investigating consciousness that could explain nothing, least of all the betrayal of comrade and following. Oh, the powerlessness of reasonableness!

Stranger in msasa-red clothes, from the beginning his wit charmed me. He knew the quips that light up an all too gloomy conversation. He knew more points of the compass than the disputatious poets and other such celebrities who congregated in the home of my owner, the rich widowed merchant, to eat my well-prepared meals and to pay for them and for the intercourse with his pretty slave girls with sophisticated conversation, even if this was limited to looking and desiring, or at most to some daredevil trying to fondle them when he thought his host was looking the other way. This one, on the other hand, in his msasa-red, in his water-green, in his flame-yellow, this one with his gold-speckled necklaces and slim gold bracelets was in no small measure well read and self-confidently informed about affairs. Without being asked he delivered a rejoinder, briefly summed up long-windedness, and time and again carried the arguments to ridiculous ends. Which made him little loved among our great spirits, who without success egged him on and tried to catch him in sacrilege or sedition. Let the gods stare over our heads. They know what they see. He asserted. Let the ancestors alone. Their intercession is not needed when you live unimpeachably.

Isn't that so? he asked. Isn't that so?

As fresh and new as lightning he put it to me.

So too the intercession of the prophets and the intercession of the family members of the prophets and the intercession of the gods combined and the intercession of god-fearing people, as well as the moral lessons to be learned from the experiences of people who elevate their tribal history to a religion – all this is interesting, and long may it be so. And invoking a deity morning and evening is beautiful music, is a resonant component of the sounds with which man attests that he not only thinks of food and propagation but considers himself immortal as well and therefore wants to take appropriate measures to ensure himself a pleasant afterlife. Let them. Let them by all means.

And let the merchants carry on. They are providing all this prosperity – and with an eloquent gesture he handed a porcelain dish of shrimps stewed with rice in sesame oil and coconut milk to the peevish poet on his right, while smiling in my direction. I thought he winked at me.

My owner's sardonic gaze rested on me. He beckoned me closer and his copper bracelets fell from his wrist to his elbow, so thin had his arm become. I picked up the palm fan to fan him. His upper lip was damp with droplets of sweat. Tonight he would again shiver with fever. He was already a sick man, probably dying, when I moved in with him and dared to become his youngest favourite. With long regular movements I tried to stir the heavy air around his face. He had left his food untouched, just tasted a dish of water. Poor creature inexorably gasping out a rich man's life with the spectacle of so much abundance before him. Influence and power slipped out of mouth and nostrils. Stored-up memories played themselves out in his cloudy eyes when the eyelids, between the spells when he sat and dozed, opened a slit and he presumably observed his guests, his slave girl servants, his sons and daughters gathered in luxury and pride. And his emaciated fingers, what were they trying to catch? A butterfly? The salt breeze? A woman's laugh?

The talk grew dull. He asked to be carried to his room. I say asked, not commanded. He asked in a whisper.

Left alone with him, I held him tight and soothed him, for he rebelled against his weakening and was far too fidgety; but then out of pity I let him be and by watching I understood what his hand was grasping for. He was trying to tear the fine web that death was spinning around him. When he jerked in spasms the web vibrated and shimmered slyly in anticipation. Tighter and tighter it was spun around him, so that the threat of sounds outside the room could not penetrate and the murmur of people with concern or concerns remained far outside the ring of his death stillness.

I let the invalid nestle between my drawn-up knees with his head on my breast. In his language I whispered lewd stories which made him smile blissfully in my arms. Shrunken baby, what an easy delivery for me. I fed you with the deathsmilk of indifference, for it could do your dried-out body no more harm and perhaps it was your way out, this being set free of any charitableness. Any pity would only delay your departure painfully.

One morning I climbed up to the highest terrace on the roof of my owner's house to breathe in the morning freshness and look out over the city and the sea, at the skiffs lying drawn up on the sand, several of them belonging to him whom I had just said farewell to for ever, that would probably now, like me, be disposed of. My future and the future of my fellow slaves, women and men, as well as that of the skiffs over there in the rosy daybreak, as well as that of the stores of elephant tusks and ambergris and iron, and that of the great house now at last plunged into mourning, and that of his fragrant garden down below me, had been allotted a precarious fate. Only those who have, have security as well. For me there was only insecurity. I waited, expecting to sigh. I waited for my feelings to well up. It was now the time for that.

I who come from the heart of the country bear the murmur of waters subliminally with me, a water knowledge preserved in my tears and saliva, in the blood of my veins, in all the juices of my body. I who knew how to extinguish attacks of fever with my water being, I found myself crying uncontrollably here in the morning stillness about so many things all at once that I would try to sob my tangle of thoughts to death rather than seek an interpretation that would amount to mourning but also a feeling of relief, anxiety about the future but also plain happiness about the purity of the morning after the oppressiveness of days and days in a sickroom.

With a corner of my robe I dried my eyes and cheeks and climbed back down to the garden. I had to find out what was going on. I walked down to the beach and from there – for my call to the solitary dhow in the bay remained unanswered – from there I walked through the neglected waterfront area, hoping that no one would notice my absence in the bustle and diminished supervision that follow such an important death. And even if they did notice it, what did I care. I was dumbfounded with grief, but more, with longing, and did not care who saw it. My longing was a hard little nut hidden deep within me. I did not care who knew of it now. Now, after my benefactor's decease, this feeling was my only certainty, and it helped me forget my fear of what lay ahead. Frivolous, perhaps, if I had been a woman who could have decided her own fate, but surely a permissible escape for the owned class to which I belonged. To fall foolishly in love and try to pocket happiness where happiness waited visible through a chink, and the time possibly favourable.

So now I searched for the man I had fallen in love with. I heard him laugh behind a heavy, richly carved teak door in secret consultation in his life away from me. I saw him disappear round a corner. I smelled him out, wherever he might stay, where he might yet walk, for he had promised to come again, and he would come again over the swell on the lee side of a billowing lateen sail, and I followed him in my imagination where the hem of his robe dragged through the mud, brushed over the fleshiness of a broken melon, and whisked over sand and fins and scales. I lingered with him where he stopped before the market women, occupied in observing how the poorest of the poor lived. Clouds of flies swarmed up from the piles of grilled fish and meat. They settled in patterns against the blue of his clothes and crawled over his nose and eyes and forehead, at the wet corners of his mouth, wherever there was moisture.

An old acquaintance came shuffling along with a flat basket of plantains on her head which she put down with a groan; then she took up position with legs stretched out in her traditional place under the shade tree. He began to chat to her and to others round about. He listened to brusque surly answers, embarrassed answers or equally embarrassed silences, to eagerly supplied information and quick-witted remarks in answer to questions from him, this presumptuous gentleman who was certainly not a client, making his own deductions. And with his inquiries about the price of crabs and clams and mussels and the availability and readiness to hand or otherwise of meat and fish and firewood, he built up cases using his own information, acquired on the spot, with which to refute other later arguments, opposing this information to the vague theories of rulers and well-meaning people. An attentive man. An inquisitive person who came to acquaint himself with the lot of the lowest, so much more complicated than the easy existence of a slave girl in a generous household, as he often pointed out to me.

My easy, indolent existence, yes, an existence now perhaps at an end.

Where did I find myself now, and was this smell of smouldering fear not familiar to me? The stench of blood. From this fear I never escaped, this trusty dizziness that impaired my sight, that made me brush with my hand over my eyes to see better and made me rue the act at once, for where I found myself, I discovered, was very near the slaughterhouse where I was sometimes sent by my second owner to buy entrails for his slaves. This smell known all too well to me, this lowing and bleating. Slippery heart liver lungs and gullet messily wrapped in leaves, a messiness too prone to slip out to carry on my head, I held it before me a little way from my body and walked away from a desolation soiled with dung and filth where animals buckled at the knee and the sad palms in their long dresses rustled dry leaves and grated, powerlessly anchored. Walked off from the joking butchers' teasing and provocative remarks and obscene gestures to go and cook the food that I would share with many mouths, and plot how to keep the liver aside for myself and mine, and how to pinch a scoopful of my master and his wife's rice in the – advantageously for me – untidy running of the household.

In two low huts with collapsed roofs we lived, the slaves, all to-gether, not separated by sex. From sunrise to late at night we toiled for him, the spice merchant. The work was what separated us. The men worked in his warehouse on the waterfront and the women in his residence. From far and wide we came, we spoke a variety of tongues, but here we got along by mangling the natives' language and turning it into our idiosyncratic workers' language. We were acquired second-hand, third-hand, even fourth-hand, mostly still young and healthy, we women fertile and rank. At night it was legs apart for the owner on his sweaty skin rug. Some of us welcomed it. Not I. He was clumsy and rough. I envied the slaves exempted from this sort of service. It brought a certain freedom along with it, after all, to be unmanned, I thought. I did not mind standing in front of the fireplace. I did not mind toiling with pick and hoe in the garden in the murderous heat to keep it neat around his mango trees and yam vines. I did not mind tidying his house under the eye of his shrew of a wife, obeying her expressionlessly, keeping my murmurs for the sleeping quarters, and even there being careful, for there were tell-tales amongst us. And to be discovered meant that your tongue was cut out.

I kept myself to myself. Lived as much uneasily as patiently. I was a coward and refused nothing.

With a stiff face I listened on his skin rug to the noise of the sea. I became a shell plucked from the rocks but kept my oyster shell of will, my thin deposit of pride, kept myself as I had been taught. I did not give in. I did not surrender. I let it happen. I could wait. I listened to the beat of the waves far behind his groaning, and it lulled me. I was of water. I was a flowing into all kinds of forms. I could preserve his seed and bring it to fruition from the sap of my body. I could kneel in waves of contractions with my face near to the earth to which water is married, and push the fruit out of myself and give my dripping breasts to one suckling child after another. My eyes smiled. My mouth was still.

Always still. Frightened mice in the middle of a great roaring, that was what we were, the subordinates of the system, apparently docile, our children taken away from us and sold while still infants, while our bodies still hungered for them, our past a past of pitiless mistreatment or the sarcasm of gifts, our present without prospect. We were all one woman, interchangeable, exchangeable. So we comforted each other and each other's children, so we shared, so we looked for lice on each other's scalps and wore each other's clothes and sang together, gossiped together, complained together. Without prospect. Once someone tried to run away. She was caught and her feet chopped off. A second time someone tried. She got away. The eunuchs deserted regularly.

There were stories current about a colony of deserters far from the city in the middle of the great swamp, where the escaped slaves lived by hunting, where they built mat huts and survived unbearable heat and loneliness to die there eventually as free people. It was said that they had developed their own system of government, with a headman and advisers, that they considered themselves safe, protected from pursuit by the impenetrable swamp infested with mosquitoes and leeches whose secret paths only the initiated knew, that they knew the authorities winked at them seeing that it would have cost a great deal of money to bring them back, seeing that those who had escaped would always be looking for trouble, would always grumble and rebel, and that it was wiser to punish such rebellious souls with oblivion in the wilderness, seeing that there were anyhow always fresh consignments of slaves coming from the interior. And that the eunuchs did not allow slave women among them.

One day a storm blew up worse than any I had yet experienced. It felt as if the heat were taking possession of me. It felt as if my eyes were going to bulge and stand out on stalks like a crab's. I pressed my palms hard against my eye sockets, for it felt as if sand and glass splinters were rasping over my unprotected stalk eyes, as if they beheld too much and too tenderly, therefore I tried to press them into my skull, but they throbbed so violently in my head, they rolled around inside my skull, and when my eyelids opened, I saw nothing, I saw only heat, and that made everything roll and heave. I could no longer hear anything. I could only feel in the pitch-black air that came towards me and drew away from me and began to push me around, to tug me in gusts this way and that way, to bring me face to face with rending lightning bolts that transformed everything into gaudiness and in a flash blacked everything out again and left me totally confused as to the direction I had been taking. I saw a bitter-orange tree where none had stood before. I saw a grey cloud consisting of crested terns and a second cloud thick with glistening sardines. I saw fishes rain and jellyfish tumble down and flotsam performing tricks and saw how a hut sucked in air till bursting point and suddenly collapsed and was flattened and suddenly began to whirl away in pieces.

Then I fled before the wind that was snatching up me and the refuse and everything that was frail, and I struggled onward at a slant, half-crawling, reeling from one support to the next, tree, pole, gate, building. That I could be blown into space, I, the peels, the tatters, go up in the whirl into all eternity. The sea beating. It fought with itself. It drew apart and clashed and balled together, it drew itself up high into the sky, it beat thunderously down on the high-water mark and rolled over and over covering the city's shanty quarter and the luxuriant woods there, and hurled pieces of wreckage from dhows and skiffs that had been made for and dedicated to it, down between the palms and rosebushes of the gardens of the rich. The wind tore the sails loose from the trees where they tried to hide like the ghosts of birds and blew them far away into the strange interior.

The sea drew back hissing over its destruction, drew in a last tortured, foaming breath, and subsided to a gloomy calm, and the wind subsided too, leaving such a rarefied stillness that a sob could have shattered it.

This brittle peace lasted only briefly. There was a patter of drops. At once it became pouring rain. Dense sheets came racing on over a sea that had totally forgotten its brief calm and heaved swollen and confused as the tide dragged it one way and the wind pushed it another. Pouring rain, gouts of water, hard and vertical, drops that mutilated the surface of the street into pockmarks, water that streamed and scoured out and washed away what the wind had forgotten to blow away and ran off in clattering furrows. A thorough, purposeful, seething rain. A storm rain with a mission.

Someone must have heard me moaning. Someone must have heard me whimpering where I lay trapped under a branch of a kudu-berry tree, a tree that, under orders from the storm, wanted to claim me as sacrifice because I had always resolutely ignored it and never tried to seek the favour of its spirit, because I ignore all spirits save that which lives in me. Probably because I did not know better. Perhaps. Perhaps I was obstinately defiant where I had brought nothing of my own with me and local rituals appeared without content, and I created my own rituals for my own indwelling spirit and without preknowledge went and picked up a white shell and a black shell. Placate the spirit of the earth, the spirit of the house, of the air, bring an offering of atonement, recite rhymes, mumble a formula, placate the spirit of the tree, he listens, he notes your gesture of sacrifice, he will watch over you, only be careful when you talk – no, that meant nothing to me. I smiled at the gestures. I walked nonchalantly past all the kudu-berry trees, which had after all been planted here and there on street corners only for their fierce autumn colours and had not come to grow here for my sake. I walked past them head in the air and offered them nothing. No, I laughed at the other women who bowed before them and reverently set down a handful of millet grains on the great leaf of a fever tree beside the silent tree trunk and muttered over them. I did not mutter at all, not for any tree spirit in the world. My tongue is meant for me, my tongue, my mouth, my whole self is mine. I pressed my ear against the grey-brown trunk of the kudu-berry and listened attentively to hear if its spirit had anything to say, but I heard only wood slowly growing, slowly expanding the chronicle of its year rings, and I knew he would not have anything to say one day about a woman who once pressed her head against him, just as little as he would have stories to tell about other simpletons who begged his blessings. This was my considered opinion long, long before I myself was looked upon as the spirit of a tree.

And then the kudu-berry punished you, my benefactor joked, he who sent his slaves to free me from the branch after he had been notified of the accident right in front of his house. He gave me shelter in his slave quarters till the broken bone I had suffered healed. But even before I was literally back on my feet he became my third owner.

So he must have found delight in me. So I must have afforded him pleasure. One evening he came to inquire about the condition of the chance patient in his care, and looked surprised when I laughed at the superstition about the kudu-berry tree, and drew me out on my short history, as self-contained and boring as the history of most of the slave girls in the city. In a brief and concise transaction he bought me, and my stay began in all humility in the high residence with the terrace roof built of stone from a far-off quarry, with a view over the low-lying city and the sea, with neat outbuildings and well-tended inner courtyards. My benefactor often summoned me. We spoke. The night came when he slept with me. He found me charming. More often than he had sexual intercourse with me, he ordered me to undress and simply talk to him quietly, while he kept looking at me as one views a pretty sunset or something like that. In the same way he looked at his son's serval cat. When his bouts of fever came over him, only I was allowed to stay with him, and I sat and fanned him.

Fellow slaves of my second owner, who had stayed behind in misery – I had no chance to grieve for you. It had happened that the hurricane elected me. I was in agreement with what was befalling me. I hankered for nothing, I moped about nothing, I could not get excited about anything in my past, and in fact was unwilling to talk about it. It was wasted time. For I was becoming possessed with myself.

Now for the first time I discovered beauty, my own and that of bunches of flowers, and of soapstone statuettes and jade clasps and porcelain glaze, and of batiks dyed with indigo, and of lovely silk, light as a breath or heavy and stiff and interwoven with gold. It was almost as if I were learning again to talk. I occupied myself in refined tasks like complicated embroidery, which was taught to me by older slave women, and the preparation of dishes for a banquet for a roomful of visitors, and the tasteful serving thereof. In the last-named I excelled. I learned to converse quite differently, with a metallic tone of irony at the tail end of a remark. I learned to make my voice dove-sweet when the conversation became pointed and too many quick remarks, like slim arrowheads, were being shot off all together. I learned to laugh with abandon.

Above all I learned to find pleasure in how to look desirable and in the power it was obviously supposed I could exercise to my own advantage in my benefactor owner's room. He gave me an ivory bracelet which fitted around my left upper arm and which I shamelessly showed off. Often I referred cattishly, when he was in the right mood, to the other slave girls' most glaring defects: to thin calves, knobbly shoulders, missing teeth, breasts out of proportion, jutting chins, fingers as rough as a chimpanzee's; and though he playfully agreed, and although he claimed that such shortcomings were limited and made little difference on the couch of pleasure, as he jokingly called his sleeping mat, I knew that what I had said remained in his thoughts. But I got only one bracelet from him.

Nevertheless. Nevertheless. My life shone. I hummed as I rubbed my skin with coconut oil. Only later did I find out that he had two kinds of slaves in service, one kind for their looks, the other kind for their readiness to serve.

So what was the source of the melancholy that sometimes attacked me? As I looked out from the terrace over the sparkling bay and saw the dhows and skiffs wink there, as I looked over the roofs towards the haziness of the horizon and grew dulled with a stupid restlessness here within me and the screech of a gull frightened me, what were my hands doing in front of my face? What could I have to feel sorrowful about? Now that the fondness of my newest owner, wealthy widower and foremost citizen, like cool moss coolly and softly protected me and I felt cosily hidden in his care, not just feeling safe but surmising the sparkle of a new time of life for me here in the looser relationship in which I now lived and in which my talents dared to unfold and there was little to restrict me – why did the tears well up in my eyes and the city tremble in refracted colours? Why did my head sink on my chest? Why did I try to make myself as insignificant as possible, look for a dark corner, pretend absence when I was called?

I sat, tiny as a beetle, and whined. I was so full of held-in whining that I was ready to burst. I wished that I had a snout with which to burrow into the earth and disappear, or into the bark of a tree where I could lurk inconspicuously, pressed flat.

This was the mood I knew best. I knew it from long back. I have known it here, too, I admit honestly to you, trusty baobab, confidant, home, fort, water source, medicine chest, honey holder, my refuge, my last resort before a change of residence over which I shall have no control at all, my midpoint, guardian of my passionate outbursts, leafless coagulated obesity winter and summer life-giving rocking cupola of leaves and flowers and sour seeds that I press to my cheek (the grey-green fur strokes my skin), that I break open to roast your kernels and devour them, hanging like fulfilment from you, directed to the earth, waiting. You protect me. I revere you. That is to say, the fieldmouse and I inhabit you, but only I revere you, I think, only I.

If I could write, I would take up a porcupine quill and scratch your enormous belly full from top to bottom. I would clamber up as far as your branches and carve notches in your armpits to make you laugh. Big letters. Small letters. In a script full of lobes and curls, in circumambient lines I write round and round you, for I have so much to tell of a trip to a new horizon that became an expedition to a tree.

Here comes a rhythmic pause. Oh, I have learned much from the poets, I am versed in the techniques, in the patching together of lyric and epic. Rhythmic pause and on roll the thoughts, round and round your trunk the poetic history of a crazy eagerness that was finally all we could cling to, stripped of material things and emaciated and tired to death of ourselves in the endeavour that transported us along, ballast of the past.

Thus I decorate you line after line with our hallucinations so that you can digest, outgrow, make smooth this ridiculousness, preserve the useless information in your thick skin till the day of your spontaneous combustion. And satisfied I put down the porcupine quill and stand back to regard my handiwork, hands on my hips. You are full of my scars, baobab. I did not know I had so many.

If I could write. Even then, melancholy would take possession of me. Wearily I take the path to the river, there in the cool to fill my being with the sounds of my sister-being, to refresh myself in the modest scents of pigeonwood and mitzeerie, to let my gaze end in a tangle of monkey ropes and fern arches and the slowly descending leaves, and to find rest, all day long, all night long.

There is always an ape to defile a sanctuary. How irritated I get when animals do not stay within the limits of their animal nature but want to address me on my level. For instance, the troop of samangos in the top of the water-berry tree. As if they were being sold short by me, as if I represented a great threat, as if I did not also belong, but had to be driven off with reproaches and deep warnings. Glare at me impudently indeed. Reprimand me indeed. Confront me and show disapproval indeed.

So too the grey parrot that my benefactor kept. Cool disapproval, ridicule, derision in the little eyes. If he wished you good morning he meant push off, and the eyes became small as dots. He turned language inside out so that the meaning fell out and nothing could be said. He fouled his cage. He woke the whole household with his noise and challenged you when you hushed him with such a clear whistle that it split the air with its purity; and he, the prisoner, triumphed. That he with his puny bird intellect could learn how to triumph while I was plagued with depression, and acted uncertainly, and showed that I felt hurt, and defended myself with acrimony, said sneering things behind their backs about the two sons and one daughter who still lived in the house, made myself unloved among the slaves.

Wholly different my relation with the tame serval of the house. How often did I not wish I could scrape together the courage to blandly slip the catch on the door of the parrot's cage so that he could fly out, the idiot, so that the serval should suddenly jump up from behind a bush somewhere and slap him unconscious in the air and grab him. Then he would carry him off in his mouth and grindingly eat him up, grindingly, till there was nothing left but one grey feather and one red. End of parrot. ·

Down below in the courtyard walked the speckled cat. He scraped his cheek against a plane bush and a scattering of scarlet, jasper-green and black blossoms sifted down on to him and grey-white tatters of bark stuck to his snout. He snorted in surprise. Then he trotted off, taking a short cut across the paving, with decidedly and certainly a most important objective in mind. He paid no attention to my call. He had pinned a gecko with his forepaw, I saw, and was considering what to do next; first he looked up at me, then with cat-specific dissimulation at his prey. I stared at him. I could stare for long into his changeable eyes and imagine we were of one spirit. He yawned hugely with tongue curled back and as he yawned looked terrifyingly cruel. Yet this illusion was enough to make me understand that we were not playmates and that there was a distance to be maintained between us, which I would keep, I promised him, and stroked his fur and scratched behind his ears. Black-snout-sweet-face, your self-sufficiency amused me. Perhaps we had more in common than you could think.

As a kitten he was made a present to my owner's youngest son, who as a young boy had apparently collected wild animals as a hobby. In the time of which I speak the son's interest was concentrated mainly on fishing and one barely saw him at home, for from early till late he was aboard his extremely expensive proa. But when he was here I enjoyed his wonderfully healthy roughness and his boyishness, and enjoyed all his pranks. Young frolicsome man, most attractive, and so serious and laughably touchy when it came to his hobby. I consciously call it his hobby because I did not believe his father would ever allow him to choose fishing as a career, unless perhaps, unless it could be administered as a subdivision of the family's business and the boy could then, as befitted a scion of the wealthy, do business and not haul in the nets like a poor simple fisherman.

Now I knew why I felt depressed. I had seen the procession. Well, I knew they were to be expected. Knew they had to turn up some time or other, and therefore went up to the roof every blessed day to keep watch, to keep an eye out to see what I had promised myself I would not look at. The terrible procession, nerve-rackingly slow. I saw them coming from afar from my look-out post and beheld, fascinated despite myself, the signs of brokenness that rent me, crushed my spirit, made me stare despairingly, made me note their fate helplessly every time and keep my sympathies in check, force myself to joke about them so that I could forget and repress. My eyes followed them from where they appeared out of the bushes and bulrushes at the seam of the unravelling residential quarters and wove through the harsh planes of shadow and sunlight on the streets, sometimes disappearing from my field of vision, but I knew the route too well and settled my unwilling gaze in advance on the point where they must reappear; at the head a few of the men in service, armed but on foot like their human prey, followed by a primitive sedan chair on which the slave hunter sat at rest, rocking on the shoulders of two of his captives, the big boss no longer half-asleep as on the immeasurably long bush path that they had all covered, but wide awake now that the moment, the most important moment was about to dawn, followed by those in chains, some with packs of leopard skins, elephant tusks, rhinoceros horns and provisions on their heads, their faces twisted as the neck irons chafed them, followed by the young women and tender little girls shackled to each other with lighter chains. So they trod reluctantly on to the place of destination. At the tail a rearguard of more armed men.

I followed them. I knew where. I took a short cut through side streets and alleys and across open unbuilt spaces and arrived at the square near the beach before them, and hid behind the tattered dusty castor-oil trees there and the scanty undergrowth around. The arrival of a fresh consignment of slaves was proceeding normally and attracted no one's attention. Only I was all unwilling eyes.

Clinking, my fellows in fate arrived. The untouched girls, my little sisters. The young eunuchs no longer men, no longer human beings, the survivors of a raid deep into the interior, my own people half-people may not be people, the compelled, the pitifully strong healthy products. They stood still. They were allowed to sit.

The sedan chair was set down. The slave hunter stood up stiffly and stretched, a pleasant long stretch, before he got off his chair and turned his steps towards the city to discuss business over a bowl of fig wine and a pipe of hashish. He was an old man, I saw. He had grey patches of beard at the point of his chin, but he strode quickly as if refreshed by the sea air and cheered up by a sense of relief that the difficult undertaking had gone off successfully as far as the coast. The guards stayed at their post. I wondered if they had been here before. I wondered if the complement of the slaves was full and how many had grown so weak from exhaustion along the road that they had been left behind as unserviceable, and how many of them had perished of marsh fever, and how many had grown rebellious and been killed. Those who were left now lay in silence on the ground. Even some of the guards had sat down.

On the beach a group of urchins were kicking sand at a dead hammerhead shark. They rushed about and barked and growled, pretending to be dogs, and laughed and jumped with exuberance over the shark. They laughed their joy out. They lost interest in the leathery carcase and careered further up the beach looking for fun, picked switches and chased each other further along the foamline of the waves, splashing in the shallows. Brief happiness disappeared from the air. The sultry stillness again closed in.

A few days ago I had seen the hammerhead shark leaping in spasms there on the beach where fish-drying racks cast their grid shadows. It was trying to lift its whole body up from the sand as if wanting to swim upwards into the sky. Sometimes one eye was buried in the sand, sometimes the other; one saw doom, the other spied hope, and in uncertainty the poor thing struggled. Spasmodic jerks, fanatical till death, eyes that till death bisected the world. Would he, even in death, have to reconcile one half with the other half to find his way in that haze? Deeper and deeper he steered himself on into death with twisting movements of the head. To the left hung death as a grey apparition, to the right hung death as a grey apparition, no choice for him, but perhaps he fabricated his own death and chose the total nothing of seeing nothing more, and nothing has neither tinge nor grain nor substance.

I was not permitted to offer refreshments to the new arrivals. I had already tried that in the past and been chased away. Nevertheless I went closer. In my worker's language I softly welcomed them and expressed my commiseration; but it seemed that no one heard or understood me. Nevertheless I talked to them because I knew of nothing else, and most of all of nothing more effective, to do.

I told them all I knew about my origins. Humbly I offered them the scanty history. My facts I patched together as they occurred to me, my memory of a journey with fear the starting point and fear the end point. I was well grounded in the knowledge of fear. I had felt him in my blood vessels, for he had come to live in me and I had begun to smell like him, and with his eyes I had seen forests and plains shift by poisonous and distorted; with his ears I had listened, and there was a growling, and even the stillness rumbled, and there was bitterness in my cheeks. Oh, fear is by no means whatsoever a connoisseur of events. He gobbles up everything. He crushes everything. He leaves no bloody trail behind because he stands still. Everything comes to him, feels drawn to him, and he knows it.

I don't know. This I know: that I allayed fear and terror in and through my dreams and that thereby I rendered harmless the nameless, the formless. But I had to learn to do that. It was the outcome of affliction. It is something I still do.

This I know: that I was not condemned as these people were, because on the day of my arrival, so I was told, I, the only girl captured, exempted from chains, wandered away from the others, shot down to the sea and picked up a white shell and a black shell. For I am of water. I know what turns the air to water. Then, so they say, it began to rain. Rain, rain drizzled down.

I turned my back on the damned. I was the head slave girl of the richest man here. I had more power than many a wife. Love of ease characterized my life. A lazy contemplation of the stupidity of others, that I could afford, with the symbol of my owner's pleasure in me around my arm like a reprimand to those who would like to humiliate me. Even if the bouts of depression came too often, too often, I gritted my teeth: it dared not get the upper hand. My existence was pomp and circumstance, was sparkle and excitement, was shining rippling water over a bed of pebbles, was secret well water's blessing upon the lips, was sea water's beneficence and power.

Like a baby laid on its stomach, curling its spine as it tries to curl upright, so the hammerhead shark had struggled.

Hurriedly, seeing blind, I went over to the dead one and buried him in the sand with my hands, and on my knees sat before the little grave and cried and did not stop. It brought me no relief. I did not stop.

I cannot remember that, since coming to live in the baobab, I have ever cried so bitterly. From rage, yes, often. From frustration, at the beginning, when I was still struggling to light a fire, the knack of the friction-stick escaping me and the spark simply not leaping. Or when, unequipped stupid civilized creature, I tried to search out tubers in the tracks of baboon and warthog, food intended only exceptionally for the human system, as I was to discover with sorrow when stomach cramps made me writhe in pain. I ate locusts – the hoppers. Exulted when I chanced on a jackal food flower that porcupine and baboon had missed. I disdained my nose's warning and in a sweat dug the fruit out, only to bring up before I could put my mouth to the gruesome brown musky bluebottle lure. I get sick when I think of it. I get glassily sick. I pulled grass stalks out of their protective leaves and chewed the juicy white lower points. I tried to steal birds' eggs, but was too clumsy a climber. I did not even get to the nests. I did not have the sharpness of vision to discern ground nests in the grass veld.

In time I grew emaciated and dulled. My weakness affected my sight. Plants, trees, stumps, stones, antheaps changed before my cloudy gaze into billowing lines that resolved themselves in frighteningly beautiful arrangements and left me floating and penetrated my sleep, for now I slept most of the time, I slept on the heaving colours, they made for rest in their restlessness, I did not try to control them, they washed lovingly over me, rolled me considerately over, I bathed in them and sighed contentedly.

Then I got up, wide awake, and wandered about like a fool in the paradisal luxuriance. This was a garden! Let me acquaint myself with it. To the eye uncared for and full of thorns, full of brambles. Let me inspect again. The berries hid mischievously. I had to learn the game better. A clusterleaf offered winged fruit. But was it for me? Was it a clusterleaf? Let me walk further in the waves of heat, in the visible unfamiliar abundance. Every tree was a tree full of whistling. It made me light-headed. The noise. The exuberance. The confidence. The crazy-coloured buntings frisking about.

I discovered a creeper with orange-red fruit full of thick spines that had wound itself around a tree, and its fruit seemed to me so pretty, so enticing, but I was sure they would be poisonous, I was sure they were not for me. Let me rather pass by. Nevertheless, I turned back and approached and picked one. Perhaps I should just try. I dared not. It was a bitter-apple of death, be warned. The fruit hung so nicely. I broke off the point of a spine. The flesh was light green. I pressed my tongue carefully to it and registered a pleasant taste. I tasted more of it. Ate it up. And for days waited to be sick. Then ran joyfully to the tree where the divine creepers grew and picked all the fruit and ate it all up, even those the birds had pecked. To this fruit I wanted to give a name. But I could not think of anything suitable. I called it the red spine fruit of the twining plant that in the winter adorns the camel's foot tree against the rise over there. I was far too scared to take honey out of the nest in the top of my home so as to store away provisions for the winter. I devised plans, oh yes, I thought myself to distraction, but I remained frightened. To be hungry and to know of a source of food and not to be able to get to it.

To be hungry like the beggars in the city were, and the other outcasts, like the lepers banned to the bush and those who got pox and were rejected, and the lame and the crippled, those who tried to get by with a wooden stump, the blind with turned-over eyes and a child to lead them and help ask for alms. I gave nothing. I possessed nothing and could give nothing. With distaste I looked away. They pursued me with the fury of the desperate and stretched out their hands to me and looked at me urgently; they were so obtrusive, so dirty and full of sores. I was not my owner, and particularly not his eldest son, who scattered handfuls of cross money in the mud, on which the beggars descended as greedily as gulls, fighting over it and kicking up a comical hubbub. An uproarious, squalid, frenzied struggle for life would then take place in the streets on the outskirts of the city. In which I had no part. It was as if they were ready to bite and tear one another, peck one another till blood came. Here I was simply an unwilling spectator. In my time of hardship earlier . . . Admittedly I was looked after. I regularly got a bite to eat, that is true. There was an airy palm-frond roof over my head that leaked miserably in the rainy season and was never repaired. I had cotton clothes, threadbare with age, to cover my nakedness. I could exist. Admittedly. Certainly. Despite. In dullness I nosed around and kept body and soul together by drudgery. In tedium went on. Admittedly, that too was life. One of the slave girls in service with my second owner became bosom friends with me, and we tried to help each other as far as we could. She preferred laundry, I cooking. We ignored the other slave girls and divided the work as it suited us, even though it made them berate us, we knew they would gain nothing by going to complain to the man who owned us. To him we were all identical labour units. The two of us had wonderful jokes about him. We discussed his ugly habits to the finest detail, for example fiddling with himself or getting up halfway through intercourse to go and make water outside. Perhaps he suffered from incontinence. My bosom friend and I went into paroxysms over him and his nose-in-the-air wife, the old dry one, the old barren one.

Our children were plump and thriving in poverty, and we made no distinction between hers and mine. She carried mine on her back, I hers. She suckled mine, I hers. I was midwife to her, she to me. A child was a child to us. A warm little body in our arms, a dribbling little mouth searching for the nipple, the one's fat little neck as pretty as the other's, the one's teething as annoying as the other's. We brought them shells to play with, plaited a reed rope for them to skip with. Such a warm community, we and the infants. When it was my turn to cook I pinched some of the coconut milk and smuggled it back to them; and she in turn took them along to the washing stones at the river where they could make a mess undisturbed. Such a satisfying, lovely fullness that made up for so much in our shabby lives.

She was some years older than me. Had been through the same as me.

She and I had been through the following:

Caught young, not yet circumcised, for just that reason sought and caught. Among screaming women and old men, among the corpses of able-bodied men who had fought to the death or could not flee in time, among the burning huts, the beaten down kraal fence, the destroyed millet containers, in the thick grass that offered no hiding place, in vain pulled behind a broad trunk by someone who wanted to save you, it was in vain. It was a vain scream of fear. It was a small commotion in a wide forest. It drew no more attention than the noise of a troop of apes. After the interruption the birds went on twittering. The hesitant bongo stepped into the open patch, cautiously smelled the odour of ash and decay and violence and the sweat of fear, and made an about turn, noiselessly. It rained. Slime and mud remained, black pools of putrefaction, of a sunken history. How hugely sighed the storms. How ceremoniously rocked the trees. Rose the sun. Turned the stars.

My friend told: How she first saw the sea, and she was afraid of the blue wall, the bank that rolled over and crashed.

I told: Here too I first saw the sea, but I was not afraid at all. I ran towards it.

My friend told: The man with whom she then went to live was very friendly. He was like a father.

I told: It was the same one. He bought the very youngest at the market. He cracked them as one cracks young pods. He was considerate and permitted you to have your firstborn under his roof, then he sold you.

He bought the very youngest. He broke the soft membrane like a blister. You were the spread-out one from whom blood flowed. You caught your breath, from pain and from what was surely ecstasy.

I told: He promised me a present. He gently pulled me closer, where he sat, till I was standing between his legs. He undressed me himself and let his hands roam lightly over my body. Then he licked me. Then he pointed to his headrest with the pretty snake bean and mother-of-pearl intarsia and promised me just such a one if I was good. Yes, I would be good. The women in his household had taught me what to do and what to answer; I nodded. He was out of breath and in a hurry.

I got my present; what about yours? I asked my friend.

Yes, she said.

Where are our headrests now? we laughed.

Mine was too big for me. My neck was still too short.

Mine too, I said.

Do you miss it?

No.

Does he still buy the very youngest ones?

He is dead.

No! When?

Long ago – long ago. His heart stopped.

What a pity! He is dead. he was actually quite kind-hearted.

Yes.

Yes, he was. Really. Funny and kind-hearted. And we could really stay with him till after the first confinement.

Oh, I was the sweetest little mother, I remember. Played at swelling for nine months, assiduously helped to make preparations, clumsy but very willing. I sucked a tamarind stone and spat it out. A mother-child, that's what I was. From my young mouth the rotten laugh of the fruit-bearing woman sounded. Full blown from now on, now I knew everything. I carried myself. I grew tired from the carrying, I could no longer, I pulsated from inside, I became more and more. How I sat on the beach lost in dreams and played with my shells, my black shell and my white shell. How nice the other women were to me. How they looked after me, like a trinket. The time I coughed so nastily, one of them went specially to the market women to buy bush willow roots, which she could luckily get, and gave me an infusion to drink. And if I complained of the slightest headache I was made to swallow a brew of horn pod leaves and they said it was good for stomachache too, since the head caught it from the stomach. Well cared for and ringed around and protected and words became knowable and I felt happy but too clumsy, and I felt everyone had to get out of my way.

No one could or would tell me to whom I called when the child's skull made its appearance out of me. It was a scream back to my place of birth. There it echoed. There it echoes.

My baby was so greedy. He had only to say *ee* and I fed him. Soon he was almost too heavy for me to carry. To my owner I no longer existed. Already there was another little thing in my place. I did not speak to her.

I was sold off a second time on the square near the sea where even then the raggedy castor-oil trees were standing. Was sold second-hand. I was a damaged plaything, my bundle of baby and myself bid for separately and disposed of separately. Simply playthings. Useful, certainly. My owner thought he had wasted his money. Someone unknown grabbed my child. What was spoiled? Another examined my head, the inside of my mouth, my pelvis, my arms and legs. He was dubious. What was skew? A merchant sent an agent to buy as many slaves as the fingers of one hand. Where did it leak? Where was it cracked? What was botched about it? The sun baked down on my head. I wanted to faint. Items of everyday use of feminine and masculine gender. One by one. I was left. On one leg. On the other leg. Biting my nails. What was missing? What had been twisted? I no longer saw my child. I spun around. Nothing to see. I screamed within myself. If I could cut open my belly, draw out my guts. I looked for a knife. If I could spit myself out of myself. My heart froze. Who was buying me?

Hateful one. You are loathing like me. Come and kindle your ill in me. I am evil and dangerous. I am dried-out ape dugs and fresh slippery ox eye and peeled-off human skin and the venom of the deadly sea slug with the sucker mouth. I am hatred and hatred's mask. I am deformed. There is a snake in my blood. I drink my own blood. I kick in my swoon. I flounder.

Men came and sang like girls to lay the spirits, but the fires would not flare up. Timbila players from all over the city gathered around me in a circle of clinking slats whose water sounds, sounds like water stars, star drops, dew of bitter stars, were supposed to cool me and, sprinkling down, extinguish my rebellion. But what was I if I was no longer my child? How could an afflicted person feel regret?

Finally the gora player. Tap the single string, a flow of thoughtful sounds gradually moving down the string, a continuous tapping of sounds, each of which immediately fell to earth and became sand and remained lying in the sand never to germinate. Down and down slipped the sounds, deep into the sand. Deeper than taproots ever go.

Deeper than the kingdom of the earthworms. It was enough. It was buried. It was done. I was picked up and, apparently for a risible sum, disposed of. The gora player stopped playing, pushed the stick into his thong belt, put the gora over his shoulder, and left.

That day my new owner bought a glittering cock with bright yellow feathers on head and throat, the neck purple-brown, the back impressively speckled yellow-brown, the wings magnificently black-green with rust-coloured tips, the breast a glitter of dark grey and green-gold, a cock with a kick and a crow, and me.

The cock walked around the yard as he wished and mounted the hens whenever he wished. He crowed us awake in the mornings but also crowed in the evenings to predict good weather, upon which it poured. We threatened him with the pot. Cock, cock, we want to eat you. Cock, cock, fly onto the roof ridge of our hut and crow the day red. Your owner is stingy with his chickens. I mean our mutual owner. You and we, cock, cock, your crowing and shitting and our chatting and our excretions and secretions, our babies, our ornaments of pod mahogany seeds and our body cloths, and the house and the ware-house full of baskets of spices and the rats there, all his. The cooking equipment, the eating utensils, our lice, the cockroaches, the ants in the cracks of the walls and the earth around the house, all his. My labour his. My sleep his. My coming and my going. My sweat. My hair. The soles of my feet. The ant can hide away. So can the cockroach. And the rat. Not I. I do not know where. You and I, cock, we are trapped.

When I was expecting my third, I visited an abortionist. My friend stopped me. Life is cheating me, life is poison honey, I complained tiredly. She threw away the seductively scented violet tree roots I had bought.

What did you pay with? she asked.

With myself.

She scolded me. Whore, she called me, which made me laugh.

If it were true I'd be rich.

Go away! she scolded.

Yes, I joked tetchily: the world stretches as far as the master's eye can see.

One day. Oh yes, one day. As far as the master's eye can see, but I wanted to go still further. One day.

My next benefactor-owner plainly had a wider world-view, stretching from deep in the bush to the sea's horizon, including negotiations with gold-miners and woodcutters and the dispatch of goods up the coast and, through the intervention of the charming stranger to whom I, an impudent slave girl, became enslaved, to lands over the sea as well.

It was far, but I wanted still further. I had a craving for distance.

Here now in my baobab I am still bounded on all sides by the horizon. So does one never break through an horizon? Life is treacherous, like poison honey. Come from afar, I thought I should perhaps pack all the landscapes that had passed before my eyes in a ring around me, that would certainly yield a wider horizon. The further I travelled, the wider it had to become. And in fact everything has shrunk to what a tree defines.

Here there is standstill. Here there are hollowness and artefacts. Here there is care – I hesitate to call it adoration – on the part of the little people who pretend they are invisible. Here there are gifts of venison and sour plums and edible fungus. My ostrich eggshell with the neat little hole breaks and is replaced. My collection of beads is added to. I acquire clothes. I feel good, I feel presentable in my leather apron and cloak decorated with spring-hares' bones, in my self-strung black and green beads and my long strings of ostrich eggshell chips. They are the clothes of a new life in which I travel all around the baobab and never lose sight of it, since what lies on the road back happened only once, and what lies in whatever direction on the other side is (bitter realization) not intended for me to tackle on my own.

I am a melancholic but I do not stop searching, said my ever-voyaging, ever-travelling, my always charming stranger when the eldest son made him the offer. I like to reconnoitre. I like to discover. I cannot get enthusiastic about humanity, but I do not stop testing and do not stop searching.

No, let me not curse him. He should have known that I had no choice but to follow him, for I was not a searcher, I was one driven from circumstance to circumstance, and whoever bought me had to keep me, and this time would keep me. Sometimes it was pleasantly advantageous and easy to be property. I was simply someone together with someone else.

Even before the death of the youngest son, the eldest son had conceived the fantastical plan and begun making arrangements for a brand new kind of expedition. No one had ever heard of such a thing, and our city dwellers were not uninformed. News from across the seas and from the interior reached them regularly. As wide-awake traders they were sceptical about whatever was supported by nothing but guesswork and whatever was, in their considered opinion, the idle talk of poets. The dream of the unknown. The enticement of the foreign. Playing games with knowledge. For such purposes the city had its marginal figures, the subtle word artists and the storytellers on the squares to whom the children listened open-mouthed and whose entertainment value, including the word artists', rose and fell according to whether they succeeded in exciting or boring listener and reader. Yes, they, the colourful madmen. And if a rich man's heir wanted to act stupidly romantic, wanted to prove that an overland route ought to exist, then it meant that there would be opportunities for preying in his absence. It meant that the trade contacts so carefully initiated and forged by his father could now freely be grabbed and taken over by whoever was sly and quick enough. No one expected competition from the middle son, seeing that he had long since settled into a remarkably profitable brothel enterprise behind the glitter and show of the gold-trading business that he had already begun to manage several seasons before the father's death.

And then there was the unfortunate accident to the youngest son, the carefree one. So many disasters struck this house. On the death of his father there followed the quarrel between the eldest son and the spiteful unmarried daughter. She left the family home fuming. Now her dried-out spirit nourished itself on thoughts of vengeance. They swelled up her whole existence as from early in the morning till late at night she intrigued and schemed to bring the eldest son to his knees, even if it meant that she and the married sisters and her two brothers should all go under. She had the look of someone on the hunt. She had the smell of someone who had become cancerous, and whatever she came in contact with she polluted with the venom and the cunning in her breath. She was contaminated with bitterness.

I stayed out of the way of her breath and attached myself with softening heart to the youngest son, to whom I had been bequeathed. He was good and kind and not interested in the slightest in the slaves and slave girls and the other duties he had inherited, and went his way unperturbed with an engaging smile and a casual greeting.

No, I did not believe the stories that he sought out his death because of a disappointment in love. Someone who knew the way through the coral reef as well as he did does not simply stumble, so whispered the slaves to each other, and the mourners in the house. Two fatalities between new moon and full moon. How long is the life of man? From one wink to another of the lightning. From the fuller swelling of the drop to its fall. So long is the life of man. From move to checkmate. And heads were shaken and hands were wrung – yes, so long *is* life. And the young tree was chopped down, and the voyage was short and the boat capsized and sank, and the mourners piously got through with all such nonsense as befitted the occasion.

No, he was not the type who wilfully stepped on a stonefish.

Perhaps one of his comrades called his name to draw his attention to a school of rabbitfish in the purple deep-sea water beyond the reef, and he looked up and staggered on a sharp coral point and lost his balance. That was more likely. That, too, was what his comrades said. They brought him home on a stretcher, in his death as slender and beautiful as he was when he left the house in the morning to go and catch fish in that remote bay. Helplessly they had had to watch how, after they had carried him back to the beach, he had thrown himself down without control and kicked, and how foam had come from his mouth, and how he had then grown still, glorious again after the brief mad interlude that had helped him from life to death, again in death as perfect and untouched as he had been in life, a youth who was contained in himself, I reckon, and in his self-absorbed charm had never experienced either sincere friendship or sworn enmity.

I counted up what I stood to lose by his death and what I stood to gain. For the umpteenth time my future was being decided on a whim. I waited tensely. For I knew this fear. Were he and I not old friends? If anyone was ever true to me, then it was he, perhaps because he had become part of me and accompanied my heartbeats as he accompanied my breathing, because he sat in the white of my eye, in the trembling of my fingers. My companion, who had come to acquaint himself with me on my forced march, who had openly made himself at home alongside me and blown his suffocating breath over me – here he was again.

The day after my benefactor's death, when I, soggy with love and confused, had gone in search of the stranger, then too the fear was with me, and it was fear and longing that propelled me forward; and uncertainty, the only certainty I could always count on, led me to streets where mould made the walls break out in multicoloured sores and the gates hung askew and rotten and I recognized a building, I recognized some of the slaves who went in and out there with baskets on their backs. It was my previous owner's spice warehouse and I decided to visit my girlfriend, and I arrived in my splendid silk robe and my new quick way of talking, my precious manners, and there I stood awkward with embarrassment, confined within my affectations.

She sat with her legs crossed on the ground in front of the dilapi-dated hut scratching in the sand with a stick. The hens and chicks scoured as before in the yard, around the huts and house, and around the mango trees where fallen fruit stank sourly. She did not seem to mind the chicken shit and the filth. A naked baby with snotsmears on its top lip crept about on one side and stuck filthy sand into its mouth. I asked if it was hers. She did not reply. She gazed at me. I wanted to pick up the baby but thought better of it. I considered what I could give him. My friend gazed at me. When I walked off, I felt that piercing gaze on me. I felt someone throw something that hit me. I turned around. I saw her picking up handfuls of sand and throwing them at me. I called her name. The baby, also hit by the sand, laughed with delight. Then he began to cry. I walked off, overcome. The baby cried with rage.

I went back past the slaughterhouse and the tall palm trees there that tried not to see anything. I walked past the market women and the slave square and the skiffs drawn up on the beach, their masts snapped back like comical antennae. I saw the sole dhow frisking on the swell and called out again my shrill inquiry about the stranger and saw again gestures saying no, and I turned back to the great dreary silent house where bundles of jasmine bulged over the garden walls and put their scent in service of the dead.

How did my benefactor come by his wealth? I once asked the stranger, when he and I were all that remained. I stroked the pea-shaped swellings of the scarification marks on his forehead. My finger glided over them. Two mad pioneers that we had become, now two devoted to each other.

How? I asked again in the intervals between a lourie's abuse. My finger glided over his lips, purple as a fig. How thin he had become, it struck me. His cheeks so sunken. He lay with eyes closed in a hollow full of soft mouldering leaves.

Busybody, he tried to hush me. I kept on asking.

Your kind made him the most powerful person in the city, the stranger then said. You ought to feel flattered, actually. Your bene-factor was a connoisseur in a class of his own and seldom bought lower-grade material. In your case he was absolutely right. Look, he indicated, your physical proportions are of a rare symmetry.

He wanted to stroke me. I pulled my arm away.

How did he come by his wealth?

Again the stranger came with evasive explanations of aesthetic considerations that had led the benefactor-merchant to seek perfection, a balance between beautiful externals and the intrinsic, and that had also led him to view his slaves as a collection of art objects, meticulously purchased with an eye to investment and sometimes disposed of individually at a profit after he had refined them through education, as he had admittedly done in my case. It was then pointed out to me that my benefactor had displayed a remarkable appreciation of my qualities, to such an extent that he had never disposed of me and even allowed me at his deathbed.

That's not how he got rich, I objected. He must already have had a lot of money to afford such a hobby. Where did this man come by the means for it?

And what if I said he was a brigand?

Then that is what he was.

A slave raider?

Everyone is a robber of something. Robbers are all I know.

Am I one?

How should I know?

What if I were?

Then you are.

I rob money, I don't rob people, said the stranger. I rob on the open seas. I rob before I am robbed, before I become booty.

Like me, I said.

Yes.

Did my benefactor hunt us in the interior?

No, the stranger laughed, that is not how one becomes rich. The outlay is not worth the trouble and the profit. Rather be an ivory hunter, for your product is something dead, more easily transported. People, on the other hand, die like flies, and have to be fed, and try to escape, and your expenditure on guards, on food, on weapons, is tremendous. Human loss is comparable to capital loss. No, it is the exceptional type who becomes a slave hunter. And then you run the danger too of being killed and robbed in turn. That is how your benefactor set to work. He had spies everywhere, and messengers. Then he ambushed the slave raiders and their convoys somewhere near the coast, when all of them, captives and guards, were tired to death and offered little resistance. That was when he was young. He put together enough to build his house, where he could live peacefully as an established prominent citizen, turned his back on brigandage, and concentrated on gold, ambergris and wood, on copper, to which the rich people of the city attached more value than gold, and on his hobby.

Then the stranger lay with his eyes shut, silent, as though exhausted by talking.

I felt helpless with humiliation but tried not to cry, or not to cry visibly or audibly. Possession and loving are concepts that damn each other. I did not want to be as he and the others, all the others in my life, from my earliest memories of huts and mother and security in a misty, sultry forest basin, from my memories of the lascivious man who bought me to deflower me, and the spice merchant whose labours I had to endure grinding my teeth, I did not want to be as they all regarded me, all of them, my benefactor with his fatherliness and this one too, this man whom I embraced with my whole body and allowed to come into me time after time so as to be absolutely full of him, absolutely convulsively full and rich and fulfilled, floating, seed satisfied, making him, self-content, part of me, of me exclusively – he too, he who had just described me analytically and disposed of me like an object in a dispensation, even he, I was different from what they all thought, utterly different from what anyone might think, I rejected all the opinions, all the observations and reprimands of all the women in my life, what did they know of who I was, what did any of them know.

I remembered the poets' sarcastic remarks about women in general, but at the time I had not taken them to heart: to tell the truth, I joined in the so-called sophisticated disparagement, and this kind of superficial display of lust did not strike me as vile and immediately to be condemned. Vain. Vainly and frivolously I participated. Clothed in luxurious fabric that enveloped me like a soft caress and with saffian sandals on my feet, quickly adept in all the little arts of seduction, I joined in the talk and laughter. I felt, I knew I was in my flower. I laughed without reserve. I sent laughter upward and outward and picked myself the pale purple double stars of the wild chestnut blossoms to stick in my hair.

My benefactor smiled. He found it attractive. When I put my arms around him it was like protecting a child. Crazy, when he was the possessor, but it was so. He propped his head against my shoulder like, and with the innocence of, a child. And in the wink of an eye he changed and became wiser than I, scolded me, took over and initiated the caresses, and when we had intercourse he was both father and son and I both mother and trustful daughter. We knew everything together, completely, wishing for nothing more. Until later on he grew so weak, so pathetically emaciated and listless as the fever got the upper hand that he scarcely made his appearance in the dining room any longer but chose to remain lying on cool palm mats in his room. Afternoon rain outdoors, the cool brought on by the evenings and followed in the nights by the sharp sparkling of stars as a bonus, the white splash of moonlight over him – all this did little to change his state of mind. In every corner of the room the eye of death glittered. Sometimes he stared absently out over the sea and declined the extract of bitter false-thorn pods that one of us held out to him in a delicate little porcelain bowl. Likewise ignored the prescriptions of the city's best doctors, uttered his thanks laconically in a hoarse voice and made no use of them.

In my perfect arms he died, supported between my perfect thighs, leaning against my perfect breasts, he and I, father, mother, child, owner, valued art object and servant, lovers.

It had happened too long ago to wish to hate him. There was no time to hate anyone and plan revenge. The veld threatened us. I turned back to the stranger whose gentle nature I had also found out about on this interminably long journey to the mirage of a city in a blooming red desert. Where I had earlier allowed myself to be charmed by

185

his wit, I learned during this time to appreciate his humanity and helpfulness. The circumstances were certainly not conducive to deep conversations embroidered with light-hearted thesis and antithesis, and in those days it seldom happened that the two of us spoke together. I think the encircling silence was too great. It compelled our respect. No, it is silly to think so, for in truth we were usually too tired to begin a conversation. I could not deny that things were going badly for us. We shuffled one behind the other through the hot region, our tired gaze measured the distance to the next spot of coolness and the relief of a roof of leaves, and though we knew we could not afford it, we lingered longer and longer in this way in the shadows of trees. Like now.

We exchanged apologetic looks. I took his hand and pressed his fingers to my mouth.

We had to be going. It was no good. We had to make up our minds. We thought of the alluring city and everything that would be awaiting us there. We filled in the scanty information provided by the hunters with our imagination, and the deeper we went into the interior, the further from home, the more desolate the bush and the slower and more unwilling our bodies, the more richly we festooned the images we had called up. We did not see that we had begun to pretend that what we wanted must exist. We referred to the city as if it were an accomplished fact that we would soon reach it, just another day and another day, just another couple of days and another couple of days, then we would see it lying on the horizon, flat and shining at the foot of mountains consisting of pure rose quartz.

I dreamed of that rose quartz. My dreams were stuffed full of rose quartz. I could barely move among the craggy pieces. The floors of my dreams were rose quartz, the pillars and the ceiling of my dreams. I peered out between rose quartz at the rest of the world. I withdrew into rose quartz and nodded contentedly.

But first we had to cross the swamp, the hunters had said.

The more burningly I longed to see the city at the foot of the rose quartz mountains, the longer I wanted to postpone the sight of the swamp between. For I did not believe the description of white and green water lilies arranged on dew-clear water wherever you looked, and golden reeds to which the tiniest red and silver painted frogs clung, and spiders that tumbled from the glitter of their webs when the dugouts bent the grass.

I had seen what a swamp looked like when we left the sea behind. I felt its oppressive air upon me and its sharp smell irritated my nostrils. Its endless green expanse stretching into the haze enclosed me. I heard a sucking and a bubbling and saw the snouts of crocodiles lying in the bruised mud. I saw mosquitoes in a mist above the pools. I saw mudskippers creep halfway out to stare boldly at me. And the worst was the silence that I vaguely recognized from earlier on. It was the oppressiveness that had been lying in wait for me on a journey of horror so long ago I should scarcely have been able to report on it. But I recognized this silence. It was the supreme wide silence that prevailed over the noisy croaking of the frogs. The silence had a width of weight that muted your appetite for life and then after a never-ending day tried to press you into the mud and bury you with the wingbeat of night. Was it the immeasurability that made yellow sweat drops burst out on your forehead and disturbed your breathing? I recognized it. There was also fear, a sticky fear that shut off your throat. I recognized the fear. In what ways could I still experience it? I knew the fear of bloodthirstiness and of isolation and of ignorance and of punishment and of bewilderment. I knew him.

This fear was part of the air. It hung as far as the coast where the city of my various owners commenced with shanties and pole fences, with herds of untended goats and spill-off channels full of nightsoil, the busy commercial city to which I was kidnapped.

I had already tried to imagine a kind of existence in which I was not a possession, but it did not come easily to me. What would have become of me in the land of my origin? Would I, for example, have walked, sat, stood differently? Would I have entered into other kinds of friendship, accepted wholly different opinions? Would I have cloven to religion? Would I have had a husband, and children by him only? Children I would have raised till they could stand on their own feet? Suddenly I thought: I would have been able to be a grandmother. Grandchildren playing around me in a yard full of tame guineafowl.

Suddenly I saw: here in this city I would never become a grandmother. Here I functioned as mother till my children were as high as my hip, then I lost all say over them. They disappeared from my life. For me there was no continuation, no links backwards or forwards. There was coming and ending, a finality as if darkness were made abiding. If it had been death, I would have had certainty. Now I did not know.

Where were the children I had brought into life? How would I be able to recognize them if I bumped into them Somewhere? And would I be able to recognize them? Sometimes I looked attentively at young faces, searched for myself in their features, their voices, their behaviour, their posture – assuming that my children were all here, I thought bitterly, and not sold into service in other cities and countries. I wondered whether I would be able to pick out a child of my own by maternal feeling, no matter where or how we met. Would I know it was he? Would I immediately feel a glow of recognition course through me, and yearn to press him to me, meticulous identification having been rendered unnecessary by a bittersweet knowledge within me, a source of certainty warmer than the sun, like mothers are supposed to have? Mothers being unfathomable, after all.

It had not yet happened. Nor had I yet heard of such cases. But I continued to look into young faces, listen to young talk.

In the house of my benefactor it was part of my duties to amuse his grandchildren when his married daughters or his middle son paid visits with their spouses and children. Such visits occurred often, at any time, unannounced, and I enjoyed the fun. I liked to see the little ones gobble down sweets. I liked it when they clambered up and over me tirelessly, and I liked telling stories; but with the older boys and girls I did not get along as well. I felt strangely embarrassed with them. It was as if I had consciously to sense their attitudes and desires, and as if my lack of intuition were noticeable in my behaviour, as if I betrayed my confusion, even as if I were afraid that they would detect a flaw in me which excessive friendliness and affability simply could not disguise. So there remained a distance between us. Fortunately some of them were already provided with their own slave or slave girl to see specifically to their needs, while the slave girls who came along to look after the small children were only too ready to leave the work and fuss to me. And I enjoyed it. I enjoyed wiping dirty little mouths and listening to terrible accusations and finding words of comfort for little hurts and big frights. Hey! Hey! I called – Don't put finger into the parrot's cage! Oh no! And I cuddled the little bodies till they were out of breath with delighted laughter.

I felt uneasy when my benefactor caught me doing this. His smile. It did not at all rhyme with the self I tried to be for him, and it was certainly not good for my self-confidence in his bedroom. Abruptly I stopped playing and waited, hanging my head, for him to go.

On the whole I could not complain about my place and the scope given to me in his household. I considered myself a lucky, privileged person, without rights but not wholly without choice. Not all slaves by far were as well cared for as those of this house, as I could attest from experience. Granted, we slept in an outside building, but it was built of stone like the main house. Our floors were not covered with carpets. We slept on thick coir mats. There were no ornately carved low tables and red-copper urns standing about in our rooms. But compared with the slovenliness and stuffiness and sour mud and the holes in the wind-torn roof of my previous owner's slave huts, I could certainly consider myself lucky. Add to this my privileged position which I knew very well how to maintain, and the spick-and-span organization of the house, and I really had little to grumble about.

On the terrace roof where, thanks to my position as favourite, I could freely repair without permission, I liked to spend the sunset, when I could fit it in. At such times I would look at the glow over the interior out of the cloudy fierceness of which I had come, and on the opposite side at the darkening sea that had called me, and I would stand caught in perfect balance in the interlight. In inescapable transitoriness I could have dissolved like a phantom into the swift black. I was marked out in peacefulness, and whole. When a dog barked, I started out of my rumination and breathed deeply, salty air, smell of crayfish, smell of damask rose, smell of clove and broadbean. I could smell the first early stars. For that reason I could not understand why I might not keep my children. For that reason I had to accept that grown children were what I lacked.

For that reason I felt relieved that I had not yet fallen pregnant again.

And thankful that I did not belong to the eldest son, whose nature was so utterly different from his father's, for the stories of maltreatment were not just stories. I myself had seen the open raw weals on the shoulders of some of his slaves, and had stealthily nursed them. It was as if the eldest son took out his annoyance on men in particular – in fact he had no slave girls. Not that he would find need for them in his father's house, but still I thought it strange. We, the slave girls, scarcely existed for this surly young man with his cane eternally in his hand. He had a blunt way of talking to us when he really had to, for example when he had to ask one of us to pass a dish at table, and he did not partake in the amusing man-to-woman pleasantries of the writers. He sat there shyly, half-leaning on a cushion, nibbling, and all that really animated him was talk about the history of other countries. Then his eyes glowed beneath the thin line of his eyebrows. And then he closed his eyes. The eyelids looked defenceless with their short curly lashes when his face relaxed so unexpectedly, and like a child he scratched in his ear with his little finger, and shook his head, and his eyes opened in a stare.

A good thing I had so little to do with him. To me he seemed clumsy, closed off. A good thing I could never have dreamed I would one day spend such a long stretch of my life in his company: and even after that, after he had shamefully abandoned us and taken along everything left over, even after that I could not fathom him. He had a habit of bumping the slaves, or tripping them and grinning when they fell with a heavy pack of provisions. Maliciously he beat the sanga cattle till the stranger intervened and virtually came to blows with him and wrestled with him. He made me shudder. Whether he left me alone because slave girls scarcely existed for him, or whether he did not dare assault me because I was at that time the stranger's property, I did not know. Do not know even now. I felt protected in the company of my stranger.

Distracted with despondency, I accosted the stranger the first time he came after the youngest son's death and begged him to buy me before I was disposed of at the market. That is what I feared would happen to me, that I would again have to go and stand in that place of shame. I remember how I gestured hysterically, how shrill my voice sounded, and later how tremulous; then I shut up. Too anguished, too tired out by struggling in the grip of uncertainty. Overconscious of being obtrusive, rash. The short interval before he answered was laden with my intensity, my violent beseechings were an indecorous wrangling with his reserve, my clammily waving hands helpless feelers before his face, my kneeling attitude a too obviously toadying trick.

When he assured me I would not be auctioned off, how lovely the flash of transition from uncomprehended relief at first to comprehension and calm. I brought a corner of my garment to my mouth to stifle my indecorously unrestrained sobs, and, to all appearances calm, thanked him while choking on my feelings and wanting to scream and rejoice crazily. Subdued I left him.

For he came again as I believed he would; but this time there was a motive I could not guess, for I assumed without thinking that he had come to do his everyday business, come to buy up iron and copper in exchange for rolls of silk and cotton, come on the trade wind at the head of the little fleet of dhows under his command as of old, come from afar across the rippling blue-green where other trading cities on other coasts shrouded themselves in a haze of strangeness – that is how I thought. That he and his crew had come to unload one cargo and take on another.

I could not know that this time he would temporarily relinquish his command over the sailors and hand it over to a subordinate in order to undertake a journey in the opposite direction from the white flutter dance of the brown-veined butterflies over mountains and plains, nobody knew whither, nobody knew why. And no one knew why he had allowed himself to be talked into it. He provided no reasons. He went. I accompanied him, his recently acquired latest possession. I became part of the extensive organization that kept him and the eldest son busy and had them doing calculations till late at night by oil lamps and had them unravelling the possible, the probable, the actual and the enigmatic and weighing them up against each other till one grew bored. The possible and the impossible fell, rose and hovered in the balance. The particulars heaped up and up, and an idea suffocated, and new ideas were sought, and eventually the question why was of absolutely no importance. Fancy and the profit motive. Childish dreams. Longing for the faraway. Elaborate estimates. A rebellious streak. Perhaps the last.

So. For that reason we departed for the frontiers of the spirit. Invertebrates about to change homes, that is what we were. Shellfish sliding over the sand. A colony of sea anemones slithering over dry rocks on their single feet. Fish walking on their fins. Wobbling salt-scaled coelacanths. Wailing dugongs.

Our procession of bearers and cattle and sedan chairs with

passengers on the shoulders of bearers wound into the interior on the way to the great ocean that booms at the uttermost limits of the world. It could not be too far, as determined by the eldest son and the stranger, rationally, with the help of their maps. It could not take a lifetime, they calculated. Taking everything into account, it ought in fact to be a short cut to the land of the able mariners who had recently called at the city and boasted of their hardships on the billows of an immense unknown sea, and who could prove on the evidence of the numerous cases of scurvy among the crew that they came from the utmost limits of the utmost limits.

To us it seemed as if they suddenly appeared out of nothing, as if they slowly came shifting across the foil of the sea, oh so slowly, in bulky caravels driven by a mass of patched sails in the tackling of which we saw the crew scrambling with apelike agility. We were not impressed. Or did not make it apparent. But in spite of this gathered on the beach or climbed to the terrace roofs. If you were rich you ordered a sedan chair, if you were a perky child you climbed the bow of a coconut tree, if you were a carpenter you dropped your tools and forgot your commissions and stood up, if you had a suspicion of new trade connections you locked up your trading house and with a small retinue of scribes sauntered, calm, chatting, exchanging greetings, pretending boredom, to the spot, more or less, where they would drop anchor in our treacherous bay. What can they offer that we do not have? Was the general feeling, and the city did not seethe with excitement, not so that it could be seen, and the new arrivals were nonchalantly made welcome, not suspiciously, but still . . . Not so that it could be seen.

The eldest son was the first to be invited aboard the flagship. He asked the stranger to accompany him because of his greater knowledge of marine matters. I remember how noble the stranger looked in his green-striped robe with green headdress, how he towered above the bearded newcomers as he stood on the commander's deck and he and the eldest son tried to make themselves understood in sailors' language, with plenty of gestures and headshaking, up and down, back and forth. We all waited on the report. We learned about a land at the other end of the earth's disc and about voyagers who had sailed as far as here all along the edge of the world and about the mighty storms with which the gods tried to drive them over the edge and plunge them into nothingness, and about voices they heard in the howling wind warning them to turn around, and about monsters on land where they wanted to fetch fresh water, about short rests to repair broken yards, about beacons they had erected and about hostile backward peoples, and they pointed, so we learned, at a red sign on their yellow sails and explained that they sailed for their king, these stocky hairy men in thick peculiar garments.

Unnoticed as the birth of a wave an idea came into being and swelled unnoticed. The city's richest merchant's as yet unmarried eldest son, he with the interest in far places because of which he felt attracted to the stranger and kept pestering him with his questions, he who now after his father's death had inherited the most important trading interests and was supposed to manage them as befitted a man of his station and prestige, and to involve himself in the city's interests, this very person hurriedly got married on the eve of his departure for a destination which according to everyone existed only in his imagination and about which he was secretly laughed at.

Only one did not laugh, namely the stranger, whom he persuaded to seal his fate thus: to cease, temporarily, one presumed, voyaging over the high seas from one land mass to another and back, voyaging across a too well-known water mass afflicted with cyclones, blessed with monsoons, and to essay the unknown of a land journey with a vague goal. A gaze accustomed to the nervous riffling of water would have to accustom itself to the green of forest and marsh, to ravines veiled in old man's beard and steep cliffs, to plains and sluggish rivers and a horizon of dome-shaped hills. The stars no longer teemed over an unstable water surface but over the stability of resistant earth, and looked relatively calmer and of surer course in the wide night. The stars of the earth would look stiller. The night look thicker. Everything would look more dependable.

I suppose it was the spirit of adventure. I can't be bothered with what made him embark upon something so silly that would provide him with a trivial death in the heart of the wilderness, lamented by his last possession, myself. I was the only one left to pace up and down the river bank calling anxiously, plaintively, urgently, hopelessly, and to feel mocked by the fish eagles that wove the strip of air above the river from tree to tree with their screeches and proclaimed it forbidden territory by order of the giant crocodile.

Come to his end in the belly of a reptile. There are times when I really can't help laughing at it. It is after all a particularly laughable death. One is so used to regarding other inhabitants of the earth as food, to accepting them, as it were, as self-evident sources of food, and to putting whatever is edible in service of one's digestion, to raising the ingestion of food to an art by adding condiments and tastefully serving up dishes that go together, to making a huge fuss of a meal and to developing customs around it that ossify into rituals, to making a whole rigmarole of the utterly natural bodily function of eating – one is so used to it that it seems terribly funny when other-consuming man is himself eaten. The untouchably mighty, revealed to be nothing but food, was knocked into the water with a well-aimed flick of the tail – actually not well aimed, actually executed with unconscious perfection – and drowned and devoured.

Did his spirit perhaps escape in bubbles? Did my companion the water spirit grow jealous and demand him as hers?

Then I grew afraid of pursuing my thoughts. I who am of water never wished it on him, and however ridiculous, he is no longer among the living, however laughable to be passed out as crocodile manure, as if it were less ridiculous to be buried and eaten by worms. He perished. He is no more.

From then on I thought carefully about the nature of his death, and I thought of it as a normal incident, I disguised it from myself, I concealed the circumstances from myself and I told myself a completely different story. Even when in my loneliness I bitterly cursed him and his nobility, or, as I was to decide, his stubborn rectitude, I used a figure of speech in which the name of my great spirit never appeared. Curse the ground that drank his blood, I preferred to say; trying to expel the abomination into the earth, or I made it stick to hyena and vulture. I brought an offering to the dark hippopotamus pool where the ruler of the crocodiles lived. Solemnly I threw my ivory bracelet in. It sank noiselessly, leaving scarcely a ripple. Harmony was restored and in the silence brought by the wind there was only the screech of the fish eagles, guardians of the stretch of water.

Could I but know whether I too am destined for a watery death! I long for it. Perhaps I had to understand that water would be his fate where he was untrue to the great water by which he lived.

I swear I will be true. Every time I plunge my ostrich eggshell into the bubbling of the stream, I mutter:

Water yes water
you live in the reed's bed
and in the hollow of the baobab
water you come out of the air
water you well up out of the earth
you cover the earth
you live under it and above it
your spirit is as great in a drop
as in flood and storms

eagerly I collect you and drink you

water you are in me

The water in the stream tastes sweet. I am thankful I wandered here after the stranger's disappearance. In humility I thank my water spirit for guiding me. And for the thunderstorms that wash the baobab nice and clean and spur him to bud and all at once thrust out all his leaves and hang up his great flowers one by one on twigs, white and crumpled, to be fertilized by the bats, white, crumpled and malodorous.

When the tree blooms, then I cannot feel sombre. Then I see the journey as a confusion I had to undergo, then I do not try to unravel it and make sense of it. I say the name of the tree aloud, the name of water, of air, fire, wind, earth, moon, sun, and all mean what I call them. I say my own name aloud and my own name means nothing. But I still am.

One time I fled from the tree. I ran aimlessly into the veld, trying to get out of its sight by hiding behind a high round rock, and I opened my mouth and brought out a sound that must be the sound of a human being because I am a human being and not a wildebeest that snorts and not a horned locust that produces whistling noises with its wings and not an ostrich that booms, but a human being that talks, and I brought out a sound and produced an accusation and hurled it up at the twilight air. A bloody sound was exposed to the air, with which I tried to subject everything around me. To be able to dominate with one long raw sound.

At night I hear lions roar. Every now and again I get up to throw wood on the fire. Sometimes I see eyes shining greenishly in the firelight. In the mornings I bake tubers that the little people have brought me in the ashes, break open a hard-shelled monkey orange with a stick and scoop the flesh with the stick into my mouth. A gulp of water, baked bulbs, and I am ready to resume my struggle against time. We fight in an endless roundabout circle. I do not manage to divide him up and segment him, so as to form a pattern and control him, in spite of my ingenuity with the beads. I sometimes get confused and forget when I linked what to what. Green and black mixed up in accordance with my mood. I cannot shake time off me. He squats continually before my tree. Everything that has been in my life is always with me, simultaneously, and the events refuse to stand nicely one after the other in a row. They hook into each other, shift around, scatter, force themselves on me or try to slip out of my memory. I have difficulty with them in the necklace of my memory. I am not a carefree little herder of time at all. Day and night pass. Summer and winter, another summer, and here is winter again. This is easy, but not the time that has made of me what I am and that lives within me with another rhythm.

Sometimes when I am washing myself in the river I regard my reflection critically in a calm pool and try to determine how much older I have become. It is not easy, for however motionless both I and the water are, there is a continual fine wrinkling distortion of my image, a water wrinkle that flatteringly replaces the possible wrinkling of age. I throw a pebble into myself. I rock grotesquely up and down and break up in lumps. Restless I. Then I withdraw myself from my divided self in the water. How my spirit struggles. I bake myself dry in the sun, dress, and take the path up to my dwelling. Soon the elephants will arrive. The sun already hangs in the baobab's arms.

At times simply melancholy.

I do not follow the little people's click language. It sounds to me just as if geckos have begun talking. Anyhow, how could I learn it? After that strange first near-meeting they seldom speak within hearing distance of me. One day I saw them bring down a giraffe. While they were flaying the animal and cutting it open they babbled excitedly, even quarrelled, so it seemed to me. I listened attentively but learned nothing. It is a language for geckos and tapping beetles.

Out of respect I stand in such a position in the opening of the baobab that they do not see me. After the time when I forced them to look at me and saw how it offended them, I never force myself on them any more, and accept with gratitude and joy every crumb of food they bring and every object of use.

And every useless object. Like the handful of little gold nails. How they shine. How pretty. I already have beads, sherds, an ostrich eggshell, clothes, and, wonder of wonders, a whole clay pot black with age but still perfectly usable that the little people found and brought to me and with which I transport water on my head. And now these lovely playthings.

I let my thoughts roam and imagine the most wonderful history of a town with bulging walls and stones packed in chevrons, of a holy echo that delivers oracles in a roar over the veld. A town more or less like the one we saw the women on our travels building. In fact we passed several such stone towns. Some abandoned and disintegrating, some half-finished and left just like that to become rubble, some in the process of being built. Walls to prop terraces and walls for houses or temples or barns, all erected by the labour of women. There was not a man to be seen anywhere, which as a matter of fact seemed strange to me.

But perhaps the men were out hunting. Are they out hunting? I asked the stranger over my shoulder.

I think so, he answered.

Do the women always build alone? Do they always carry the stones themselves, do they always pack them themselves, do they draw up the plans themselves?

Strange, strange, answered the stranger.

From the sedan chairs that carried us swinging from side to side past them, we regarded these zealous women workers curiously. I held a big leaf over my eyes to keep the sun off. Like a real lady I sat and watched the multitude labouring in the scorching sun, and made remarks and observations in a light, contented mood, I felt so good. Never before had life been so pleasant.

Perhaps the men are out at war. Perhaps they are planning an attack on us, joked the stranger.

What does our leader say? I asked.

Oh, he's always in a bad temper. He is too intense.

Yes.

I felt myself to be a peculiarly elevated, untouchable, temporary spectator always on the move, and thought out something else pithy to utter from my seat. Perhaps they are . . . I wanted to say slave women. I choked the word down.

Perhaps among them were some of my unknown family members who had remained behind. Perhaps I came from here, or from near by. It was wiser not to ask questions and to let things pass. Or were the men perhaps out on a slave raid, and must the women do the men's work? The women were bare from the waist up. They wore snail shells and multicoloured amulets decorated with beads around their necks and ankle rings of copper wire. So I rode on in perfect privilege, in the security of being preferred, in the status lent to me on this trip by virtue of being the select maidservant of one of the leaders. No, not the maidservant, not at all – the mistress. I had the freedom of finding myself in strange parts with a man on whom I could have doted and a crowd of servants and a surly leader, but him I easily forgot. And no chance of escaping. To throw myself on the mercy of the inhospitable? How foolish that would be. Foolish even to want to make contact with these women when no sure welcome was guaranteed to me and help would not necessarily be offered. So I swung on haughtily but eager-eyed past the brown stone walls in the green grass. No right angles here but soft curves connecting with the earth's curves. Thus women build.

For a while I had been noticing something in my front bearer's hair. Now I saw he was keeping cross money coins there. Stolen money, therefore. Tonight I would warn him to hide it better, for the bearers were continually changed to spread the burdens better. Before long he would have to help carry the eldest son and it was to be doubted whether the latter would let such a glaring offence pass unpunished. Poor devil. Did he want to run away one day? Did he want to flee one night, and in his flight call at villages to buy food? Did he want to take to his heels, his head heavy with metal, his heart light with rejoicing, his insides hollow with fear?

In fact, he was our first loss. Apparently he managed to disappear. Our second loss was a much more telling blow. The beautiful gentle sanga cattle disappeared overnight as if an earth spirit had made a cavern open and one by one they had all walked in, and now stood lowing in the belly of the earth and clashing their long horns and tramping miserably around.

We found that we had posted no sentries for the night, since we had never done so. We also found that we had no tracker in service, and we ourselves spotted nothing in the rain-polished veld, just our own muddy prints, traces of frivolousness, proofs of ignorance tramped far and wide.

It was a serious loss. Not only had the cattle carried the heaviest packs, but they were a last resort if hunger were to stare us in the face, and in addition it had been our intention to exchange them with tribes of the interior, in case of need, for food or information or, if need be, protection. That was how it had been planned.

The first quarrel between the leaders of the expedition resulted in uneasy silence. A momentary display of indignation, a knife-grinding of reproaches, and both withdrew from the conflict impatient and dissatisfied and stalked around as if a glittering crane crest of aggrievedness were tightly settled on their heads, and their stiff faces betrayed no desire to be reconciled. Stubborn, arrogant, could not sit still so long. A sailor is always on his feet, always on the go. The sea, his road, never rests. It pushes you, pulls you, whisks you up and down, throws you to port, to starboard, it splashes against you, sweeps past you, it takes its form in accord with its whims, it comes rolling mountain high, it becomes a whirlpool and spins you in a deep blue vortex, it stretches itself out flat and holds you imprisoned on its calm green mood, it changes and remains the same in its changing and makes of change a permanence and of unpredictability the only predictability. It is not fickle, it is always thus. And therefore he preferred to walk, the stranger explained, mocking himself. In brief, he had neither rest nor peace. In brief, he walked to make the slaves' work easier.

I too, some days, usually in the early mornings. My garment drew a wet trail in the dew. There was faint daybreak to give light. I tried to catch up with my long long shadow with greater and greater steps. To be able to walk on my head. I never catch up with myself, I sighed happily. Birds whirred up from the grass. I noted: a steenbuck skipping away – whizz, gone; a troop of redbuck ruminating expressionlessly;

a white rhinoceros bull, firm as a rock; a restless red jackal; and a lion with caked mane and flies around its snout yawning the yawn of the satiated and rolling over comically. Till the sun made its nest in my back – then I beckoned the bearers nearer.

Long ago abandoned trying to hold a conversation with them. My requests were fulfilled in silence. No answers. No questions. It was like trying to get through to zombies. More than in the city where I necessarily had to work with this type, it struck me here in untouched nature how inhumanly they were behaving. Whether unwilling or to appearances obliging, their actions were those of fellows of the tikoloshe-spirit, it occurred to me. Their eyes were peculiarly empty, their motions automatic as if they were obeying built-in commands.

We have people bewitched among us, I whispered to the stranger.

Didn't you notice it before?

I stared at him in surprise. We were relaxing in the heat of noon under a splendid cucumber tree on the bank of a full river. The eldest son had gone for a walk, as usual without mentioning it to us, without saying where he was going; he would probably reveal nothing when he came back. And we two, we felt too happy in each other's presence to care about his morbid reserve, we two were a self-sufficiency and, jealously eager for each other's attention, let the sourpuss go his way.

We had just finished eating what the slaves had prepared for us. Had it not been for the handfuls of flying ants that one of them had collected the previous night and turned into a tolerable sauce, we would have had to choke down the thick millet porridge just like that.

As we had been doing for several days. For with the disappearance (or was it the theft?) of the cattle and the redistribution of the packs, some of the goods had of necessity to be left behind, and thus, by mistake, we had to assume, the rice, the dried shrimps, the mango chutney, the dried fig cakes, the coconuts, the dates and much else was left behind. There were no accusations of carelessness thrown back and forth, but the discord smouldered. One leader formed the vanguard, the other leader and I the rearguard, and we were separated by mistrust and by a train of slaves.

Sugarbirds clung to the bunches of purple-red flowers that displayed themselves above our heads. There was a languid cooing of doves. A virtual stasis reigned. Water shining among plumed reeds. A caressing breeze. I am listening, I said. Tell.

At night I call all my familiar spirits, whispered the stranger, pretending to be mysterious. Have you not yet heard the hyena snuffling? Just as well you sleep so deeply. Have you not yet heard the faraway bark of the baboon?

Have you not yet seen the aardvark's hump stand out against the moonlight and the long snout with which he sniffs out the corpses? Poor inhabitants of the villages along our route, they don't know what hits them. They have no knowledge of wizards who make an appearance now here now there and make their familiars violate their graves. Have you not yet seen the eyes shining in the night, eyes red as fire, half-eyes, squint eyes? Have you not yet heard the growling and the scrabbling and the shuffling, and the cracking of bones? I send my familiars into the kraals to the graves of the chieftains. The cattle are too terrified to low. They stand aside. The next day the cows drop calves with two heads and the golden-red acres of millet through which the familiars galloped with their enchanted riders lie flattened and cannot be harvested, and the great famine comes to all the regions through which we travel. The storage baskets are emptied. The livestock die. People look at one another with eyes red as fire, with half-eyes, with squint eyes, and fall upon the weak and eat them up. They cut off their lips and fingertips, they let them bleed to death in pots of water, cook them and eat them up, the tastiest bits for the strongest, the offal and the gravy for what children remain.

The stranger went and lay flat on his back and stared up through the latticework of branches and dark green insets of foliage to the tatters of blue sky.

Pretty stories, he said. He supported his head on his hands. I have tried to live, he said, without religion and other such superstitions, without escapism of any kind, and now I find myself in the greatest illusion of my life. Now I seek consolation in shortsightedness and look no further than the night of every day.

There followed a mumbled rumination that I could not follow properly. I thought I heard him ask me for forgiveness. He stopped the mumbling. He sat up and looked at me narrowly.

I shall have to live the story out to its end, he decided. All stories end. For a moment he was still, his attention drawn by a swarm of starlings flying round and round the cucumber tree.

All I know is that I wanted to, he said sharply, as if answering an unuttered question of mine. I wanted to. Then he added, with the slightest trace of a smile in the furrows at the corners of his mouth and in the narrowing of his eyes: I think one can be ridiculous with dignity. Or try to.

Something broke through the underbrush on our left. Flapping, waving and shouting with fear the eldest son came racing towards us, stumbled like a clown and slipped over the tussocks of grass. The hem of his clothes caught on a num-num bush and held him back; jerking and pulling desperately, beating the bush flat with his cane, he tried angrily to rid himself of the thorns' grip, but only got further entangled, and eventually had to tear his clothes free. All the while he hoarsely commanded us and the slaves to fall flat, to hide, to crouch, to creep away, to make ourselves scarce.

Instead of making ourselves scarce we all stood up straight and gazed dumbstruck at the spectacle. With a muffled curse he freed himself from the num-num thorns and stamped over to us and explained that there was an army on the way, on the river.

Fall flat! Fall flat! he exhorted us panting. He must have run quite a distance in the hot sun.

He himself fell to his knees behind the dense reeds and hushed as if in prayer. I considered whether to follow his example. The stranger and I exchanged amused looks, though no longer exactly beaming with self-confidence and boldness, and when one of the slaves silently gestured that he saw something coming, we did indeed fall flat with our noses to the ground, each on the spot where he had stood.

I managed to turn my head carefully to one side and peer at the river, but detected nothing as yet. The plumes arched so calmly. The waterfowl had not let themselves be alarmed. I could see brown ducks drifting in the shallow water and also a giant heron's motionless head and neck sticking out above the reeds, and as I lifted my face slightly higher I saw the tense blue hovering tremor of a kingfisher at diving distance above the water and could also see the far bank walled off from the veld by a rampart of fully grown wild figs.

My ears helped me. I heard the thump of oars and concentrated on listening very carefully. I thought I could recognize human voices. Tatters of speech came to us where we lay quiet as wild animals, waiting for danger to pass. Later I saw through jagged cracks in the reeds several hollowed-out tree trunks sailing past in pairs in a kind of formation from left to right, each with a team of rowers rowing upstream with great effort. The oars came up dripping and sank rhythmically. Their progress was very leisurely. Probably the speed of the current was badly against them here. In about the middle of the formation one hollowed-out tree trunk larger than the rest glided past alone, with, it seemed to me, a larger crew wearing tufts of animal tails around their upper arms, and in the stern there seemed to be a kind of throne on which a man sat with a silvery apeskin cloak around his shoulders, and next to him stood someone holding an object like an umbrella plaited from palm leaves or grass or both over him to protect him from the sun.

It was not fragments of speech I was hearing, I realized. It was the groaning of the rowers as they laboured.

The giant heron cocked his head. He took one step, another, made sure that his shadow was not falling on the water, and stiffened. The ducks, on the other hand, drifted blandly, quacking, rocking, wagging their tails. The kingfisher had disappeared. Against the pale green background of the wild figs only the tree trunk fleet stood out, edging forward in painfully slow motion.

I began to get cramp from lying so still and wished that the warriors, if that was what they were, would hurry up. Also I wanted to sneeze. I doubted that they would hear me so far across the water, but held out for safety's sake. If they were warriors and if they were hostile to us, then all would be up with us. And before I was caught – this I had vowed to myself – before I was caught I would snatch the stranger's dagger that he carried in a girdle around his waist and kill myself. Warriors or not, it looked like a show of force of some kind passing us on the way upriver. From where? Where to? It had been a long time since we had seen a village or one of the ruins, or cultivated lands with platforms on which boys sat making a great noise to scare away the swarms of red-beak finches, or herds of sanga cattle with their child herders, or women come to fetch water or to bathe sitting on flat rocks and scouring their soles with stones and joking and laughing boisterously.

We had long since left the beaten track of the gold and slave routes and followed a course determined by the stories of those seafarers and the desire to be the first to discover a shorter, easier way to their cities and open trade possibilities. The first to discover. To be first. At the forefront of innovation. First to return with an impressive report. What would we sell? Slaves? Ivory? Tortoiseshell? Gold? First find out, before anyone else, before all competitors, what commodities these people needed and what they could offer in exchange, and find out on the spot so that you could speak with authority and be the first to celebrate the victory of big easy profits. That was what it meant to play the discoverer.

I think the two of them had underestimated the game. It also seemed to me that they realized this but were absolutely refusing to acknowledge it. Now it was a matter of pushing on, pushing through. It was a fact that somewhere in the distance lay cities that carried on commerce. It was known that the earth was ultimately ringed around with water. One day, one day, suddenly, unexpectedly, there would loom up before our eyes a blueness which, as we approached, would grow distinct from the blue haziness of the sky and announce itself as a separate entity, as being composed of water, as being water, as being water in motion with waves with foam backs and splashing foam flakes. As being the watery firmament on the edge of eternity. And we would hear a pounding and perhaps seabirds. And the last stretch we would all run.

Ah, how pleasant to meditate ahead, to listen, see, smell, feel ahead. To imagine experiences.

Our stock of food was diminishing and gave cause for concern. We grew dependent on the skill of the slaves and the knowledge of the wilds they had acquired as children to supplement our food. Thus, for example, they picked out a round orange fruit full of big pips with a thin layer of nice sweet flesh. And they picked out edible grubs: they pulled them off the leaves and pinched their heads off and baked what was left – which was not much – in the hot ashes.

I was imprudent enough to compliment them foolishly and long-windedly. I looked them boldly in the eye, created a relationship of familiarity, then cupped my hands and got a share of their fruit, berries, grubs, roots. Then I went and sat down with my gift halfway between them and the stranger and the eldest son. After a while the stranger came to join me and I gave him some of what I had. Then he shared his little with the eldest son. A complicated system. But the situation was not yet critical.

Funny incidents, like the time the eldest son caught a freshwater turtle and tried to roast it in the shell. It gave off such an intolerable stench that we all retired and no one would let it pass his lips, including the catcher and roaster.

Less amusing the incident with the sable antelope hit by lightning. Looking back I can in fact laugh bitterly. I can still see the stranger bringing out his elegant little dagger with the handle inlaid with jewels – emeralds and carnelians polished till they glittered – and trying to slice through the skin of the antelope's belly. He must have begun there because he thought the skin would be thinner in the groin.

Some distance away the slaves stood grimly looking on after unanimously deciding not to touch what seemed to us a lavish gift. A first sign of mutiny, perhaps? I don't know. The eldest son contributed by holding the antelope fast by the horns. The animal anyhow had no kick left in it. The stranger gave up the struggle. No one thought of looking for butchering equipment among the goods we were carrying. Or an axe or a spear or something of the kind.

The antelope's glassy eyes were looking at me wherever I circled around him, I thought fearfully. Perhaps the lightning bolt had merely stunned him. But no, he was really dead. We had chased pied crows away from him. These had not yet gone. They were hobbling about here self-righteously. Waiting. Waiting. Till the tedious humans left. When I looked up I noticed a vulture in a treetop. The stranger gave a snort of laughter when I approached and asked why he did not look for equipment in the supplies.

Both he and the eldest son had from the very beginning pushed their weapons into one of the packs because it was too much trouble to keep them continually at hand. They were simply in the way. What prevented the slaves from overpowering the two of them, doing away with them, and making off? Were they then so unmanned? I thought I detected a glint in the slaves' eyes. They were watching like the crows were.

From the tiny slit the stranger had made with his dagger in the belly a slow dark fluid oozed on to the white hair. The air smelled wonderfully fresh after the rain. I wished we would leave. One could see a rainbow. There, far away at its foot slept the lightning. I wished a lightning flash would make the sable jump up and storm us.

Summer was starting to grow full and ripe. It was in winter that we had last seen the sea. Vague salty damp memory. Grown so used to this routine.

After an evening's consultation the two leaders decided we should cross the great river along whose bank we had been walking for a while now, so as not to lose our course yonder towards the sunset. Their joint fright at the prince or commander and his subjects or troops in the hollowed-out tree trunks had moderated the discord between them. This nearly flared up again when the stranger teasingly asked the eldest son whether he would be able to pick out a hissing tree for the building of a vessel.

Would you? asked the eldest son sullenly. Then they both laughed with embarrassment. Here, so far from home and hearth and from the sea, they sensed their relative powerlessness and saw only too well that they did not always have the situation under control. The eldest son slapped his calf with his cane, but listlessly, as if confessing impotence. I saw in their eyes that they did not know what to do. Men look so funny, like disappointed children, when they lose control of something but dare not openly acknowledge it. And I in my peculiar position as parasite hoped fervently that they would find a solution and get us shortly to those cities that were our ostensible goal. Every morning I blossomed at my most beautiful, for them to admire my orchid-like nature for its colourfulness. I gave no less attention to my appearance than in town. My private torments were increasing too. I was utterly dependent on him to whom I was joined by deeds of sale as well as (I hoped to myself) by affection. But utterly dependent like a parasite.

Time passed and the plan of crossing the river was not carried out. Neither of the two had the inner strength to stand up, call the slaves together, and track down a hissing tree and set to work. In spiritless silence we lingered on the nearside bank. The food supply was now rapidly becoming dangerously low, spurring the slaves to set game traps of raisinwood and one festive day to cook a bustard for us.

What I could not understand was that the leaders' obvious lack of resolve did not make the slaves think of quitting us. Every night they meekly allowed the eldest son to chain them together, a measure taken after the one with the money in his hair had escaped. Every night I would hear the rattle of their shackles as they turned over in their sleep. In the mornings the chains would be removed, and no longer neatly rolled up and stored away – no, they were simply thrown in a heap. It was as if we had all become dream beings in a transition to we knew not what. The days unfolded and closed again one after another.

The river remained a joy to the eye. We were in a place where there were saf-saf willows growing. The eldest son, or perhaps the stranger, had remembered that this was an indication of firmness underfoot should one wish to wade through the river. For such an undertaking we should most certainly have had to wait for winter, even the end of winter. I say so because one of the slaves was ordered to enter the water and see how deep it was. He walked unenthusiastically in till the water reached to below his armpits, then began to swim, and shortly thereafter we heard him cry out and saw the current bearing him along and fellow slaves of his running downstream to keep up with him, calling to him to struggle towards the bank. I saw his head bobbing further and further off on the surface of the water, and the further off the more it looked as if he were floating at his ease. Later his fellow slaves returned. Precisely where he drowned they could not say with certainty.

It was nice to observe the bee-eaters as they shot across the water after flying insects. The water itself was a brownish green and muscular, and lapped at the banks where rocks or tree stumps protruded. Of the willows only the tops stuck out. The limp branches hung half-drowned. I felt like the willows and let time flow through me. It was nice to hear the bush shrike whistle and never see him. We also grew accustomed to the cicadas.

The eldest son and the stranger recited poems to each other in solemn tones and asked each other riddles, me too, and once the eldest son sang in a wonderfully deep, rich voice. The stranger wanted to clap him on the shoulder in sincere admiration, but it was as if he did not like being touched, and jerked his shoulder away. He told of yearning for his bride. He called her name over and over like someone throwing a jewel from one hand to the other.

The stranger said: If the sky were now to smash down on us, we would scarcely make a dent in the turf.

He plucked a handful of lush grass from where he sat and chewed on it, and his eyes closed. He was dreaming. I put my arm around him. It no longer disturbed me that the eldest son could see our caresses. The slap of the water soothed me like a refrain. I touched my ivory bracelet. Luck bringer. I kissed it. I had a swelling on my heel that was very painful, and of course mosquito bites all the time. What was that lonely bride left behind doing with her days where she sat without any tidings? What were people doing now in that city? Was there anyone besides the bride who remembered how we had departed?

Yet we did get to the far bank, and perfectly easily. A day's journey upstream we floated a roughly carpentered raft out from among the reeds and finch nests, and seeing that an island divided the river into two courses at this point, neither flowing so fatally strongly, we arrived without loss of life or goods first on the island and then on the far bank, where we spent a day to get everything properly in order, to inspect and check over everything. One of the slaves killed an oribi, throwing a knobkerrie that he had carved for himself during our halt from the light yellow wood of the bush willow. With this welcome addition to provisions the expedition once again got into its stride.

Our pace was quickened. There was a noticeable air of urgency about the two leaders, an alertness long last seen, as if they had undergone a personality change under the effect of the scrap of news about the city in the red desert retailed to us by the hunters. Both now walked at the head of the procession, each taking longer steps than the other, striding more smartly than the other; one even heard them laugh. Their good humour infected all of us. It encouraged industry among the slaves, who, dividing the work more readily in an atmosphere of co-operation rather than supervision, in no way fell behind their owners. We felt jointly attracted by that promised city at the foot of the rose quartz mountain.

Still, I could not help noticing how untidy we looked. From above, from my litter, last of all in the line, I was struck by our slovenliness. It could not be disguised that we looked dirty, worn down and shabby, dusty, our clothes full of fat stains. One of the slaves was no longer even carrying a pack on his head. How was that? What did he think he was doing here? Another had tied rattling round yellow seeds around his ankles that made suru-suru as he walked and one revealed himself to be a notable imitator of bird language, so that sometimes, after hesitating a while, birds whistled back to him in response to his call. It was funny to hear him talk.

I wonder how I looked to the others. A sorry sight but full of life at least?

How insignificant our little line of human beings among the tall rough grass stalks, a wholly inconspicuous phenomenon in the midst of frisking herds of zebras and wildebeest and redbuck, and the ever-amazed ostriches. We entered upon highlands where the air was fresher and the wind unceasingly bent the tops of the grass and bush and trees, a billowing in the grass, a jerky nodding from the bushes and a stately response from the trees. The loose hanging stems of creepers swung helplessly about. Their magenta trumpeter flowers peered tremulously yet archly from every level of the host tree. In these more open plains the clouds floated in the blue independent of each other and came together only at odd times, as if called, to manufacture thunder and lightning and dissolve in rainshowers. We took shelter under trees and waited till they passed. It was colder here. We moved on, a shifting tableau through the days.

After the city in the distance which must be the intended city, which would have to satisfy all expectations, on which we pinned our hopes, for whose sake we exerted ourselves, mustered our forces, had reorganized ourselves, where we would find shelter, meet people, streets with people, buildings, markets, squares, windows full of smiling women, children in gardens.

The city – so said the hunters who had advised us to use the raft they had made for themselves from tree trunks and rushes and left lying among the reeds where the island divided the great river – the city lay swept by the wind in a red desert. Sunbaked red walls. And behind it on the horizon rose the rough jagged rosy peaks of the mountains.

And behind them? asked the stranger.

And behind them the sea.

Ah . . . The sea.

A slave had been the first to notice the hunters. We felt embarrassed that we could offer them so little in the way of food and drink. Actually they were better off than we were, as we soon noticed, and also much better organized. They were carrying their booty of elephant tusks back to their kraal and were in a hurry because they had been away longer than they had planned. Summer was marching on. The elephants, they explained, had migrated further than usual, thus they had had a long search for them, but patience and endurance had been rewarded. Contentedly they indicated the bundles of tusks. This raw form of ivory looked rather ugly to me, particularly the blunt ends cut out of the flesh, and the texture of the tusks did not look at all like what I wore on my arm. Yet it was claimed that the ivory of this region was of far higher quality than the ivory of elephants hunted beyond the sea from our city. How should I know?

The hunters were surprised to encounter a woman. One laughed so much that all his tooth stumps showed, and I got furiously annoyed and withdrew. In contrast our two leaders carried on a lively conversation with them. I understood that they wanted to gain as much information as possible, but I could not help feeling the hunters' stealthy glances on me. After a while I went and hid behind a bush. I heard the eldest son trying to arrange a barter and trying to buy provisions from them. I heard him take cross money out of his embossed leather bag with long soft tassels and let the coins tinkle through his fingers back into the bag; but the hunters were not interested in such a bargain, for, they explained, they had only enough meat for themselves. The eldest son had to put away his heavy cash with nothing achieved.

The stranger was more interested in the precise direction we should take. The city lay in the sunset, he learned. Still many plains, then the vegetation grew thinner, then the ground between the grass tufts turned to sand, then there was more sand and the tufts would quiver silvery here and there, then the sand would become dunes, they would loom steep and rippled, perfectly formed humps with perfect stillnesses in between, and behind dunes after dunes after dunes which we would wearily climb, there would lie the city.

But first the waters, said one of the hunters. Yes, confirmed another, first the waters, the great shining, profuse in flowers, profuse in shadows, profuse in game, the reflection that would seem to be a reality out of which tiger fish leapt viciously, where the honeybirds called one on without cease and at dusk the kudu stepped out of the mopani forests and the marabou storks flew up like ghosts to cover the moon with their wings.

Messages were communicated to the hunters to pass on, when they got back to their kraal, to the ivory traders from the city who would come and buy the tusks. Thus the stranger and the eldest son tried to restore a connection. I had nothing to say. The other slaves were silent too. We existed where we found ourselves at the moment, and they, the stranger and the eldest son, existed from the coastal city as far as here and further as far as the desert city and the other desired cities, and they existed even further than that, they existed as far as over the seas that lay between the lands, and in those lands too they existed. But I was without connection. I was solely I.

The hunters had barely disappeared from sight when the eldest son and the stranger leapt to work, filled with a feverish zeal that infected the slaves as well, and in a jiffy everything was ready and we could push on, after all the many days of drowsy bewitchment when we had been like sleepwalkers each spun into a cocoon of pleasant absent-mindedness. When the water spirit enchanted us and bound up our thoughts.

Secretly I was relieved that the hunters had left, for their lecherous glances felt as if they stuck to me, and I felt that I was struggling to pull the cloying streaks off me, from my breasts and nipples and from my belly; but worst was the feeling of ruttishness they had aroused in me.

Thus the summer moved on. The great river already lay far away, the city of our desires still in the remote distance.

One afternoon we halted at the foot of a koppie with a cornice of round rocks. We had by now several times come upon these koppies with tremendous rocks on top. In our coastal region we never saw such formations and we could not help remarking on them. It was almost as if we were discussing art works. We praised their proportion and splendid balance, as it were the craftsmanship and sensitivity with which they were so arranged that it looked as if they would have to roll down and rumble across the veld till they found a little hollow of rest where the sun could crack them open or perhaps till they smashed into another of their sort and splintered.

Now we wanted to examine such rocks from closer by and climbed the koppie, the eldest son, the stranger and I, while the slaves got supper together unsupervised and made our beds ready. The one who no longer carried anything was the one who gave the orders, I noticed.

Strange that he, so unattractive, with his slight build and unremarkable features, had never seemed to me a potential leader, though I must add that till now I had never thought of possible leaders among them. They were simply the slaves, the eunuchs who did the hard work without getting any choice and obeyed the expedition's leaders without answering back. Could he possibly be of royal blood? One could easily get soppy in one's speculations. Perhaps he was simply the smartest of them: to judge by his organizational ability that was the most likely explanation. He wore a great white snail-shell about his neck. Still, I thought, he deserved to be watched closely: but I hesitated to express my suspicions to either the stranger or the eldest son.

Once I caught the slave leader opening a pack and taking tools out, adzes and gouges and awls and so forth, which had presumably been brought along to hollow out a tree trunk somewhere where that seemed necessary, a problem that had been surmounted by the use of the hunters' raft. I saw how lovingly he handled the tools, just like a craftsman. I saw him absorbed in arranging them in categories according to use and size, and saw how he then packed all the tools in again, very neatly, very skilfully. Then he put the pack down with the others.

There was a surprise for us on top of the koppie. Two surprises. The first was remnants, limited but nevertheless there, of stone walls of the same design we had encountered several times previously, only more badly destroyed, or longer in disuse. More dilapidated. No single length stood intact, there were only weathered knee-high fragments overgrown with thorn bushes; but one could infer the builders' plan from stone block to stone block. In the afternoon sun the stones shone with the same honey colour as the blocks against which and over which they were packed. If one could have stayed longer one might have discovered other objects. Where had all the inhabitants gone? We wondered and guessed. Were their skeletons squatting under the earth of the plain around us, undecided whether to rise and brave the dangerous journey to the land of the ancestors, or did they feel abandoned by their descendants? No one left to make a libation. Only wind and hyena laughter. Here something was utterly annihilated. Here was nothing but sorrow, nothing but meaninglessness and battered traces of glory. From below a thin trail of smoke ascended into the sky in confirmation of our entirely superfluous presence. Ah, I sighed, how long are we still to journey?

The second surprise on top of the koppie made me even sadder. The stranger was the first to come upon a cave on the east side, but I was the first to notice the curious drawings on the rock walls. They seemed to look like people, but also like stick insects, painted aimlessly sometimes in a bunch, sometimes singly, sometimes one on top of another in rust-brown and white. Very faint. Who in the name of the creator of all things would have come here to immortalize himself, and in so unfinished a way? It was too odd. Surely not the inhabitants of the walled town. The stranger and the eldest son were just as nonplussed. The stranger complained about the lack of finish and the obvious absence of artistic rules in these clumsy attempts. Obviously backward painters from a backward society. Totally amateurish. The work of adult children. Yet not quite. No explanation occurred to us. The little figures so free of all connection, exiled here in the heart of the wilderness. There were too many questions here, and the dreariness of no answers. Here people had come and gone, again come and gone, dreary, to all eternity.

Here, said the eldest son, is one that looks like a buck.

The stranger expatiated tastefully on paintings on parchment and silk that he had seen on his travels in other lands, the richness and subtlety of their use of colour and the fine balance between trees, birds and people – recognizable as trees, birds and people, he emphasized – painted by trained artists and classifiable in schools and trends, and valuable possessions too. With the blade of his dagger he scratched at one of the ridiculous drawings. Someone's way of passing the time, he decided. It has nothing to do with art. It records nothing, it does not mean to communicate anything, or to satisfy aesthetically. It is functionless. The more the stranger spoke, the more heated he grew about the rock drawings, and in fact now he began to scratch them off.

Here is something that looks like a woman, said the eldest son. It has breasts. Here is a snake, I think. And look here! An elephant with a scalloped back!

He went into an uncontrollable fit of laughter.

I turned my back on the two of them and stood in the mouth of the cave looking out over the darkening veld at the glimmering evening star. Far away I heard the voices of the slaves, but always against the noise of the wind, which sounded now louder, now softer, like breathing. I felt so depressed. I felt as if my throat were about to constrict, I felt as if the incomprehensible were about to choke me and I had to hurl a cry into the wind which would vanish in the wind.

It is all meaningless, I thought, and walked off and descended the koppie alone. I went as far as a jutting rock, and as I stood there I heard myself say something. Not say. Mumble. Stammer. I heard the words fall from my mouth in snatches over the cliff to be swallowed by the wind filled silence, words that spoke of a jackal that would run through the air with a burning tail and set all the air afire. So there sprang a jackal from my mouth. I heard myself prophesy feverishly of languages that yet slept, of strange trees that would one day march out through valleys and over hills and along the mountainsides. I prophesied that there would be a walking around inside the earth. I prophesied that huge grey breakwaters would be thrown against the sea and that vessels would hide under the water and that there would be migrating back and forth and extermination over and again, and when it was all out of me, when all the fibrous sounds were off my tongue, I felt as if something had been gnawing at me, as if I had been gnawed full of holes and no longer obstructed the wind and had become without resistance; and afraid for myself I climbed down the last stretch as quickly as I could and hastened towards the slaves and the conviviality of the fire.

Once there, I asked them if by chance they had heard me. They stared at me stupidly and went on with their tasks. The one who no longer worked, the so-called leader, did not even look at me, did not deign to reply. Nor had the stranger and the eldest son heard me, it seemed, as I inferred after discreetly inquiring. I felt annoyed and very tired and not relieved.

Now it so happened that the stranger and I slept a short distance from the others near our own flickering fire, while the eldest son slept further away, though near the bearers and a big fire. After the sanga cattle disappeared watches had been set nightly. This practical measure had however lapsed and remained forgotten once we had been bewitched by the water spirit. The laxness of these times had certainly given way to enthusiasm and industry once we were on the near bank, but it was diligence that had required neither urging nor supervision. Even the chains had been left behind on the other bank, and the slaves slept free as we did. To tell the truth, they kept watch in turn over the sleepers on their own initiative, and over the ever-dwindling goods, and took decisions ever more independently. Of course their leader.

Now it so happened that the stranger and I never detected signs of conspiracy between the eldest son and the slaves; and yet one morning when we rubbed the sleep out of our eyes, both he and the whole bunch of slaves together with the goods were no longer there. Vanished. Completely. The stranger climbed a termitary and stared all around without success. The veld was simply veld, with veld-noises – a rustle, a twittering, a chirping.

We tried to track them, we urged each other on and had no success. We noticed flattened grass and footprints in the immediate vicinity of the fires, and that was all. We naturally assumed that if the eldest son and the slaves had decided to proceed with the expedition without us, they would have walked in the direction of the sinking sun, but that way too we detected nothing that looked to us like traces of people on foot. The hard earth showed no tracks and there were grass stalks askew everywhere. We wasted a day wandering about because we secretly hoped that they would come back. That did not happen. When darkness fell a great and horrible realization came upon us. We went to sleep in silence and rose the next morning in silence and set off walking at a reasonable pace. I must add that my sedan chair, the only one of three brought along from the city that was still in use, had been left behind. Without implements we could not chop it up for firewood and the useless object remained beside the ashes of the little fire for which we had gathered together the skeletons of brushwood, all in deathly silence.

We took our direction from the sun, but were forced by the course of rivers to diverge from it. Without slaves to carry us through the water we were helpless. We had no waterbags. We lived on the veld foods that quite by chance I had learned to pick out by keeping an eye on the bearers. It was hard work. I did my best, but we found barely enough to keep body and soul together. In our time of testing in this place of desolation we nevertheless felt of good heart and tender towards each other. But the terrific grandeur of the nights left us dejected.

One day, seeing vultures, we limped along to where they were circling. A revolting stench struck our nostrils. I knew we both had the same thought, but the stench was much too awful. Furthermore the vultures did not give way to us. They hobbled about the rib cage, presumably that of a wildebeest, and pecked each other. They ate greedily as if we, just outside their circle, did not exist at all.

We walked many days. The veld did not change. Sometimes we talked. I expressed my surprise at the eldest son.

They would kill him, take his money, and seek their freedom in the city in the desert – that was the stranger's opinion.

To this day I do not understand the eldest son's behaviour, this foremost heir of the coastal city's most prosperous merchant who, because of his father's influence and power, had been given nothing but the best since childhood, nothing but the finest that civilization could offer, and who had become an eccentric, short-tempered dreamer and fantasizer who had taken out his bad temper on the helpless yet could also dispense alms lavishly. The last time I had seen this happen was on the outskirts of the city on the day of our departure. He took a handful of money out of his leather bag and hurled it from the raised level of his sedan chair at the leprous beggar sitting at the side of the road, without looking at the fellow. Some of the coins struck the man in his tense face. There was nothing for him to do but duck and then creep around after the money on all fours, since his feet were already too blunt to walk; and with hands deformed into dried-out mopani worms, as brown too, as grey and black, he tried to pick up the coins. To manoeuvre them up.

Rocking from side to side I disappeared around a corner. I think that outcast was the last city dweller on whom my gaze fell. Why don't the creatures drown themselves? They just keep rotting till they return to the earth. It made me feel sick. More than once we came upon suicides in the woods. We saw pairs of feet, some bare, some still shod in rough sandals, turning around at eye height or hanging motionless, and among the branches glimpsed the contorted faces of old women who looked as if they were hurling abuse at us. Outcasts too. Childless women, or women convicted of witchcraft and shunned because they could not prove they had not let loose the mysterious deaths among the cattle and caused the bad harvests.

Of course I often wonder how long a person keeps on till. Surely there must be a boundary somewhere that becomes clearer and clearer to you, towards which you then reach as towards the greyness of sleep and thence towards the grey dream in which, as in a smaller death, you meet good and evil, the inseparable pair, the twins who defy death.

My dreams fill me and help me eat time. It no longer matters to me that I cannot neatly dispose of time and store it away and preferably forget it; for now I perceive that dreaming and waking do not damn each other, but are extensions of each other and flow into each other, enrich each other, supplement each other, make each other bearable, and that my baobab is a dream come true, and when I see the little people I know they are dream figures that really hunt and really provide me with food and that they really see me but also do not see me because I exist in their dream, and they feed their dream by caring for me. We meet each other and know nothing of each other. We go our ways separately and depend on each other, they on me in that I am as I am, and I on them in that they act as they act.

Nowadays I laugh ruefully at my spasmodic attempts to use the black and green beads I picked up to measure what is so ridiculous to measure and record. I attribute it to my education, random but education nevertheless, in which division and counting and classification played such an important role as to inspire people to undertake a journey that ought to progress so and so, and bring in such and such, and therefore for this and that reason ought to be set about in this way and not another, in this season and not another, in this direction and not another, with this equipment and not that – in which every last factor was taken into account, and when the day of our departure arrived with late-summer laziness, when day slipped into the realm of night and we forgot our sleepiness and our yawns, when for a last time, purely out of habit, we looked at the sea and saw the dhows and the skiffs heaving and the sky begin to burn with colours of fire in the kudu-berry trees, none of us noticed that we were entering a dream. so treacherous are the adventures of sleep.

It is clear that when I have finished drinking this last gift of the little people I will gain entrance to a new kind of dream. The brew is unknown to me but I do not have to know it to know that crocodile brains are the main constituent. Perhaps that is what I have been expecting. Will a dark mumbling wind come and fetch me?

What will I do with the golden nails and the beads, with the near-black water pot and the ostrich eggshell, my possessions? I would like time to reclaim them. The nails were the most useless present. I could do nothing with them, and how to show gratitude for them remained a riddle to me. Here they lie in my palm like seed that might germinate advantageously.

Everything I do is discreetly watched, and even my last gesture, the lifting of the ostrich eggshell to my lips, will be observed and (hopefully, presumably, probably) approved of. I will do it respectfully, slowly and stately in a last vain effort to satisfy demands I do not understand.

But for them I would long ago have starved. I was in a precarious state when the meeting occurred.

Scorching sunshine early-winter, but I remained asleep in the belly of the great tree. I remained asleep from hunger exhaustion, delirious and slowly withering away, with too little strength to change my habitation, to move to better grazing, simply grateful for the roomy hiding place, bare and robbed of its foliage, uncomfortable colossus with its probing fingers. I remained lying half-asleep, half-awake, and did not know if what I heard was really taking place outside or was in my mind, for I became aware of people talking, but as in one's sleep they talked so that one understood nothing. These phantoms busied themselves around the tree and I wondered whether they would enter my own dream reality and bend over me. I smelled something. I smelled smoke. It frightened me. I was not prepared to believe I would be consumed in the flames of my delirium. Through the crevice I saw floating forms pass, and sat upright on one elbow. Smoke. Human voices. The phantoms carried long branches stripped bare and joined to one another in a rough way to resemble a ladder. I understood nothing of what was going on. Nothing of the events being played out around my dwelling. I saw faces. Through a haze of smoke and incomprehension I saw the ladder being leaned against the smooth trunk, men climbing up it with bouquets of burning twigs, I heard shouts of joy, I saw ghostly people dance, men and women and children, I saw them gorge themselves and lick their lips and heard them laugh, and I stepped out of the baobab, the meagre remnants of me, stepped out of the shadow mouth of the opening into the blinding winter light, clad in the tatters of a silk robe, my eyes huge, my lips open, my hands stretched forward in helplessness. I spoke.

Only the next day must one or two of them have returned, for when I came back from my drinking-water stream there was a dry hollowed-out monkey-orange shell filled with honey waiting for me at the crevice opening. Dark brown, almost black honey with the coarseness of bee grub.

How to show thanks? I held the monkey orange in my outstretched hand and stood a short distance from the tree trunk so that I was easily visible. For a while I stood so. The bees in the disturbed nest above buzzed busily, hummed as they tried to repair the damage against the assault of the cold. In the movement of light and shadow it looked as if they were swimming around, falling and rising. Thus I paid tribute to the bees and to their accomplices.

Every day there was something waiting for me. When I went to drink water they came with their gifts and set them down before the opening. Out of curiosity I spied on them one day. I pretended to go into the river undergrowth but did not at once go to the water; I hid in the thicket and watched the vicinity of the baobab. I saw two men approach through the long grass. They were short, and the grass made them seem even smaller. They had a light skin colour and short hair like lichen spread over the head. They had crude clothing and weapons. First they gazed at the tree, then quickly went nearer, put something down, and scampered off. The long grass swallowed them.

A ground hornbill came up, walking. I saw that he was heading for the baobab opening. I could clearly recognize the calculating look in his light-blue eyes, coquettishly veiled by stiff eyelashes, and I got cross, and before he could get to my present I burst out of my hiding place to chase him away. The next day nothing was brought to me. Only the day after that. Thus I learned to behave according to unknown laws, though I burned with curiosity and would have given anything to learn more.

Particularly welcome were the serviceable hide clothes that they gave me, with an eye to the premonitions of winter which was so much harsher here than the winters I was used to, harsher and drier and more yellow. The earth crumbled and turned to powder. The branches of deciduous trees showed confused silhouettes against a sky become much lighter. And the bauhinia flowers decayed into a frenzy of shooting seeds. Everything seemed to me as if abandoned. The ibis community looked dusty and untidy. Even the elephants looked dismal.

It affected me. Again a sombreness came over me. The mischievousness of a mongoose, the water games of an otter failed to cheer me up. The head-wagging rock lizards did not divert me. I slouched aimlessly around.

Chased somewhere by the intimidation manoeuvre of a baboon sentry, I had picked up the first beads somewhere where a crack in the rocks turned into a crevice, somewhere in the dust among intertwined dry dead tubes of stalks, grass tassels, calices, petals, roots, somewhere not so long ago.

Humanware. Humans been here. An incalculable distance between me and those who had left behind beads and potsherds, irrecoverable time, unbridgeable estrangement, insuperable my loneness intensified by this small discovery, interminable the continuation of solitude, surrounded as I am by those who keep themselves apart and for whom I exist, but only as an apparition.

As an apparition I throve, became rounded and plump again from eating fungi and carrion flower stalks, python flesh, marulas, livelong berries, waterbuck liver. Whatever a winter and a summer had to offer to the eye and gathering bag and the bow and arrow of the little people, I too was fed on. There was no question of hardship any more, rather one of lazy overabundance.

Whom to thank, I sometimes ask myself. My water spirit is silent. So I thank the honey-bee. I thank the tree that houses him. I thank the earth that gives the tree its footing, with great difficulty, because it grows upside down. I thank the rain that descends to the very roots of the tree so that it can drink water and grow leaves and flowers. But the water spirit is silent. Baobab around whom the bees dance by day and around whose sensitive flowers unfolding like moons so many bats flap by night, in whose forks the rain pours rainwater for me, my water spirit is silent about you. Once I found an injured bat on the ground beside the daylight-filled crevice. At first I thought it was a funny flat frog shuffling backwards out there. Then I noticed it had fur. Then I saw the ears. And went down to the water. When I came back it was gone.

I searched for the place where I had picked up those first beads. Continually, naggingly I searched.

The bat was gone. A necklace of ostrich eggshell fragments the colour of wild pear blossoms and a handful of medlars were waiting for me.

Then latish one afternoon I discovered the pale knot of a rock fig in an overgrown cleft, and overhastily climbed the stone ridges, hauled myself up on loose hanging roots, and arrived on a small plateau. The steep side I had scrambled up was at an angle to both sunrise and sunset and offered a view across a long, virtually empty slope with clumps of trees. A few giraffes. The dust of a mixed herd of snorting, barking wildebeest and zebra. At the time I noticed nothing more. A flight of birds, yes, that too, swiftly dissolving into the distance. The wind was present everywhere. It rustled steadily as if it were the companion of silence. That was all I found in a thorough investigation of the plateau: wind and the background of wind, silence. I made believe this was the guardian who had wiped out everything, and woe to him who came sniffing around. Why scratch open, dig up, expose, reflect and deduce? Let be, just let be. Here there had been perhaps.

A city, perhaps, with ruler and subjects. I did not know what they came here to seek, what made them build their houses here of all places, with a view over endlessness, and whether they knew of the great sea that lapped around the horizons, and whether they imagined their various gods in the heavenly bodies or elsewhere, whether they observed ceremonies in their honour from which they departed, eyes glassy with faith and hearts full of good intentions, and whether they knew beforehand of their certain death. Or was death a game of chance to them, sometimes complicated by sicknesses, sometimes coming at a stroke, but in any event the actual beginning of life without the nuisance of a body and the time-consuming needs thereof, and if death is life, then they still live. Here. Right here.

The wind died down. In the unbelievable silence one of the big stones rolled down the cliffside, bouncing, leaping as if performing a trick, fantastic and soundless, and came to rest on the level below. The soundlessness gave me a fright. Now I no longer heard anything. Suddenly I knew that if I were now to speak, something tremendous would happen. The dead would arise, or no, they would become visible to me, and time would somersault, the earth would tilt, capsize, and hang upside down in the direction of limitless darkness and the spirit of the water would voyage into eternal space and forever be lost.

Then I felt something creeping in my ear. It tickled and itched and I shook my head. An ant. Something. An insect. I crushed it with my finger. And as if I had spent some time in a swoon, I now noticed that the sky had clouded over and that it was going to rain at any moment. Pell-mell I cleared out, possessed by fear and determined to get to the baobab before the lightning began to flash, but above all determined to be back in time in the time in which I belonged, for as I ran and sometimes stumbled too I felt behind my back another world growing, I felt that what had existed was extending its realm faster and faster, and felt that soon, in the very act of running, I would move in a wholly other time.

I reached the baobab with beating heart and a stabbing pain in the spleen that doubled me over, and I squatted in the opening and saw the rosette patterns that first raindrops make as they hit the dust.

So I yielded to the powers of my environment, or, to put it less despondently, I learned to live with them, as I learned to live with the veld and the animals and insects, with the choice of paths in reality and in my sleep, and with the presence of people who kept me apart. It is a strange experience to share a life without contact, and I often ask myself whether they are displaying charity towards me or bringing tribute. I try to behave fittingly. Acknowledge to myself that there is nothing for me to do but accept my fate as pampered captive and show myself grateful accordingly. It is as if the presence of others aggravates my loneness, as if the distance between myself and other people has become greater now that they exist in tangible proximity. I see them walking in the distance, I see girls playing with a monkey orange, throwing it back and forth to each other, I see women carrying babies on their protruding buttocks, men with wrinkled stomachs and legs thin as sticks, all of them yellow as a tortoise's belly, and I hold my hand over my mouth to prevent myself from calling someone nearer. I hear the click sounds they utter, I mutter something to myself that sounds like the language of my childhood days. Words that had got lost take on dim shape. Mother I see before me, father, brothers, sisters. I see huts and very high trees with trunks pleated like billowing skirts and green foliage. Mother I see again. Warmth and softness, a slimness, long breasts with sturdy nipples. Voices I hear vaguely and other noises too, a chopping, a crackling. I remember suddenly dogs that never bark, and noisy apes, and there was gaiety, I remember, when meat was portioned out, ape-meat too, yes, and I had had a doll made of bark fibre, the doll had beads around its neck, the head was a club, and I had the doll with me when everyone fled from their huts into the dense underbrush, my mother yanked me by the arm but she was killed, her head was split open and I was jerked out of her grasp and driven into a knot with other women. There were a whole lot of male captives too. I held on to my doll. I kept it with me in my arms. We travelled and travelled and then came to a village. The male captives were herded together and something was done to them. Later we set off and travelled further and further and came to a city on a terribly big, immeasurably broad dam, blue from this end to the far end.

Now I have the names for everything: slave, castration, commerce, coastal city, sea, forced labour. Yes, now I have it all.

I have the names and I am not listened to. There is nothing I can do with the names. They are nothing but rattles.

Borne from far on the wind I hear the little people making music. The sounds seem to me like beetles jumping over a fire. Also I hear them singing and clapping their hands.

Now I will force a confrontation.

When they next come to pick baobab seeds to suck the sour white flesh off the stones, I vow – then. Then I will confront them naked. Then I will undress. I will lay aside my skin apron and my skin cloak with the spring hare bones, as well as the necklace of ostrich egg fragments, and I will confront them, challenging them, though with my challenge tempered with acquired grace, shy but queenly, seductive but aloof; and I will look them right in the eyes and force them to look right back at me and acknowledge me, as a human being and nothing more than a human being. That is all I am.

I did it. They approached talking among themselves, and I guessed they were coming to pick seeds as they had done a few days before. I took off the clothes, removed the necklaces, loosened the sandals from my feet and kicked them off, and before doubt and hesitation overcame me went and stood in the opening of the baobab. And they walked past, and up the same home-made ladder they had leaned against the trunk to get to the bee nest one of them now climbed, picked seeds and threw them down to his comrades on the ground, who nimbly caught them. Unconcernedly the picker then climbed down, carried the ladder around to set it on the other side, and harvested there too. Then everyone walked off, each with a gathering bag on his back chock-full of the fruits of the tree.

I was deliberately not seen.

In this dream in which I am forced to live, I take refuge more often in the city of rose quartz, for thus have I already adapted the hunters' story. Not only does the mountain glitter rosily, but also that city in which I wander in the company of many others like myself. We do not have to talk to each other, we understand each other naturally. I notice the stranger there too, but detect no need for his companionship, for I am of a self-sufficient crystallinity, transmuted into pure bliss. I am one whole, and divided too and present in everything everywhere.

Strange that the water spirit sends me to a desert, but I understand, for, see, the water too has become quartz, everything has, stone and water and man have the consistency of quartz and the glory and the glorious knowledge of splintering and remaining glorious. Then when I awake, whether in the night or the day, I feel crinkled and stiff.

The insult of not being allowed to be human, that I have overcome. All ugly visions too, of hairy huts and skew door openings that try to entice me in and lock me up, all false solutions, all wrong exits; for I myself determine appearance and reality. I rule. I dream outwards and with the self-assurance of those who have long ago discerned that it is all just appearance I smile to myself, follow my own path diligently, will drink this parting poison gift in the nourishing awareness that dream leads to dream.

There is no other termination. That I concede. I am used up. To myself as well; but whether that makes up part of their deliberations is barely relevant, and why should they in their grief make room for the feelings of someone who let them down, who so lamentably failed where she should have been able to offer a way out?

Let the gods stare over our heads, the stranger once said. They know what they see.

That was precisely what I did not know. Wanted to join in. So I thought.

The stranger had stories to tell about many gods and religions, about the strange customs of priests and enthusiasts and prophets in the cities where he touched in the course of his trading voyages, and about their mutual malignancy and their competition for the blind obedience of the masses and their competition for the favour of the rulers, which could lead to being financed by the rulers, and the acquisition thereby of positions of power for the preaching castes, and all, all just because man feared death, all just to exorcise these fears. Promises of the cycle and promises of resurrection, promises of a paradisal hereafter, of the friendly community of ancestors, of salvation through abstinence but also through investment and bestowal; and every religion recruiting shamelessly and rejecting every other shamelessly.

And death a commonplace! the stranger said, and fell silent, and waited for someone to contradict him. Stories to scare children, was his conclusion. A bore at best, sometimes amusing, like adventure stories. Let us tell each other fables rather than try to rend each other over religion. Who believes me that there is a land where people ride on elephants? Who believes me that there is a land where people ride on an animal with two humps? Who believes me that there is a land where people yoke buffaloes on their ploughed lands, that there is a land where people use milk to make light? But you believe, you philosophers and manipulators, in paradise?

The stranger laughed scornfully.

There are enough wonderful things in life that arouse my curiosity. I am avaricious out of eagerness to know. Look!

He took off one of the necklaces he wore around his neck, a gold chain with a huge bloodstone pendant like a beetle on it, artfully engraved to look like a ladybird, only crueller and bigger.

Which of you believes that this jewel was stolen from the neck of a dead man who is still alive? he asked.

I can still remember the startled exclamations and gestures of aversion and the growls of and the forced smiles on the faces of some of our foremost citizens, those who could not afford to display ignorance and so had to conceal it behind airy smartness.

I wish, sighed the stranger, I could travel to the outer limit of the world. I am so greedy.

I also remember that the eldest son was present on that occasion, and how he listened attentively and slapped his calf with his cane but as usual said nothing. My benefactor, too, seldom took part in conversations like this. Too sick. Too dazed by fever. My heart was with him and with the stranger. My benefactor's hand trembled when he slowly brought a spoonful of beans to his lips. What did he think of all the chatter about death, he who was touched by it? His eyes, deep in their sockets, betrayed nothing.

Of all the sorts of conversation carried on after his dinner parties, the ones that interested me least were those dealing with war. To be honest, when war was brought up I found a reason to dish up or clear the table or attend to something else of a domestic nature. There was talk of sea battles and of land battles, of armaments, piracy, of celebrated victories and the division of spoils, ransoms and extortion, raids, punitive expeditions and suchlike matters about which the men argued and tried to impress each other, and about which they could come out with the most divergent theses and get extremely spiteful and sarcastic about each other's theories. The supreme game of profit, that was what the stranger called war, and he was at least one of the few at table who could speak from experience.

The little fleet of dhows under his command had already been on the attack and also been attacked by pirates. He had already, in contrast to the cityfolk, been in fierce combat with warriors. He had killed. Had himself been wounded. He knew what he was talking about when he referred to a bloody slaughter, for to him memories clung to such incidents and every battle meant more experience for him, cumulative knowledge of a reality with which, against his own wishes, he was professionally concerned, and not fiction. Not just stories of heroism.

He had seen injured men tumble overboard, seen hacked-off limbs floating, blood and commotion in the water that attracted sharks from near and far, and had heard the wretched drowning men defend themselves roaring against the monsters' slashing bites, in vain. As calm and refined as he sat there talking, so barbaric the naked language he used. Chop, stab, mutilate, kick, stalk.

While the city folk, fat with prosperity in an uneasy peace on the edge of history, chattered about defence and building forts and ramparts, and simply chattered and did nothing out of laziness and envy and lack of mutual trust and above all out of stinginess, I suspected, and also because they themselves did not feel at all threatened. With the many dhows that came across the sea laden with wares they maintained excellent relations. Their own skiffs distributed the goods to smaller coastal towns and in exchange loaded leopard skins, ivory and ambergris, tortoiseshell and rhinoceros horn for shipment back to the coastal city and its wholesale merchants; and so long had this favourable arrangement lasted that they would not believe anyone who might predict a plot to ruin their flourishing trade. Who, after all, would be so stupid? It was to everyone's advantage. There was no question that these strange caravels that had latterly begun to call constituted any danger. Besides, relations had quickly been established with these newcomers. There was no question that they were capable of snuffing out a long-established trade. No, not these simpletons who had to beg for water and fresh meat and fruit.

To everyone, myself included, the stranger's reports sounded romantic rather than instructive and insightful. I took the heart-shaped palm fan and fanned myself. I nodded and smiled and passed a dish and made a witty remark and tried first with one guest, then with another, to shift the discussion into a lighter vein. I flirted and laughed naughtily and practised my calling faultlessly. My benefactor looked satisfied. The scent of myrrh and the scent of rich foods, the scent of the multitudinous jasmine, the scent of the water I had washed myself with, the oil with which I had rubbed myself, the particularly complex composite aroma of civilization, that was what we breathed here. That was what the sultry city offered us.

That was how far my knowledge of warfare extended.

That it is innate in woman to have a spontaneous approach to atrocities, is a lie. Though I had already held death fast in my arms, though I had taken in my own hands a stillbirth strangled by the navel cord, and rolled it up in an old torn cloth like a parcel, and carried it off from our slave childbirth hut, though I had already heard sick people in delirium and heard the moans of slaves being punished, none of it has been of any help to me.

In the deepest, darkest, farthest corner of the baobab I hid. These screams, these war cries, this floodwater of fear dark over my head; this fear that cut through me, this bestial death rattle. I was cornered; like a rock rabbit in fear of death I trembled.

For days I did not dare go out. Then the stench of decay drove me out.

The wild rejoicing of the hyenas at night. I was too frightened to make a fire for myself in case it served as a beacon for those who had come to massacre. I crouched in the belly of the tree and understood the flickering train of thought in my baby who had chosen darkness over the light of life. It was an ecstasy of never being. It was the only true victory: neither death nor life had meaning. It was equilibrium. It was the perfection of non-being.

The stench drove me out. The fighting had raged nearly to the baobab, I could now see; for while I had been hiding both far and near had sounded the same, the same and everywhere, and I could not make out at all from what direction the attackers had come.

When the slaughter began, I caught a glimpse of the attackers. I had just started back from the stream, swaying along with the blackened waterpot on my head and my scoop, my ostrich eggshell, in one hand – that is to say, I imagined I saw someone, or more than one person, looking at me, and realized with fear, quietly walking on, that it was strange people staring, not the little people whose peeping, if I may call it that, was of unparalleled subtlety, in fact never noticeable. While these . . . Too clearly I felt eyes upon me, too clearly saw dark beings disappearing into the long grass. They must have been spies. And that same night. And it kept on. So long. The merest chance that I had a tree hiding place. Which they must not have observed and noted, for I was still quite a distance from it when I became aware of being pointedly watched. My self-trodden footpath seemed to me irritatingly long. With one eye on the tree I kept it in sight all the time. The distance between me and it refused to lessen though I lengthened my stride. There were spies. There were others here.

Others overwhelmed us. Who were these others? And from where?

It is disheartening to remain spared.

On the day when I at last dared to investigate, I picked out among the gnawed corpses those of the little people. The other were bigger. I do not know how to assimilate horror.

How the scavengers must have feasted. There was too much for them to consume. The offering was too great.

Most remarkable the spectacle of one of the other up in a tree, stretched out over branches, the berries of the eyes already neatly pecked out, the fruit of mouth and tongue rubbled at. Decay that turns form fluid.

The ants went mad. There was far too much. They would never be able to break down everything and transport it fibre by fibre to their store places, where there would anyhow not be space enough. The ants scurried on all sides.

The bluebottle flies swarmed with delight over messed entrails, formed green patches like dangerous flowers, larger and larger grew the shiny flower, till suddenly the disc divided itself into multitudinous floating parts. These settled and caked together to make a new flower. They were everywhere.

The corpses had been torn apart by jackal and hyena and vulture and dragged far and wide and rearranged in an order that suited them; but everywhere bluebottles swarmed.

It was not possible to determine who had been the victor in the slaughter. I could pick up as many weapons as I wanted and build up an arsenal in my baobab. I could pack it full of ironware, feed it on iron to satiety, reinforce it with iron from within, install spears like staves in the opening.

I could not find out whether there were more corpses of the attackers lying around than of the little people. It was so quiet, aside from the usual birdsong and the breath of the wind, and in the late afternoon, as ever, unperturbed, the arrival of the elephants, their expert insertion of trunks in a row into the water, and leisurely bathing and sand-throwing and tranquil retreat with the oldest cow in the lead after everything had been achieved that they wanted to achieve. I greeted them.

First of all I went to fetch myself a load of wood. For now I wanted to make myself a huge fire. For I did not care in the slightest if I were seen or by whom. For even if the long grass were to bring forth just as many attackers again, I did not care. For let death come, let the death blow fall. For nothing mattered any more. For it was the end.

On the return trip, the long bundle of wood on my head, I heard a groan, or imagined I heard it. Or was I not imagining? I listened intently and heard nothing more. I concentrated, turned my head carefully away from the direction of the wind to catch the sound, and heard nothing. Remained standing there a long time, then went on and set the wood down in front of the opening. But I knew I had to go and track down the groaning. I had to track it down.

The knowledge drove me on. Carefully I inspected all the remains of people, and forced myself to do it systematically, to scrutinize systematically and to watch carefully for the slightest sign of life. I searched and searched and searched. I forgot about the stench and the flies and the vultures watching the spectacle from the trees and the horrible appearance of human beings destroyed, and searched over and over all around the tree as far as there was anything to be seen that looked like a human figure, human remnant, and I arrived at an ant-heap and again heard a groan. Now I searched feverishly all about, and further, and back again. There were interjections from a lourie, but I knew, I was convinced I had heard the groaning of a human being. It was as faint as could be, only just audible, only just. If I could only hear it again. Distance is deceptive.

I went back to the tree and drew a stick out of the bundle of wood. Using it I now searched around the anthill, poking with the stick in the tangled grass and dense ground cover; but what did I think I was actually doing? Was my sense of relation totally disturbed, that I imagined what I was searching for had shrunk to dwarf size, to foetus size – was that what I was searching for? Why was I churning around with the stick? I was searching for a groan, a groan without a body. A groan got lost here. That was what I was searching for. A groan had sounded in the air and I wanted it for myself.

Now I began to laugh. Half-sobs, half-laughs came from my throat. They came from my insides like moans. One after the other I forced them out like clods, and when they were out I felt like someone who had vomited. With my stick I returned to the baobab.

I made a fire. Spark. Flame. Fire. It flared high, for I threw more and more wood on it; I considered fetching even more, getting an immense fire going that would crowd out the smell of human death with the more pleasant smell of plant ash, and I also envisaged announcing my orphan presence via the fire. Let it be seen that I am. Let woodpecker and tapping beetle see it, let the leopard stay away from me, let kudu and duiker sniff fire and stay away, let what human beings remain see it and make up their minds. Do with me what you will. In godly impotence I walked among your corpses and achieved nothing, I whom nothing befell in the shelter of a tree, I who am not from here, do not belong here, do not want to be here. I heard your war cries, your child moans, your last sounds, and quietly remained in hiding, and when everything was over stepped out of my baobab. Had eyes seen me?

Had they seen me shudder at what I saw?

If there are more of you, little or big, light or dark, come.

Gradually I got going again. It is winter again. Spent a summer, a winter, a summer, a winter here. Winter of hardship now, where I again have to rely on myself and have only the wind and now the phantoms too for company. White bones around the tree. The baobab clutches and claws at the sky. The grass stands pale and stiff. An aloe sucks the blood up out of the earth and wears it gaudily in a cluster of red knobs, splendid against the clear blue sky and only too attractive to the sugar birds. White skulls around the tree. Little by little the wind brings in dust to fill up the brain hollows and the pelvises.

I have to make new paths where skeletons block my way with their rib bones. I can do without the company of hyena and vulture.

Gradually going again.

A long time since I noticed baboons. Warthogs with upright tails often.

In fact gradually more and more slowly as if I were about to come to a halt. My territory contracts as my powers decrease. The humiliation of not being able to care for myself. Though I know what I can eat, I do not know how or where to look for it, and drift around again as I did right at the beginning; but resigned now. Why hysteria, after all? To what purpose fierce concentration? I let things go their course. On some days I find something, on others nothing. It does not matter.

There always remains the balm of the stream behind a ravelwork of lianas, its murmuring refreshment, the mood of coolness it creates, and there always remain the samango monkeys who announce their disapproval of my penetration with funny growls. In spite of all there is something familiar for me here. It has so happened.

The clattering stream and then the river into which it quietly and timidly debouches. The river runs towards where the sun and moon rise, towards where I once began to travel, towards the sea of the city from which we departed in search of a city on the sea at the other margin of the world.

I long for nothing any more.

Once, only once thus far, have I again undergone the pain of expectancy, when in the distance I saw a fire which developed into a veld fire that windingly sailed over the horizon and gradually devoured it. Fire snake, I earnestly willed, sail around me too and swallow me up. It continued to burn in the far distance and the smoke persisted as a pall in the air long after the flames had died. I got the smell of it, and I noted soot freckles on the bark of the tree.

Would whoever might be responsible for that destruction be aware of my nightly fire?

My answer is the poison that was set down for me one day during my customary trip to fetch water. Someone knows about me now. Someone has always known about me. But who? Here I can play a neat little game with my golden nails. I can count them out and simply accept what they say. Why not? I count them according to the rhyme. Ultimately useful, little nails that have joined together what was bygone and mysterious to me, precious little signs of a disappearing meaning. Now you help me to make my last moments amusing.

Good. I have counted them out and behold, the upshot is that I was not forgotten, which is as I thought all along. I will be thankful that my surmise agreed with chance. I no longer procrastinate. Recklessly I throw the nails up in the air. Let them fall where they will and lie and never rust. I was really a mistress and mother and goddess. Enough to make you laugh.

I stand before the crack and hold up in outstretched arm the last gift so as to be seen. Then I disappear into the dark interior.

Baobab, merciful one. My baobab.

I drink down my life. Quickly, water spirit. Let your envoy carry out his task swiftly.

Yes.

As a bird takes leave of a branch. Fruit falls. A bat. Like a bat, black and searching.

I dive into dark water and row with my wings toward the far side where in descending silence I am no longer able to help myself and deafly fly further and further. I will find rest in the upside-down. I fold my wings.

图书在版编目（CIP）数据

去往猴面包树的旅程:汉英对照 /(南非) 威尔玛·斯托肯斯特罗姆著; (南非) J.M.库切英译; 李斯本汉译. -- 成都: 四川人民出版社, 2019.10 (2020.5重印)

ISBN 978-7-220-11548-6

Ⅰ.①去… Ⅱ.①威… ②J… ③李… Ⅲ.①长篇小说—南非共和国—现代—汉、英 Ⅳ.①I478.45

中国版本图书馆CIP数据核字(2019)第231396号

四川省版权局
著作权合同登记号
图字：21-2019-209

The Expedition to the Baobab Tree by Wilma Stockenström, translated from Afrikaans by J. M. Coetzee
Copyright © 1981 by W. Kirsipuu
English translation © 1983 by J. M. Coetzee
First published in 1983 by Faber and Faber
This edition published by arrangement with Big Apple Agency, Inc.
Simplified Chinese translation copyright: © 2019 Ginkgo (Beijing) Book Co.,Ltd.
本书中文简体翻译版版权归属于银杏树下（北京）图书有限责任公司

QUWANG HOUMIANBAOSHU DE LÜCHENG

去往猴面包树的旅程

著　　者	［南非］威尔玛·斯托肯斯特罗姆
译　　者	［南非］J.M.库切（英译）/ 李斯本（中译）
选题策划	后浪出版公司
出版统筹	吴兴元
编辑统筹	朱　岳　梅天明
特约编辑	宁天虹
责任编辑	杨　立　罗　爽　邵显瞳
装帧制造	墨白空间·杨雨晴
营销推广	ONEBOOK
出版发行	四川人民出版社（成都槐树街2号）
网　　址	http://www.scpph.com
E – mail	scrmcbs@sina.com
印　　刷	北京盛通印刷股份有限公司
成品尺寸	143mm × 210mm
印　　张	8.25
字　　数	165千
版　　次	2019年10月第1版
印　　次	2020年5月第2次
书　　号	978-7-220-11548-6
定　　价	49.80元